I0680682

THE
vanishing
dragon

THE
vanishing
dragon

ROBERT A. NEWTON

FREEDOM STREET PRESS
HILLSBORO, OREGON

Freedom Street Press
Hillsboro, Oregon
www.freedomstreetpress.com

Copyright © 2016 by Robert A. Newton
All rights reserved, including the right to reproduce this book, or
portions thereof, in any form. Published in 2016.
Printed in the United States of America on acid-free paper.

Editor: Sharon Eldridge
Interior Design: Jennifer Omner
Cover Design: RockingBookCovers.com

PUBLISHER'S CATALOGING-IN-PUBLICATION DATA
Newton, Robert A.,
    The Vanishing Dragon/Robert A. Newton
    Library of Congress Control Number: 2016912721
    ISBN: 978-0-9905036-2-0 (paperback)
    ISBN: 978-0-9905036-3-7 (Kindle ebook)

Acknowledgments

The author is grateful for the help he received from the United States Customs Service and the United States Fish and Wildlife Service for background material utilized in the creation of this story.

And to the World Wildlife Fund, Save The Elephants, Wild-Leaks and the Elephant Action League, who are leading the fight to save our most noble species.

Part One

EARTH AND SKY

Dragon Revealed

The dragon is the spirit of change; therefore of life itself.
Taking new forms according to its surroundings, yet never
its final shape.
It is the great mystery itself. Hidden in the caverns of inaccessible
mountains, or coiled in the depths of the sea, he awaits the time
when he slowly rouses himself to activity.
He unfolds himself in the storm clouds, and washes his mane in
the blackness of the seething whirlpools.
His claws are the forks of lightning. His scales glisten in the bark of
the rain-swept pine trees.
His voice is heard in the hurricane which, scattering the withered
leaves of the forest, quickens the new spring.
The dragon reveals himself only to vanish.

—Okakura Kakuzo, 1905
The Book of Tea

Chapter 1

Hannah Song lay hidden behind the gothic spire of a termite mound and focused her field glasses. As she scanned the approach to the water hole, a gigantic shadow emerged from the acacia scrub. Lured by the smell of the water over the grasslands, the great bull elephant drew near the pool. He paused warily before stepping into the red mud ringing the shore. His magnificent crossed tusks gleamed brightly in the mid-day sun. With a cautious sweep of his trunk, the beast pushed forward and began to drink.

"It's a huge bull," she said to the Tsavo ranger lying beside her. "His tusks must be at least seven feet."

Transfixed, she held her view on the scene of eternal beauty. But the cross-hairs had found a target. Song saw the elephant shudder in response to an invisible shock to the base of his trunk. The crack of a distant gunshot roiled through the air. She gasped sharply and tensed her grip as the bull lifted his head dully into the wind as if to plead for divine grace. The force of a second cruel slam to the brow collapsed his forelegs and rolled him to one side. He lay still, half in the water, as the image of a faint cloud crossed his open eye.

Song bit down on her lip, staring in disbelief. Cold and sick inside, she watched silently as a covered lorry approached the fallen form. Two men jumped out into the swirling dust. One carried a large bore rifle. The other jumped from the truck bed, juggling an axe and a chainsaw. The man with the rifle stood watch while the other attacked the tusks.

1

"There's only two of them," she whispered to the ranger.

She shifted her glasses toward a droning sound over the low hills to the northeast. Beyond them was the Somalian frontier. Song followed the twin engine cargo plane as it drifted into an approach and dropped onto the dry lake bed nearby.

The ranger worked the bolt of his ancient Lee-Enfield, chambering a .303 round. Song scanned back to the truck at the edge of the water hole. One of the poachers pulled back a canvas flap and heaved the precious tusks onto a pile of ivory collected in the bed. Their work finished, the poachers climbed into the lorry. It started with a puff of black smoke and headed toward the waiting plane.

"They're going to transfer the load," Song said. "You'd better call for the gunship."

The ranger grabbed the field radio. In a tense, high-pitched voice he began to recite the call sign. "Seven, Mike, Kenya, November, this is..."

His transmission was interrupted by the thud of the bullet impacting the middle of his arched back. Instinctively, Song scrambled to the far side of the mound just as a following shot ricocheted off the edge of the mound where she had just been lying.

She called out to the ranger. His rigid form lay propped against a jagged rock.

No answer. She could not reach the radio without exposing herself to the sniper. He must have circled behind them. The sniper had the advantage of plunging fire. She was caught between him and the poachers on the lake bed below. Her Rover was secluded too far away to risk a run for it.

Song tried to reach around the mound for her own rifle, but a bullet fragment caromed off a rock and stung her hand. She pulled her arm back at the shock and heard the radio crackle with static from beneath the body of the ranger. Reaching again, she caught the sling of her Remington 700, attached its tripod and drew it into position.

The others now gathered around the plane pinpointed her position and began to unleash curtains of AK-47 fire at her. As the automatic rounds popped above her head, Song wrapped the sling over her forearm and lay prone, legs wide apart. In a fluid motion, she worked the bolt, raised the scope slightly and eased it to her eye. She found her target and squeezed the trigger. The explosion from the rifle made her ears ring in pain. One of the men hunkered down beside the tail of the airplane pitched backward, raising a wisp of dust.

The pilot started the engines and the plane rolled forward to take off. Shells kicked the dust all around her. Song adjusted her weapon to fire again, but a round from above and behind narrowly missed clipping her boot. The sniper had changed position.

A loud crackle emanated from the ranger's radio. The voice calling on the radio was drowned out by the rush of the plane as it gained the air. Song rolled to her left and felt a pulsing vibration. The steady beat of rotor blades echoed from a plateau to the west. Looking up, she noticed a glint from the sun off the glass cockpit of a helicopter as it swept with a wide turn, arced upward and then screamed down like an eagle diving for prey. It was an AH-64 Apache gunship on loan from the United States Government. She had only heard about its capabilities. But they were formidable.

The gunship was armed with a 30 mm nose cannon, an M230 Chain Gun hoisted between its landing struts and hellfire missiles mounted on its stub-wing pylons. It had the combined firepower equivalent to a jet fighter, with the added capability of hovering over a target.

The poachers went to ground as the streaming electric pulse from the chain gun struck every square inch of the earth below. As the unmerciful shudder of its gun momentarily ceased, the craft changed position to re-engage. It hung in the air and seemed to skip backwards as a flight of rockets blasted from the deadly pods.

Song saw furious currents of blinding light. She heard the screams of the men above the roar of the chain gun. The truck below lifted, exploded and splintered apart. Then, most abruptly, it was quiet, except for the finishing echo of the gun, the low whine of the twin engines and the whoosh of the four blades cutting the air. Nothing moved below.

The peace did not last. Another shot from behind clipped the lowest spire of the mound, showering her with brick-red dust. She pushed her face into the sand and inched toward her right. Song rose up slightly. The reflection from a distant acacia tree caught her eye. It was the sniper's scope. Song paused to slow her heart rate. She rolled the rifle against her cheek, aimed and fired. Her first shot missed. Too far left. Song had to adjust for wind distance and temperature without the help of a spotter. She studied the motion of the clouds and the grasses for the right windage. Five inches for every mile an hour of wind. Song judged the wind as just under three miles an hour. Slowly, she again eased her rifle into position, framing a line leading to the solitary tree. She adjusted the scope and froze. The reflection appeared again. Song hesitated for a moment and decided that shooting a sniper through his own scope had long since become a cliché. So, the next blast from her rifle removed the top of his head. In an instant, the corpse tumbled from the crown of the tree as if in slow motion.

The gunship suddenly loomed overhead. As it swept by, the pilot offered a wave, then pulled about and landed the craft in a clearing. The gunner dismounted and ran toward Song, carrying his helmet in one hand and a canvas bag in the other. She gained her footing and scrambled over to the fallen ranger, placing her fingers to his throat, checking for a pulse. She shook her head at the approaching gunner.

Although he was smiling, there was an air of danger about him. A knife in a leather scabbard was strapped to his ankle. He dropped his helmet, pulled a light blue beret from his back pocket and placed it on his head at an angle. He was well-built, sunburned and badly in need of a shave. As he reached for her bleeding hand, he said in an unmistakable Australian drawl, "G'day. Here now, let's have a look at that."

He grabbed a towlette and a dressing kit from his bag and began cleaning the wound. Song brushed back a strand of sable hair from her face.

"You don't know how glad I am to see you."

"My pleasure. I hate these poaching ratbags."

She surveyed the smoking devastation on the plain below. Song turned and tried to look him in the eye, but he kept looking down while he wrapped her hand.

"You sure made short work of that bunch," she said.

He smiled slyly. "Yeh. Out here if you want security, you've gotta make your own."

The gunner relaxed the pressure on her wrist and reached into the bag.

"We knew you were in this sector and figured there was a bit of trouble when your transmission was cut off."

He sliced an extra length of gauze with his teeth.

"Name's Duffy Weede. Mates call me Duff. What's yours?"

"Song. Hannah Song. Special Agent, U.S. Customs. I'm here as an observer."

"Oh, a diplomat, eh? Well, welcome to Kenya. I'm a diplomat myself. Without portfolio, I'm afraid."

Weede finished wrapping her hand. His own hands were surprisingly delicate. "It's just a scratch. But you'd better get a tetanus shot. In this climate you can die from the most ordinary things."

The gunner helped her to her feet. She looked at him closely and for a moment his eyes could not leave hers. They walked to the distant rise marked with a single tree.

A .308 caliber rifle lay beneath the acacia. The crumpled figure of a man hung suspended in the branches just above their heads like a resting puppet. One arm of the corpse dangled pitifully. The index finger of the hand curved inward. He was wearing a fatigue uniform with a curved tab on the shoulder. His brown beret with a gold flash was folded under a leather strap. The sniper was a park ranger!

Weede shook his head as he looked up at the dead ranger. "Poor devils don't make spit. Not enough to live on, anyway."

Song reached up for the beret. "Well, this poor devil tried to kill me. I had no choice."

Weede averted his eyes and walked past her. He picked up the sniper's rifle, which was intact except for its scope, which had cracked in the fall from the tree. He looked at the sniper missing the top half of his head and whistled, "You got him right in the apricot. That one was at least 800 yards. Where'd you learn to shoot like that?"

Song tucked the beret into her pocket and smiled coyly. "Finishing school."

Chapter 2

A lonely tropical moon illuminated Twin Lion Cliff on the northeast shore of Orchid Island. It rose above the edgeless waters like an unstrung bow pointed toward the distant heavens. Bright beams of light fell upon the rocky steps ascending from the craggy point that jutted into the shimmering sea. Within the nearby shadows, shivering waves roiled against iridescent boulders. The essence of exotic flowers drenched the air.

The great house and its cluster of outbuildings had been raised on the highest part of the tapered peninsula. Built in the nineteenth century by a Chinese monarch as a summer retreat, the complex was surrounded by a low stone wall. Bent palm trees dotted the interior grounds, while ancient evergreens skirted the gravel roadways. Armed guards paced the perimeter at irregular intervals. A new lord had taken up residence.

From his southern balcony, Shang T.K. Au watched the flickering torches of a ceremony in the Rapao village below. Colorful lanterns twinkled among the reclining pine trees, signaling the arrival of the honored guests. The hamlet rested on a coastal plain stretching inland from the sea like an open oriental fan. He owned the countryside as far as the eye could see. Or cared to see.

The harsh moon glow flooded the terrace, bathing him with a ghostly light. Au swirled the ice in his tumbler and downed his second gin and tonic. He raised his arm slightly and, within

seconds, a servant approached with a fresh drink. Without speaking, the servant removed the empty glass and placed the new vessel
at Au's fingertips. He bowed low from the waist to his master and
glided back to his assigned station.

Weary of the view, Au gathered his silk dressing gown and
surged from his high-backed chair. He passed through the house,
with three servants in tow, headed for the north-facing balcony.
His mood had changed. The shift of positions would suit him
better.

He smiled at the bird flittering in a bamboo cage at the edge
of the porch. It was a yellow oriole which had fallen from its nest
in a recent storm. Au had rescued the bird and kept it warm and
well nourished, as specified in the textbooks he had ordered. Soon
it would grow too large for its enclosure. It would have to be freed.
But not just yet.

Au opened the cage, gently grasped the bird and pulled it from
its perch. He held the creature on its back within his palm and fed
it vitamins from an eyedropper. The bird pressed its grey tongue
against the glass and worked its beak to take the liquid.

A car door slammed at the gatehouse of the compound. Au
replaced the eyedropper in the bottle and returned it to its place in
the special rack. One of the attendants whisked into the enclosure
and stood silently beside him. Au looked up at him. "Yes, what is
it?" he asked impatiently.

"Mr. Mitoma is here, sir."

"Very well. Show him in."

"Yes, sir."

Au returned the bird to its cage and meticulously fastened the
door. At the sound of clipping footsteps, he turned to face his guest.
A short, thin man with an acne-scarred complexion and a cheap
haircut entered the enclosure. Crashi Mitoma smiled, advanced
swiftly across the deck and embraced his host. "My dear Chairman, how is business?"

"Most fortunate," Au replied. "*Yoku irasshaimashita*," he added.

"And I am glad to be here," said Mitoma.

He drew back, still holding onto Au. The scent of decayed fish upon Mitoma's breath was overpowering. Au pulled away diplomatically.

"My Chairman, may I take it that you now have available the merchandise which we discussed?"

Au nodded and turned toward the shrouded vastness of the open sea. Mitoma followed, edging closer. The lights of a fast ship sparkled just off the point. "One of yours, my Chairman?"

"Undoubtedly."

They followed the freighter as it negotiated the crescent reef. Au extended his arms and rested his fingertips on the railing. "You know, Crashi, we have finally completed the transfer of our entire operations here. Once the Communists assumed control of Hong Kong in 1997, certain of our entrepreneurial activities were not as readily tolerated."

Mitoma dipped his head repeatedly in knowing approval.

The two men watched the ship's lights disappear over the horizon. Au thought of his own father, a poor fisherman. Like him, his father had been both a stern and kindly man. Trying to feed a wife and seven children, he had ignored the storm warnings and set out at dusk for one last try. He had never returned. Au's mother had been forced to sell her body for sustenance. Her pimp had beaten the boy, so he had run away at the age of fifteen. Hardened by the streets, Au had supported himself through petty criminal acts.

Au found work as a longshoreman and soon became the foreman of a shipbuilding crew. By the age of forty, he had become president of the company. Now sixty-four, he owned one of the largest shipyards in Asia. His merchant vessels plied the waters of the world. Au's brilliant rise to the top had coincided with the phenomenal growth in Pacific Rim trade. His toughness and mettle were legendary. He had amassed more money and power than most people could dream about.

For years he had believed that his father was still out there somewhere. Lost at sea. Au bit his lip with the memory. "We're all lost at sea," he whispered.

"Excuse me, my Chairman?"

Au grasped Mitoma's arm at the elbow and urged him toward the house. "It's nothing, dear Crashi. Nothing at all."

Mitoma had been the overseas representative for a major Japanese manufacturing conglomerate when Au first met him. Now, he was an agent for other interests. The Japanese were his best customers. They paid handsomely and on time. In short, they were thoroughly reliable.

Au picked up the bamboo cage, peered in at the bird, and carried it toward the portal. As they crossed the threshold, Au raised his head, discreetly signaling a hovering lieutenant. The attendant moved out at a brisk clip in the direction of the annex. He returned moments later, lugging a leather salesman's case. The orderly placed the valise on a low credenza. He unlatched it and stood at attention. Au dismissed him, opened the case and withdrew a polished, mahogany box. He set it down before Mitoma and snapped it open with an exaggerated motion.

Mitoma could barely contain a gasp at the wondrous, small carvings arrayed on black velvet. Nestled in vertical slots were *netsuke*, ornamental ivory buttons employed to fasten a purse or other articles to a kimono sash.

Mitoma's eyes danced to the edge of the display holding the most important pieces. They were *hanko*, or chops. The personalized name seals required for all official documents in Japan. *Hanko* made of ivory were status symbols. They had rocketed in popularity during Japan's emergence as a dominant trading power. Now Japan alone consumed 40 percent of the international ivory supply and *hanko* were the single largest use of ivory in the world.

Au feigned inattention as Mitoma lifted the pieces one by one and turned them over and over with his fingers. He appeared to be mesmerized by the display of artistry. Au toyed with the bird, watching and waiting for the perfect moment to set the hook. When he was sure that Mitoma was thoroughly enchanted, he waved his hand at the orderly. "This, of course, is but a tiny sample of what my artisans are capable of producing."

Mitoma looked up expectantly. Au moved toward an adjacent dining table. The attendant returned from the anteroom with a mahogany box the approximate size and shape of a footlocker. Obvious strain creased his face as he struggled to gingerly set it on the table. He deftly placed it beside Au, wiped his forehead and left the room.

Mitoma scampered over. His breathless attention was riveted on the box as Au slowly unfastened the closure and teased it open. He opened his eyes wide, blinked and gulped.

Set within clumps of cotton batting were flawless ivory effigies of the favorite Chinese gods. Mitoma was speechless. Au had realized the impact the pieces would have and saved them for last. He waited while Mitoma massaged the carvings and continued to marvel at them.

Au sat down beside Mitoma. "You know, it's amusing. I've never been to Africa. The only elephant I've ever seen was in the Paris Zoo."

They both laughed. Mitoma absently handed Au a bulging envelope and continued caressing the objects. Au pushed a fat finger into the cage. The bird moved indifferently to the opposite end of his perch.

"When can the balance be delivered, my Chairman?"

"One segment has just been completed. It should be delivered soon. A new shipment will be leaving the African Continent momentarily. My carvers are most anxious to begin work."

The bird padded toward Au's finger and pecked it. He grimaced and turned back to Mitoma. "Also, I am pleased to inform you that we are tracking a large Kenyan herd. Your entire order should be filled in three months."

Mitoma's lip curled upward, exposing a silver tooth.

"Barring any complications," Au added.

Chapter 3

The Golden Gate Promenade skirted the entrance to San Francisco Bay from Fort Point to the Marina District. A heavy east wind had made the water too choppy for pleasure craft from the St. Francis Yacht Club. Only a single U.S. Coast Guard cutter had ventured out from its station. The cutter turned menacingly toward the inbound freighter before sailing by on the starboard side and heading for the open sea. Screeching gulls riding the air currents whirled in the cutter's wake. They followed it until it reached the Golden Gate Bridge. Then they floated upward, turned and glided back into the bay.

Surging waves convulsed against the hull of the rusting container ship. Its bow pushed steadily into the wind as it made for the harbor. The lookout on the flying bridge studied the shore. That had been a close call. No other cutters were preparing to get underway. All small craft remained anchored snugly in the marina. Clusters of cyclists and joggers leisurely traversed the length of the promenade. They migrated in both directions. No one was fishing. The water was too rough. There were no suspicious-looking vehicles parked along the bank. All was quiet and secure. The *Ganbei* would dock soon, two days late.

"Have you been through here before?" the mate asked.

"Yeah. Six months ago."

"Where do we pick up the harbor pilot and the tug?"

"Right below Alcatraz. Just stay in the channel."

"Thanks. I'll go tell the captain."

A sudden gust of wind blasted the hatch door shut behind the mate. The lookout watched the shadow of the ship as it knifed through the water. He was entranced by the motion and looked up to avoid getting dizzy. The spattered white rocks and structures of Alcatraz Island loomed on the horizon.

Just the thought of surviving in such a place sent a shiver down his spine. He felt the engines slow. The cargo ship plied another twelve hundred yards before shuddering violently and slowing to a stop. An ancient tugboat, rolling on the swells, bumped alongside. The harbor pilot came aboard and took the con. He navigated for The Embarcadero, and with the assistance of the tug, guided the freighter into a berth at Pier 31.

Specially designed cranes went to work hoisting the corrugated metal containers from the ship to the dock. It was nearly sunset by the time the unloading process was completed. Customs officials opened the rear doors of each container, checking for contraband. They found none. The search had not been thorough. It had been rushed due to the dimming light and the impending shift change. As it happened, the regional office was shorthanded due to budgetary cutbacks and the annual staff conferences in Washington, D.C.

At the Bayshore Truck Stop south of the city, Jasper Grogan had just lost another quarter in a well-worn Donkey Kong Jr. machine. The electronic beep of the dispatch phone blared over the loudspeaker. The owner answered it in the adjacent office.

"Hey, Grogan, phone, line one," he yelled.

Grogan slapped the front of the machine. "Thanks. Be right there." He made a mental note of his point total before tearing himself away and grabbing the courtesy phone. "Grogan."

"Yeah, Jasper. This is Art Fong. Remember me?"

"Sure do. How could I forget? You still owe me for that last trip to Benicia."

"Well now, that's a difference of opinion. That cargo was damaged."

"Yeah, sure. One carton out of a hundred. When you gonna pay me?"

"As soon as the claim's resolved."

"Yeah, right." Grogan fought the urge to hang up.

"Listen, Grogan. I have a deal for you that'll more than make up for it."

"Yeah? What's that?"

"Good customer needs a container pulled out of the harbor tonight."

"Where to?"

"Chinatown."

"Chinatown? Short trip. Won't pay squat. Goodbye."

"No. Wait, Grogan...how about double?"

Grogan pressed the receiver closer to his ear. "Double, huh? Why?"

"Let's just say it's seasonal merchandise."

"How seasonal?"

"Toys."

Christmas had been nearly two months earlier. Grogan knew that merchants did not begin stockpiling and building inventories until summer for the next season. Yet, he hadn't handled a shipment for a week and his truck payment was coming due. Grogan couldn't very well refuse any job. The truck had to be kept working. Still, he didn't trust Fong. Not at all.

"Okay. I'll do it. But I get half up front. Cash. The rest on delivery."

"Fine, fine, Grogan. Just get down here ASAP. Pier 31."

"Bye," Grogan said as he was hanging up.

A half hour later, Grogan rumbled into the harbor. Fong was

standing beside an orange, forty-foot container mounted on a chassis. Grogan pulled the tractor around and backed under the chassis for the hook-up. Before doing that, though, he meant to be paid.

He hopped down and swaggered up to Fong. "Where's the money?"

Fong looked like a shorter version of Richard Loo, the Chinese-American actor who always seemed to play John Wayne's Japanese nemesis in Grade B war movies. He sneered at Grogan and shoved a manila envelope at him. "Here it is, Grogan, and the paperwork, too. Just get this box outta here."

Grogan opened the flap and counted it out. "Well, it's all here. I guess you're for real."

Fong looked around furtively. "Yeah, yeah. Just go, will you?"

Grogan held up his beefy hands. "Okay. Okay. Just relax."

Fong turned his back to clamp a numbered aluminum seal on the rear door latch. Grogan shifted to the front of the container. As Grogan grappled with the hook-up, a rumpled man with an irregular rolling gait approached him.

"Hi, Jasper, got anything today?" the man whispered.

"Hey, Wally. Long time no see."

The man wiped a grizzled chin. "How about it, Jasper?"

"Nah. Not today, Wally. This load is sealed. We won't be breaking it down, so I won't be needin' any swampers."

The man looked over at Fong and back to Grogan. "What're you pullin'?"

Grogan noticed Fong edging closer. "Toys. Say, listen, Wally, I got to be going, okay?"

There was a note of urgency in his voice. He slightly raised his eyebrows and cocked his head in Fong's direction. "If you know what I mean."

Wally took the hint. "Yeah, sure, sure, Jasper, don't worry about it. Be seein' ya."

Grogan waved as Wally pivoted away on his good leg and moved off along the wharf. Fong rushed up. "Who the hell was that?"

"Oh, just some local guy looking for work. I told him I didn't have any this trip."

Fong eyed the departing man with suspicion. "Well, just hurry it up."

Grogan finished the hook-up, raised the landing gear and climbed into the cab. He released the brakes with a metallic squeeze of compressed air and started the engine.

The moon had blackened and disappeared by the time the tractor-trailer left The Embarcadero and crawled up Broadway toward Chinatown. The base of the hill was already gripped by fog. Grogan shoved the rig into low gear and gunned the engine. His cab inclined sharply as he tried to increase speed. But the pressure on the accelerator had little effect. "Too heavy," he mumbled to himself. A creeping shroud of fog suddenly engulfed the truck. He squeezed the wheel tighter and flashed from high to low beams and back, trying to make out street signs. Grogan flashed once more and heard the frantic squeal of tires. An abrupt shudder lifted the rear of the trailer from the ground. A tinny munch of metal rebounded from the street.

Grogan spun to the side of the road to inspect the damage. He opened the door of the cab, heard the tires squeal again and caught the shadow of a bobtail truck as it disappeared into the hanging fog.

"Sonovabitch," he said, giving the other driver the finger.

He walked to the rear of the rig. His survey of the trailer revealed slight damage to the frame. But one of the container's rear doors had been sprung open by the impact. Grogan snapped the seal to check for damage. When he opened the door all the way, he was astonished to see a plywood divider immediately behind the first row of boxes. The container was loaded high and tight. But the final tier between the wooden divider and the rear doors was for show. Or was it? It dawned on him why the load had handled like a heavy. Grogan shuffled the papers on his clipboard, hunting for the bill of lading. He found it attached to a manifest and began to read.

"'7,500 pounds.' Bullshit. More like 25,000. 'Classification: Toys, plastic, NOIBN—not otherwise indexed by name.'"

Strange. No consignor, consignee or country of origin was listed. Fong had instructed him to drop the chassis and container at a toy warehouse on Sansome Street. Grogan had long suspected that Fong had been cheating him. He had been pulling heavies and was not being paid for the extra weight.

Grogan secured the doors and decided that he had better get off the fog bound road and report the hit-and-run later. He climbed into the cab, started the engine and crept through the fog to a side street. After turning around, he headed for the public scale.

Twenty minutes later, the public scale came into view. He slowed down and pulled into the drive through lane casually marked with orange cones. The weigh master waved him onto the scale and, after a moment, signaled "o.k." through the glass booth and indicated he should pull out. With the weight registered, Grogan parked the rig and walked into the enclosure to receive the weigh ticket.

The weigh master finished his reading and announced, "Looks like 23,368. What're you hauling in that thing anyway?"

"Toys."

"Must be made out of lead."

Grogan paid the fee and, clutching the ticket, rushed outside. He suspected that it was not just a weight issue, but given Fong's urgency and the plywood divider, there had to be something sinister about the cargo. He wasn't going to lose his operating authority for Fong. Grogan found a pay phone, pulled the decaying directory toward him and thumbed through it. Finding the after-hours number, he dropped two quarters in the slot and hurriedly mashed the buttons. "Gotta get a cell phone one of these days," he muttered.

"U.S. Customs," said a woman.

"Hannah Song, please."

"One moment while I transfer your call."

"Special Investigations," a man said.

"Yes. Hannah Song, please."

"I'm sorry, but she's out until late tomorrow. Can I help you with something?"

"No. Just tell her that Jasper Grogan called about a problem with a load. She'll remember who I am."

"Sure," the man said as Grogan was hanging up.

About a half hour later, Grogan was still lumbering through the narrow caverns of Chinatown, searching for his drop point. He had been confused and distracted by the colored lights, parked cars and throngs of pedestrians. At last, he located the darkened novelty shop.

Above the front door arch of its crumbling brick façade, he could barely make out the letters "T YS". The "O" had long since faded. Also on the brick, just beside a drawing of a snake, were some Chinese characters which he could not decipher. He backed the rig down a narrow alley, rolled down the short incline and made contact with the loading dock behind its adjacent two-story warehouse.

Grogan released the air pressure, set the brakes and climbed down from the cab. He hopped up onto the dock and banged on the roll-up door. No answer. After a moment, he banged again. Still no answer. Grogan decided to wait until the consignee showed up. He wanted his money and would stick around as long as it took.

An hour later, Grogan's curiosity overwhelmed him. He was determined to vent it by having a look-see at what he was carrying. Once Song called back, he would be able to fill her in.

Grogan threw the latches, opened the doors and removed the first tier. He opened one of the boxes. It was stuffed with shredded newsprint. Grogan loosened and pried away the plywood divider.

Behind it, the container was stacked floor to ceiling with cartons of uniform size. Grogan judged that there were at least two hundred.

He pulled a carton from the top row and examined it in the weak light cast by a solitary lamp over the dock door. The stylized imprint of a snake glared at him from one side of the box. He tore it open, shuffling past the packing material.

Grogan was staggered by what he took into his hands. Ivory! A delicately carved figurine. He opened a second box, then a third. More ivory figurines in different designs. "Plastic toys, my ass!"

A sudden sense of dread caught him. Grogan repacked the figurines, closed the boxes and neatly replaced them.

As he started to back out of the trailer, a small cold hand covered his mouth and snapped his head back. A knife flashed in a shaft of light. An intensely hot pain raced from one side of his throat to the other. Grogan could hear tearing vibrations in his ears. He tried to yell, but could not. The fabric of his vocal cords had been cleanly severed.

Chapter 4

Hannah Song marveled at the intricate detail of the ivory figurine she held in her hands. It was a flying horse motif from Chinese mythology. The evocative horse captured in flight was exquisite. But the carved cylinders were still her favorite pieces. They depicted scenes from ordinary Chinese life in ascending carrousels.

She returned the figurine to its place on the counsel table. The carvings were exceptionally clear, pure and spiritual. But a terrible price had been paid for such beauty. According to the report at her fingertips, organized poachers had decimated the elephant population in Kenya. Their numbers had declined 82 percent in the last twelve years alone. She knew that an estimated three to five million of the great beasts had roamed the continent of Africa in the 1930s and '40s. Now, in Africa, an elephant was being killed for its ivory about every fifteen minutes. The black rhinos in Kenya were at even greater risk of extinction and an estimated 10 percent of the population were being killed each year. Right now, her focus was on interdiction of the illicit trade in elephant ivory. To the poachers and their customers, elephants only represented a $50,000,000 a year business. To her, they were a symbol of freedom.

Song had witnessed the brutality of the poachers first hand. They had to be stopped. Somehow.

The Convention on International Trade in Endangered Species had banned trafficking in elephant ivory. But only if it was less than one hundred years old. Mammoth ivory and elephant ivory more than one hundred years old or obtained from authorized sport hunting were still legal. The problem was proving the age and source of the ivory. Quantity importers avoided the issue by smuggling ivory into the country. Customs agents had found ivory and whole tusks in crates marked "BONE MATERIAL"; "MARBLE"; "JEWELRY"; and "BEESWAX". Certain rogue nations ignored the ban and continued to feed the anxious market regardless of the impact on wildlife populations.

Naturally, art importers claimed their ivory was old elephant ivory or mammoth ivory. Fine arts dealers and their well-heeled customers were not known for environmental consciousness. They were only interested in the objects themselves.

The flying horse, along with other carvings, had been seized by customs agents from an intermodal container imported by Shih Jen. He and his customer, Benson Wicklow, a Nob Hill art dealer, had been charged with violations of federal import laws, the African Elephant Conservation Statute and the Endangered Species Act. This preliminary hearing, now in recess, would determine the sufficiency of the evidence and whether the matter should be bound over for trial. It was standard procedure. Song had been called as a witness. She had already testified about the seizure. There was no question that the defendants were guilty. Proving it was another matter altogether.

The buzzer under the court clerk's desk sounded, drowning out the final words of a spectator's conversation with the U.S. Marshal. Recess was over. The court clerk jumped to her feet and commanded, "All rise."

Song exchanged anxious glances with Victoria Moy, the Deputy U.S. Attorney, and carefully adjusted the exhibit tag attached to the horse so that it could be read easily. Moy was twenty-eight and had recently passed the California bar exam. This was her first solo case representing the government. Previously, she had only conducted research and carried the briefcase for the attorney in the "first chair." Tall and large-boned with coarse features, Moy had accepted Song's teasing with good cheer. Song had claimed that her own lithe figure had been derived from the aristocratic origins of her family. Moy's ancestors had all been peasants.

Moy and Song stood up together. As they did, the defendants and their nattily clad attorney crawled to their feet. Song took special note of defense counsel's alligator shoes. All faced the bench.

The heavy wooden chamber door behind the bench creaked open. A robed figure ascended the steps to the platform and stood perfectly straight behind the high-backed chair. The clerk waited for a moment, then intoned most deliberately. "Facing the flag of our country and recognizing the principles for which it stands, the Court of the Honorable Cramer Mallison, United States District Court for the Northern District of California, is now in session."

Without comment, the Honorable Cramer Mallison took the bench. Mallison had been on the bench for thirty years. He had taken his appointment for life seriously. A strictly-by-the-book type, Mallison had been repeatedly overlooked for elevation to the Court of Appeals simply because he was apolitical. In short, he didn't believe in doing anyone any favors.

"Be seated," he said.

Mallison waited for the slap of chairs and shuffling to diminish.

"The United States vs. Shih Jen," intoned the clerk.

The imperious Mallison grabbed the stack of documents placed before him. Moy looked tense. The judge thumbed through the files and frowned. "The Court has thoroughly weighed the evidence presented as well as the motion of the defense to dismiss the Government's motion for a continuance."

Mallison coughed loudly before proceeding. "The Court takes judicial notice that under present law, elephant ivory that is more than one hundred years old, and mammoth ivory, may be legally imported. Further, the Court finds that the Government has, to date, failed to introduce sufficient evidence to refute the testimony of Shih Jen, and the affidavit of one Howard Ju of Singapore, that the ivory seized by Customs was, in fact, mammoth ivory from Siberia. The government of Malaysia has certified the legality of the source."

The defendants' attorney smirked at Moy. Song shot him a glare, forcing him to avert his eyes. Shih Jen smiled, revealing bad teeth. Benson Wicklow breathed a sigh of relief. Song desperately wanted to jump out of her seat and choke them. But Mallison was not finished. "However, due to the seriousness of this issue, the Court is also disposed to grant the Government a short continuance of two weeks to produce further evidence, if it can. Barring such evidence, the Court's order will be to dismiss this case."

Mallison dropped the file sharply and stood. Everyone in the room rose with him. The courtroom was quiet until the chamber door slammed behind the judge. A digital clock on the clerk's desk glowed 2:44 p.m. Moy absently shuffled her files and placed them in an open briefcase. The defense attorney stuck out his hand in a snake-like manner. "Hey, until next time."

Moy ignored him. He withdrew his hand with a feigned hurt look. He received no reaction, so he waved his hand in dismissal. "Forget it. You're going to lose and lose big time."

The defense attorney walked briskly to the leather wrapped doors with his clients. Looking bored and impatient, the U.S. Marshal waited with his keys already in the lock. They could hear the derisive laughter of the defense attorney and his clients in the hallway.

"C'mon, Vickie, let's grab a late lunch. I'll buy." Song grabbed Moy's briefcase and tugged at her sleeve, pulling her toward the door.

When they reached the high-speed elevator, the defense attorney stood blocking the doors. He carried a hand-tooled briefcase that looked like a saddlebag. His cellular phone hung at the ready.

Smiling sweetly, his eyes dropped to Song's breasts. She felt immediate icy revulsion.

"Going down?" he smirked.

"Not with you," Song shot back.

The defense attorney disappeared as the doors mercifully folded together.

Song and Moy exited the courthouse and walked towards the Powell Street Grill.

"A dismissal would be disastrous," said Song. "We've got to find a way to prove that the ivory streaming into this country is illegal."

Moy looked pensive. "Hannah, I have an idea that might help."

"What is it?" Song asked.

"I'm not certain yet. But I remember reading about a new forensics technique in a wildlife memo. I'll check it out and let you know."

They arrived at the restaurant and were ushered into the bar to wait for a table. Song used a pay phone in an alcove by the bar to call her office for messages. She'd flown in from Kenya the night before and hadn't had time to stop by headquarters. Song scribbled her messages in a small spiral notebook and returned to the bar. Moy had ordered white wine for them. She was intensely watching the television above the bartender's head. Madonna's "Material Girl" on the sound system was drowning out the newscast. Song started to hum along then noticed Moy's concentration on the set. The scene of a truck cab being lifted out of the bay by a crane appeared on the screen.

"What's so interesting?" Song asked.

"Shhh. Can you turn it up?" Moy asked the bartender, motioning toward the T.V.

A mosaic of camera shots filled the screen. The sound blared on. "The trucker, by the name of Jasper Grogan, was found in the cab of his truck here in the harbor," the announcer's voice said.

There was a close-up shot of the isolated Kenworth in the parking lot surrounded by yellow tape. "His throat had been slashed by an unknown assailant," continued the announcer. "The police agencies have no leads as to who committed this crime, or why, and they are requesting help from the public." There was a tight shot of the reporter. "From San Francisco Harbor, this is Daren Bell for Newsday 8."

Song stared at the message in her book. She covered her mouth in disbelief, having just remembered who Jasper Grogan was.

The year before, Song had saved him from doing hard time by clearing him in a drug smuggling probe. A cache of narcotics had been found on a single pallet in the nose of the trailer he had been pulling. Her thorough investigation had absolved Grogan of any involvement. Grogan had tried to call her. Now he was dead.

"He tried to call me last night," Song said.

"Who did?"

"Jasper Grogan. The dead guy."

"What for?"

"That's what I need to find out."

Song clutched her purse and stood. "Vickie, I'm sorry, I have to go now. I have to run this down. I'll call you later."

"Okay," Moy said.

Song paid the tab and marched out of the bar.

Chapter 5

The halo of the late afternoon sun circled San Francisco Harbor. Temperate winds blew offshore from the bay, signaling the change of seasons. Young clouds rose from the water in a mass of glory and rubbed against the mountains. Gentle waves lapped against the rust-stained docks. A lone gull cried as it wheeled overhead in a zealous search for sustenance.

Song glanced at her watch and wrote, "Harbor. 4:13 p.m." in her log book. She had checked in at the office and driven straight to the harbor. Her superiors had authorized a preliminary investigation since the overnight call to Customs had been within two hours of the fixed time of Grogan's death.

She stretched a supple leg from her Dodge Charger and drew to her full height. Buffed a deep blue, the car's chrome trim shone in the fading light. It was her pride and joy. The breeze tossed her shoulder-length hair as she took a deep breath of salt air and scanned her surroundings. In a remote corner of the wharf rested a yellow Kenworth tractor. It was cordoned off as if on display at a trade show. Two police cars were parked at odd angles nearby, both of the same make, but one was unmarked. A police photographer moved around the cab like an insect trying to corral a catch, snapping pictures of anything and everything. A stocky, but distinguished-looking, figure of a man in plain clothes stood off to one side, studying the scene from a distance. Song shut the car door and strolled across the landing toward him, spiral notebook in hand. As Song approached from the east, she swung her arms with an easy athletic grace. The man glanced at Song, turned away, looked again and immediately pivoted to face her. A double-take. He had a confident, warm and ready smile. Something she did not encounter often in law enforcement. Song noticed the SFPD shield clipped to his belt.

"Jeez, are you another cub reporter?" he asked.

"No. Mind if I have a look?"

He adopted a mock haughty stance. "And just who might you be?"

"My name is Song. Hannah Song. U.S. Customs," she said, flashing her badge.

The man stuck out a ham-sized hand. "Rand Brooker , Inspector, SFPD. Pleased to meet you."

"My pleasure," she said, extending her own.

As they shook, Song noticed the captivated look in his eyes. At least he had not tried to overpower her with a crushing grip as some he-men were prone to do.

Brooker gestured at the truck's cab. "Sure. Go ahead. The rig's already been dusted for prints and the photographer is about finished."

Sea water still dripped from the frame and engine compartment. He followed her toward the partially open driver's side door. "Customs, huh? What's your interest in this homicide?"

"I'm not sure just yet. All I know is that Jasper Grogan tried to call me before he died."

"About what?"

"Something about a problem with a load."

"Looks like he had a helluva problem." Brooker brushed the door all the way open. Song grasped the cab rundle, wedged her heel into the bottom step rung and climbed into the tractor. She deftly tucked her skirt as she scaled the ladder like some delicate spider.

She slid into the air suspension seat and tested the wheel. Song peered out through the windshield half-expecting to see something overlooked. The cab reeked of stale tobacco smoke. Its vinyl trimmed interior was cracked and split in places, revealing yellowed sponge rubber. The gauges, dials, lights and switches reminded her of an airliner cockpit. She snapped open Grogan's CD case, revealing Hank Williams, Jr.'s Greatest Hits.

Brooker remained on the ground looking up at her. "Where do you know this Grogan from?"

Song leaned out toward him. "Last year he was arrested on suspicion of smuggling drugs. My investigation confirmed his innocence."

"Yeah. I picked up that arrest on his rap sheet. You sure he was innocent?"

Song nodded forcefully. "Positive."

Brooker looked out over the bay and back at her. "Know of any reason why somebody would want to do him?" Song thought for a moment. "No. It just doesn't make any sense."

Brooker grimaced. "I'll say. Whoever it was meant business. He cut this poor guy from ear to ear."

Song winced and resumed her search. She checked above the visors, looked in the door pockets and then adjusted the seat and looked under it.

"Do you know what he was carrying or who he might have been hauling for?" she asked.

"No idea," Brooker said.

"Any leads?"

"Not a one," Brooker said. "Some divers working on a pipeline ninety feet down spotted him this morning floating in the cab. I hear it was pretty gruesome."

"Yeah. I can only imagine."

Song ran her petite fingers along the underside edge of the seat. She caught an upholstery staple in her finger. "Ouch," she said, squeezing a drop of blood from the tip.

"Whatsamatter?"

"Nothing. Just poor workmanship." She stuck the finger in her mouth and sucked it.

"Do you know anything more about the victim?" Brooker asked.

"Only that he was an independent owner-operator. I think he usually hung out at a truck stop down on 101 until he found a broker with a profitable load," Song offered.

"Well, he crossed paths with the wrong people somewhere." Brooker held the door open.

"Listen, we've been all over this cab's interior. You're not gonna find nothin. Why don't you come down and we'll try to make some sense out of this."

Before she could reply, Brooker was summoned to his car by a uniformed officer. Song could hear him heatedly arguing with someone over the radio. Something about priorities. Just like her office. She shrugged with exasperation. Song glanced around the interior. What had she missed?

Song was about to give up when she eased her fingers into the crevice between the console and the passenger seat. They touched something soggy and pulpy. Wet paper. She caught a corner with the tips of her nails and gently coaxed it from the fissure. She laid it on the console and gingerly unfolded it. Brooker stormed up to the door. "Did you find something?"

"Uh huh. This." She handed the paper down to him. It was a leaf torn from an old Thomas Brothers map book. The page for Chinatown.

Brooker held it close to his face and studied it. "Well I'll be…"

"What?" she asked.

He laughed. "A little more thorough next time. I owe you one."

Song climbed down while kept analyzing the page. Brooker looked up.

"Chinatown drop, maybe? " He looked at the truck cab. Where'd you find it?"

She had a demure look. "Wedged between the console and seat."

"Could've floated under there or been there a long time," he said. "Who knows?" Brooker spread it on the hood of the patrol car to dry out. "What do you suppose he could have been pulling into Chinatown?"

Song shrugged, and bit her lip in concentration.

"Could it have been a load of produce or meat?" Brooker offered.

"No. That wasn't his style," Song said firmly. "He was strictly a dry freight hauler."

She looked through him. "No. I'd have to rule Chinatown out. He couldn't make any money on a drop or pull that close. He liked to be paid time and mileage...or..."

"Or what?"

"Or by the weight."

Brooker nodded approvingly. "Sounds right to me. Still, it's damn funny. My instincts are working overtime."

"I know what you mean. Too bad the map hasn't been marked."

"Yeah. That would be too easy. But that's what we're paid for."

A uniformed sergeant walked over to summon him again. Brooker looked irritated. "Will you excuse me, Ms. Song? Please?"

"Certainly." Song rolled a chunk of gravel under her shoe. She rocked on her heels with her arms clasped behind her back. She could hear talking excitedly to the radio dispatcher. He seemed more agitated than before. He returned a moment later and loosened his collar. "That was an old friend of mine," he said sarcastically.

Song said nothing, but looked at him expectantly.

"Captain wants me to clock in on another homicide over in Golden Gate Park. Boy, I love this job," he said, shaking his head. "I'm a popular guy anymore."

Song winked. "I can see that."

Brooker smiled wistfully and refolded the map. He tucked it into a plastic evidence pouch and noted the date, time and location on the adhesive tag. Brooker pressed it against the bag and slipped it into his pocket. He gave it a soft pat.

"I have to take off now." Brooker pressed his card into her hand. He looked up at the cab, turned and saluted Song. "It's all yours. Call me if you find anything else. Knock yourself out."

"Okay," Song said, as turned to go. She walked with him to the unmarked car. His driver pushed the passenger side door open. hung on it. "Oh, say. One more thing. You might want to check with the harbormaster."

"Thanks, I'll do that."

Brooker hopped into the car and opened the glove compartment. He pulled out a bottle of Maalox, unscrewed the cap and took a long shot. "Peptic ulcer," he explained. "Let's grab a pizza on the way," he told the driver. Brooker gave Song a boyish look. "You've been very helpful. I hope to see you again."

Song toyed with her earring. "You will."

The driver looked impatient. Song shut the door. Brooker waved goodbye through the glass. She waved back and watched as the cruiser fishtailed through the gravel parking lot toward the exit.

Song continued searching until well after dark, but found nothing else. Once she had looked up and detected the streaking movement of a car beside the adjacent cannery. She had looked again. There had been nothing there. Still, all the way home she kept checking her rearview mirror.

Chapter 6

Decorative banners hung along the streets flapped in the gentle breeze bringing dawn to Chinatown. Dots of pollen carried from distant trees drifted and dispersed through the square. Produce trucks had arrived from the wholesale mart to discharge crates of exotic vegetables at the myriad shops and restaurants. Merchants hurried and struggled with hoses to spray debris from the sidewalks in preparation for the day's trade.

On Sansome Street, beside a popular restaurant, stood an unremarkable novelty store. It was rarely open. Passersby often stopped and peered in the window at all hours of the day for signs of activity. The window displays were never changed. Nobody knew who the proprietor was. He was never in. The business license had been issued to a corporation, which was, in turn, owned by another corporation. No daytime deliveries were made to the warehouse behind the store. Its roll up doors were never left open.

Beneath the novelty shop rested a cramped basement storeroom. Sunlight sifted down into it through a single, rectangular window. It was so coated with grime that vision in or out was obscured. The pungent smells of baking glazed duck and cooking pig's knuckles permeated the air within the cellar. Muffled voices and clanging kitchen pots could be heard through the bare lath walls.

Within the room, the members of a guarded assembly sat before a low wooden table, murmuring quietly to each other. Art Fong sat alone on the perimeter. Seated behind the table in meditative repose was a craggy-faced man with wisps of grey beard suspended from his chin. He was wearing a cowl, which partially veiled his eyes. An iron cauldron the size of a mixing bowl rested on the table to his right. It held arcane implements, including needles, inks and dyes. To his left sat a ceramic bowl filled with blood. On its side was the raised impression of a serpent with ruby eyes.

The single narrow door creaked open, then slammed against the wall. Cheng Lao Wah, also known as "Fat Wah," stormed into the room, followed by two severe-looking bodyguards. Wah was a huge, brooding man with a cruel, sardonic air. He carried a red burlap bag, held well away from his body. Wah scowled at everyone in the room. No greetings would be spoken. The ceremony would begin now. It was the conclusion of a two-day initiation rite.

Darwin Lau, the figure in the cowl, drew back the hood, opened his eyes and stood. He touched the bowl with his fingertips, looked out over the group and nodded. A shirtless initiate stepped forward as Lau extended his hands over the bowl, palms down, and passed them from rim to rim. He whispered mystical incantations and snapped his jaws three times in supplication. Lau raised his eyes, lifted the bowl and handed it to the initiate, who quickly gulped its contents. The initiate reeled for a moment before replacing the bowl on the table. He did not wipe his mouth, but lowered his head and extended his wiry arms.

The other celebrants extended hairless forearms, all marked with blue and red tattoos. Their tattoos depicted vertically stacked Chinese characters. Each permutation was unique, except for one identical, ominous symbol: a striking serpent.

Beads of sweat formed on the initiate's forehead as Lau reached for one of his arms and stretched it across the table. Very deliberately Lau selected a chromium steel needle and dipped it into a vial of blue dye. He deftly etched a character into the man's arm, repeatedly returning to the jar for more color. Lau added red

imprints at strategic points in the design and swabbed away glob-
ules of blood with a swatch of ceremonial linen. Lau drew back
from time to time to study his work. He imprinted each ideogram
in turn, with measured skill and purpose. The initiate closed his
eyes and grimaced with the anticipation of each deep prick.

Last, Lau created the image of the snake. It came to life slowly.
Each turn of its tail was added with an expert flourish. Wah stood
off to one side with his bodyguards. They watched impassively as
Lau strained with the final puncture. With a delicate swipe of
cloth, the serpent was finished. It was like all the others.

After returning the implements to the cauldron, Lau clasped
the shaking hands of the initiate in his own. The ceremony was
over. Perspiration streamed down the length of the initiate's torso.
Now visibly relieved, he took his place with the others.

Lau wiped the ceramic bowl clean and sat down. He glanced
knowingly at Wah and dipped his head. The immense man twisted
the burlap bag in full view of the audience. It twitched violently.
Wah looked directly at Fong with a perverse grin. Fong trembled
as Wah stepped forward and started to untie the sack. His chilling
eyes moved from face to face. "There is some other business we
must attend to," Wah said matter-of-factly.

He continued untying the bag. "One of our group has betrayed
us by his stupidity."

Each man looked at his neighbor. More than a few gulped.
Several shivered with fright. Wah continued to deliberately toy
with the string. "This individual sought to make a profit at our
expense."

Wah dropped the length of twine to the floor. He looked at
each man again. Those closest to him began to shake. "As a result,
one of our more lucrative enterprises has been placed in jeopardy."

There was a long silence. When Wah was satisfied with the
effect, he shouted, "It is our policy not to tolerate treachery or
self-dealing!"

Wah stepped back and looked fiercely at Lau. The others relaxed slightly. "The traitor who did that has made a fatal miscalculation." He whirled with blinding speed and pointed directly at Fong. "That traitor is you!"

On perfect cue, the two bodyguards seized Fong and dragged him away from the group. One of them pulled the writhing man by his hair and shoved him down on his knees. The other kicked him in the face, dislocating his jaw. Fong looked from face to face with stark terror in his eyes. He tried in vain to wrest free.

They tied him down with his hands and arms twisted tightly beneath his back. Fong squirmed from side to side and tried to scoot away from the invisible approaching horror. Wah bided his time, savoring the agony.

The others drew back as far as possible. With reverent deliberation, Wah shook the sack. The life within leaped and wrenched in the bag, distending it. He yanked it open, but did not look inside. Wah gauged the reaction of the others before tossing the bag into the air with a flash of his hand. With a swift following movement, he grasped the bottom, flipped it over and dumped the creature beside Fong's anguished face.

Fong's gaping maw screamed as the snake uncoiled and buried its fangs into his writhing head, again and again. Eyes wild, the hapless Fong lay twitching and convulsing for several seconds, until his heart stopped. His work finished, the snake lay still for a moment before moving off to a dark corner of the room.

Wah tracked the serpent and recovered him with a flashing swipe of his hand. He held the twisting snake at bay, then gingerly returned it to the sack held by a bodyguard. Wah tied the top securely and flauntingly placed the bag on the table near Lau. He glared at Lau with barely subdued loathing. "That will keep your man from making any more mistakes."

"But..." Lau started to meekly protest, but Wah cut him off.

"Why did you permit that imbecile to deviate from the planned arrangements?"

Wah moved closer. Lau edged away from the table, watching the bag from the corner of his eye. "We had to act quickly. Our regular drayman met with an accident. This customs broker…"

Wah jabbed a fist within a speck of Lau's nose. "Customs brokers are a dime a dozen. You have jeopardized everything with stupidity. First, your selection of this idiot, then your failure to dispose of that trucker's body so it would not be found quickly."

"But the broker was one of us and…" Wah's hand flared out and seized Lau by the throat. He twisted the collar of Lau's cloak tightly around his neck. Lau gasped, wheezed and dug his fingernails into Wah's hand. He turned purple before Wah released his grip.

He collapsed, gasping for air and massaging his windpipe. Wah pointed an accusatory finger at him. "Customs officials are already snooping around. Find out what the authorities may have learned. You are to then eliminate any threat to our organization." Wah shook his finger in rage. "Do you understand?"

Lau struggled to his knees and nodded vigorously. "Yes," he rasped. "Please extend my profound apologies to our great leader."

The others maintained a respectful distance. Wah gave them a long, contemptuous look, clutched the sack and marched to the door, trailed by his bodyguards. He stepped over Fong's body, spun around and again pointed his finger at the cowering Lau. "Just be certain that you do not permit it to happen again."

Chapter 7

After breakfast and a quick call to the harbormaster, Song showered, brushed her hair and applied minuscule touches of makeup. She didn't use or need mascara. Her lashes were already long, with a soft upward arc. She looked at herself in the mirror, but without approval. Song stared in disbelief at the tiny crow's feet around her eyes. They had not been there yesterday. She rubbed at them and tried different expressions to make them disappear. It couldn't be. She was only thirty-one years old. A faded flower. Alone, and no immediate prospects. Song had always avoided entanglements, but didn't know why. She didn't like thinking about it.

She shoved her shades on in disgust, grabbed her purse and headed for the parking garage of her condominium in Telegraph Landing. She slipped into her Charger and allowed the engine to warm up sufficiently before revving it. With a light touch on the stick, she coaxed it into reverse, backed out and made the short throw into drive. Still dwelling on the crow's feet, she rolled slowly to the exit, then punched it with a screech into the boulevard traffic.

Eight blocks later, Song glided into a "Reserved" slot at the Embarcadero office complex. She twisted out in time to see a new Lincoln with an Asian driver make the corner. He drove slowly past her and glared in a menacing manner. Song did not recognize him, but he had the look of a local hood. She kept walking and the Lincoln was soon out of sight.

After a careful look around, she crossed the lot and came to the harbormaster's module. As Song started to climb the stairs, she heard forceful mumbling coming from a niche beneath the staircase. Someone was having an animated argument with himself. Probably just a wharf rat, she thought. Song decided to ignore the mumbler until she heard the slurred words, "Poor Jasper."

Song swiftly rounded the base of the stairwell and saw a morose, disheveled man slumped in the corner. His long grey hair was stringy and matted. He had at least a week's growth of beard. The man's skin was tanned with a baked in grime. An aura of vigorous and competing odors emanated from his body. He stank ten feet away.

The man wore an ancient tattered work shirt and dingy khaki pants. His socks were mismatched. He sported scuffed oxfords, without laces. One of his hands jealously guarded a bottle of cheap wine. The other was folded at an odd angle across his lap. He looked up and noticed Song staring at him. He raised the bottle over his head in an exaggerated gesture."Ish wine and dine for $2.59. Have some."

"No, thank you," said Song, stepping back a foot.

He held the bottle toward her and shook it. "C'mon, have a lil' red heaven," he implored.

"No," she said sternly. "But I would like some information."

"Wha'? You wan' information? Wha' kind of information?"

Song moved two feet closer. "You mentioned someone named Jasper."

The man drew back the bottle. "Yeah. Wha' 'bout it?"

"Jasper who?"

At first he looked puzzled. Then the man slapped his forehead sharply. "Grogan. Thash it, Jasper Grogan."

"Where did you know Jasper from?"

The man wiped his eyes. "Me and Wally was his swampers. You know, help load and unload the truck."

She nodded knowingly, as the man put the bottle down. "He was my goo' friend. Now he's dead. Kilt. Someone kilt him." The man broke into tears and scuffed the heels of his shoes on the concrete. "Why? Why?"

He buried his face in his hands and sobbed. She waited until he had finished. "What's your name?" she asked in a motherly tone.

The man looked like he was striving to remember his own name. "Bill," he said at last.

Song hunched down. "Bill what?"

He acted slightly irritated. "Just Bill. Well, Crazy Bill, on the street."

"Where's this Wally you mentioned?"

"I don't know. I haven't saw him since last night." His face was streaked by tears. "Hell, I'm a Iraq war veteran, man. So're Wally and Jasper." He struggled to unbutton his shirt. "Here, look at these scars, man."

Song extended a soothing hand. "That's okay, Bill. I believe you."

At the sound of her voice, he quit tussling with the buttons.

"Listen, Bill. This is important." Song searched for the right words. "Jasper tried to call me the other night. I just don't know why. I'm trying to find out who killed him. But I need your help, okay?"

Bill shook his head combatively. "But how? How can I possibly help? I don' know who kilt him."

Song framed her question carefully. "Do you know what he was hauling that night or who he might have been pulling for?"

Bill looked beyond her as if in a deep trance. After a long pause, he wobbled his head from side to side. "No. No. I can't be pacific."

"You don't have to be specific," Song reassured.

He looked away.

"You don't have to be specific," she repeated.

His smudged face brightened. "Wait a secon'. Toys! Thash it! Jasper told Wally he had a load of toys. He didn' need no swampers 'cause they were sealed up."

"Anything else?"

"No. Thash all. I jus' don' remember no more." His voice trailed off as he started to pass out. He opened his mouth wide and snored with relish. Song tucked a twenty into his shirt pocket and patted his shoulder. "I don't think you're so crazy, Bill."

She walked upstairs and entered the harbor control center. She opened her badge case for the receptionist as she approached her desk. "Hi, I'm Hannah Song from Customs. I called about an hour and a half ago."

Song had interrupted the receptionist's intimate phone conversation. She covered the mouthpiece and barely looked at Song's identification. "Yeah, sure. Go down the hall to Room 204. That's our records section."

"I know. I've been there before. Thanks for your help."

She signed in at the records desk and filled out a file request form for cargo manifests, vessel movement reports and harbor activity summaries for the past two weeks. The records clerk gave her a look of officious disapproval and went into the file index room, clutching the request. The woman returned half an hour later with an eighteen inch stack of documents and slammed them on the counter.

Song gave her an "I'm sorry" smile and set to work organizing the files for her search. After two hours, the clerk took pity on Song and brought her a cup of coffee.

Four hours into the search, and bleary-eyed, Song found what she was looking for. The merchant vessel *Ganbei* had entered the port two days earlier, near dusk and during a shift change. The freighter had discharged its cargo of toys and general commodities and left the port empty. The ship was of Liberian registry, but it was based in Taipei. She stamped her foot when she read that it had sailed for home just the day before.

There was something else. The toys had been shipped from the Dockside Export Trading Company, Taiwan. Her eyes were drawn to one toy manifest in particular. Under "Country of Origin" it was marked "Unknown."

Song asked to use the phone. Within an hour, she had traced the consignee and found that it was a fictitious business. The address was nothing more than a mail drop in the South of Market area.

As she was filling out the praecipe for copies, Song partially overheard a conversation between the supervisor and the records clerk. The man had been flirting with the clerk on and off all day. It was a wonder anything at all was accomplished in the office.

"Excuse me," said Song.

The supervisor turned to face her with a put upon look. "Yes?"

"Did you say something about a body being found in the harbor?"

He raised his eyebrows slightly, but decided to answer. "Yeah, sure did. Second one this week. Fishing boat found a transient floating face down off Pier 9. Name was a...let me look." The supervisor pulled a piece of note paper from the pocket of his short-sleeved shirt. "Yeah. Wineman. Wally Wineman."

Song barely concealed her surprise.

He swallowed hard. "Damndest thing I ever saw. Both guys, throats slashed open like pumpkins."

The supervisor rubbed his own throat and resumed flirting with the clerk. Song elected to leave before he got too familiar with her.

She walked outside, grabbed her cell phone and tapped Brooker's number on the scroll down in her contacts. After she had called to relay the information, Song hopped into her car and drove home.

Chapter 8

The lights of the shipyards and petrochemical plants twinkled along the banks of the Shimonoseki Strait. Situated at the western entrance to Japan's Inland Sea, or *Seto Naikai*, it anchored one end of an elongated conveyor belt stretching to Osaka. The *Seto Naikai* bustled with the ebb and flow of global trade. A sea within straits, it was a natural highway 300 miles long. Within its cradle, Buddhism had first taken root in Japan. Until the Middle Ages, bands of pirates had terrorized its shores. Now, vessels bearing the commerce of the world steamed through an artery bounded by a teeming megalopolis.

Three freighters were moored in the languid waters of the strait. Soon, a fourth would join them. Its cargo would be transloaded in darkness to lighters bound for Hiroshima, Kobe and Osaka. Crashi Mitoma had come to Shimonoseki to confirm the necessary arrangements. He also had certain business of his own to attend to.

Mitoma strolled through the fish market well before dawn, side stepping a battalion of flopping mackerel. The market hung on the lip of a concrete dock. It was shadowed by corrugated tin shacks crowded among tenements with prefabricated walls and blue tile roofs. Faded canvas awnings stretched between bamboo poles shielded the main walkway. He breathed deeply. The redolence of ancient catches mingled with the scents of brine and perspiration.

Boats just returned from distant waters bumped in the lingering darkness. Octopus, yellowtail, squid, eel and vermilion ribbons of tuna waited in wooden crates crammed with melting ice. Mitoma politely refused a sea bream thrust at him by an excited vendor.

Officious auctioneers, trailed by knowledgeable buyers, shifted from one crate to the next. Bidding was accomplished by touching hands beneath the auctioneer's dangling sleeves. Purchased consignments were quickly loaded into idling vans. Mitoma passed the pachinko parlor at the market's perimeter and skidded on a forgotten slice of squid. He swore to himself and furtively glanced around before pivoting into a narrow alley.

When he was certain that he had not been followed, Mitoma approached a wooden door painted with the rays of the rising sun. He banged on the door once, waited a prescribed interval and banged again. The door opened and Mitoma was welcomed by a slight, toothless man wearing a wool cardigan and fisherman's overalls dangling from one shoulder.

Mitoma was ushered into a windowless anteroom. The host excused himself and closed the door behind him. Three ships' masters were seated at a low table, sipping green tea. Animated greetings were exchanged as Mitoma joined them. He produced a bulging envelope for each captain, containing currency and falsified customs documents. Mitoma next unfolded a detailed chart of the *Seto Naikai*. Three positions on the map were marked in red. "These are your landing points. Memorize them," he instructed.

A half hour later, Mitoma had left the flat alone and returned to his *ryokan*. He had reserved a spacious room with eyes on the sea. Throughout the day, he waited.

By sunset, the last fishing boat had straggled in. Mitoma was growing impatient. He had grown weary of television reruns and kept glancing at his watch as if that would help somehow. The abrupt knock on the door startled him. Mitoma drew the drapes closed before answering it.

He opened the door for a soaking wet man with close-cropped

hair and over sized hands. They did not bow or offer one another the customary courtesies.

"What kept you?" Mitoma asked.

"I ran into rough seas northwest of Masuda and took on water. I'm lucky to be here at all."

Mitoma studied the rugged face of Junji Tsuchiyama. Intense, coal black eyes glared from sunken sockets. The veins in his temples bulged from taught, flushed skin anchored to the skull by grotesque ears. His sparse mustache failed to conceal the specter of a cruel mouth. Mitoma hated him and did not trust him. Still, business was business.

"Never mind," Mitoma said at last. "What news do you bring from Hokkaido?"

Tsuchiyama did not respond but brushed past Mitoma to a serving cart. He filled a sake cup and gulped the contents. He filled the cup again and flopped on the couch, giving Mitoma a defiant look. "My people are ready," he said. "We just need to negotiate the price."

"The price has already been negotiated!" Mitoma screamed.

Tsuchiyama shook his head. "Was negotiated."

"What is this, a double-cross?"

"No. Call it our sudden recognition of market forces and risks." Tsuchiyama paused before continuing. "That and the fact my people are the best carvers in the world."

"Damn you and your Ainu," Mitoma fumed. "I won't submit to this extortion."

Tsuchiyama chuckled and reached into the side pocket of his tattered pea coat. He withdrew a bundled object and tossed it to Mitoma. "There. Maybe that will convince you," he said with a softened tone.

Mitoma bristled with fury. He glared at Tsuchiyama and vowed within to avenge this insult. Returning to the business at hand, he strode quietly to a table, sat and unwrapped the weighty object.

Mitoma drew back and stifled the gasp rising in his throat. Before him was an ivory motif depicting a procession of a family of elephants. The massive African bull in the lead stretched his serpentine trunk out to its full length. Mitoma could almost count every wrinkle of the 50,000 muscles needed to operate it. The mother followed a pace behind, her head cocked warily toward the infant bumping close against her flank. Mitoma was most astounded by the detail of the baby's face. With its half-closed eyes and a mouth seemingly fixed in a crescent smile, it bespoke death-less serenity and the freedom of the wild. The creatures didn't just look realistic. They were alive.

Perhaps Tsuchiyama was right after all. The Ainu of Hokkaido were world renowned as highly skilled woodcarvers. It appeared to Mitoma that they had now mastered ivory as well. He had never seen anything to compare with this. Mitoma had no doubt that their carvings, particularly the favored *netsuke* and *hanko*, would establish the market model for years to come. Such savory pieces could command double the going rate. Mitoma would deal with Tsuchiyama's treachery later, from a position of strength.

Now conciliatory, Mitoma gestured for Tsuchiyama to join him at the table. He tried to maintain a poker face, even as Tsuchiyama smirked with contempt. "I thought you'd see it my way."

"Let's talk business," said Mitoma abruptly. "What are your demands?"

"Simple," Tsuchiyama said. "Double for each piece."

Mitoma fought to restrain himself. "That's not feasible. I have carriers, customs officials, brokers and politicians to buy. You must be more realistic."

Tsuchiyama glowered, but did not respond. Mitoma appealed to reason. "We need each other. I have the supply and distribution network in place and you have the production capabilities."

Mitoma looked deep into the savage eyes of his adversary. They were oddly disconcerting in the bony face. Yet, it was Tsuchiyama's calm arrogance that kindled his ire. He had not been moved. Mitoma tried the nationalistic approach. "We can rid ourselves of the accursed *gaijin*." He could say the word for "foreigners" with thirty different nuances of contempt.

He saw a flash of recognition in Tsuchiyama's eyes. "Our destiny will be in our own hands," Mitoma quickly added.

Tsuchiyama reached for the carving and pretended to examine it in detail. He looked up at Mitoma. "What are you willing to do?"

Mitoma replied without hesitation. "An additional 25 percent for each piece."

Tsuchiyama returned the carving to the table and appeared to contemplate the offer. "Thirty-five percent," he said at last.

Mitoma knew he could make an unimaginable profit even at that rate, with little or no additional effort. He was anxious to inaugurate his business coup. Mitoma rose and bowed to Tsuchi-yama. "Done."

Tsuchiyama climbed to his feet and returned the bow. "Good." He did not engage in pleasantries. "I must be going now."

"Return to Hakodate and await my instructions," said Mitoma. "You'll be hearing from me within the week."

Tsuchiyama nodded his consent and, as he reached the door, turned and looked toward the figurine on the table. He smiled wryly, spun and left the room.

Mitoma waited a few moments and bolted the door. He walked to the picture window and pulled back the drapes. A freighter was steaming into the strait from the Sea of Japan. Right on time.

Although his relationship with Au had been profitable, he did not like depending upon him. Sooner or later, Au's protracted system would be exposed. Mitoma would not rely so completely upon the ponderous ocean freighters and the carvers always beyond his reach. He would gradually supplant Au's operation using a vastly more effectual air freight system with immediate delivery direct to Hokkaido.

The *netsuke* and *hanko* would bedazzle the local market, while the finished figurines would fan out to the world from Tokyo's Narita Airport. Poachers and smugglers had no home and would serve the highest bidder. Au's foray into the ivory trade would be overcome by stealth and Japanese efficiency.

Mitoma was aware that, not far away, Kubla Khan's Mongol invading forces had been destroyed by a roaring typhoon. The "divine wind." He watched for a long while as the shining waters of the strait merged with the black, open sea. The more things change, the more they remain the same, he thought.

Chapter 9

Retreating clouds disgorged a bright moon as the C-130 Hercules transport climbed relentlessly through the heavens. Streaming sparks from shooting stars sprinkled the edges of the tranquil night sky. The turbo prop engines of the massive plane droned with a numbing whine. Weede stood staring vacantly out the miniature cabin window. All in all, he would have preferred a moonless night for the jump. Still, with the planned high-altitude, low opening drop, he had an excellent chance of avoiding detection.

The jumpmaster brushed up beside him, cupped his hand and yelled into Weede's ear. "We're at 25,000 feet! Time to depressurize! Better get your oxygen mask hooked up." Weede motioned "o.k.," and dropped down onto the metal bench seat. He fumbled with the mask and adjusted the straps, clamping it in place over his mouth and nostrils. Weede turned the inlet valve and gestured to the jumpmaster that he was receiving oxygen.

The jumpmaster plugged in his headset to converse with the cockpit crew. He walked to a bulkhead panel and flipped back a metal cover protecting a lighted red button. The jumpmaster looked back at Weede and pressed it solidly with the palm of his hand. With a high-pitched whir, the tail ramp of the C-130 dropped open and locked at a forty-five-degree angle. Rushing air roared through the cabin as the jumpmaster signaled Weede to get ready.

Weede lurched toward the tail and made a final check of his harnesses and jump gear. The jumpmaster shook Weede's hand, then raised his arm, waiting for the word from the navigator. The wind howled and blasted their bodies. Weede watched and waited. He cleared his mind, trying to focus only on the mission.

The jumpmaster cupped a hand against the earphone, then dropped his arm and screamed, "Go!" above the barrage of wind. Weede saluted and dived off the ramp, five miles up. Thunder roared past as he stretched his arms and legs and sailed for the peaks of the clouds below. Down, down, he sailed, at an airspeed of 132 knots, more than 150 miles per hour.

Weede breathed easily through the mask, carefully checking his wrist altimeter as he fell. The luminous dial wound down to fifteen thousand feet. He could see the lights of a settlement and make out the dark curve of a river snaking below. Weede used his leg as a rudder and clamped his arms to his sides in order to steer slightly east.

He checked the altimeter again. Four thousand feet. Weede ripped the mask off, fanned his arms out and cocked his wrist to watch the dial. He wanted to release the chute at the precise moment.

At three thousand feet, he grabbed the rip cord, slowly counted to five, and then yanked it. The canopy erupted from his back and filled with air, jerking him upward. Weede drifted and turned noiselessly through the African night. He pulled on the harness to bank left. The earth rushed up to greet him a moment later.

Weede splashed down into a muddy depression. A late gust of wind filled the chute before he could collapse it. He was dragged face down through the muck. It covered him from head to toe. Judging by the scent that assaulted his nose, he had fallen into a buffalo wallow. Evidently, it had been used often and recently by its contented patrons.

He weighed the possibility of drawing his automatic to immediately translate himself. Weede decided against it, reminding himself that he was a soldier, used to extraordinary hardships. Besides, it was no worse than some of his experiences working at the family sheep station just outside Alice Springs. Lord, how he hated sheep. Now he hated water buffalo, too.

Weede gathered the chute and buried it, his oxygen mask and coveralls, beneath a cluster of acacias. He had wanted to bury his clothes, too, but elected to find a pool to wash them in. Weede checked his watch. It was 1:12 a.m., commando time.

He held a tiny flashlight with his mouth, took a compass reading and checked his topo map. Weede calculated that he had landed two klicks southwest of the target. Not bad for dead reckoning. He had not wished to come down too close in any case.

Weede re-checked the bearing and set out into the bush. A half hour later, he reached an isolated pond. He listened intently for a few minutes for the splash of a croc. Let sleeping crocs lie, he had always said. Nothing. The pond was clear. He dropped his gear, slipped out of his clothes and waded into the water without making a sound.

When he was satisfied that he could stand himself, Weede immersed his BDUs and scrubbed them vigorously. He wrung them out, dipped them again and squeezed harder. He dressed quickly, checked the compass and moved out.

By 4:00 a.m., he was in position behind a baobab tree. He heard a cough coming from the outbuilding to his left. A drowsy man stumbled down the steps, walked to a fringe of brush and relieved himself. Weede was grateful that he had not selected that fringe of brush for his observation post. Finished, the man zipped his fly, hawked and spit before lurching back to the structure. Weede waited, listened and continued his surveillance.

By mid-afternoon, his clothes had dried except for lingering stains around his neck and armpits. The morning had been uneventful, but things were already starting to pick up. A cargo plane droned in from the west and landed in a surge of red dust. It turned on the runway and rolled to a stop beside two covered lorries.

Weede watched the poachers unload ivory from the cargo plane. It was a vintage C-47. The same type he had glimpsed in Kenya, four days ago.

He had found a flap of crate blown free of the lorry wreckage bearing the name "Dir Somali Banana Cooperative." Weede had tracked them to this plantation along the Juba River, knowing that this was the only estate within the province of Jubbada Dhexe with a landing strip.

A banana barge swayed at the loading dock. Its load was partially tarped. The stench of foul water was overpowering. In vain, Weede swatted at the black mopani flies invading his eyes, ears, nose and mouth.

Parked next to the runway, a Russian BTR 152 armored personnel carrier guarded the skies. It was armed with twin 23 mm anti aircraft guns. A formidable weapon, it was a real "people's deterrent." But the guards milling about made Weede even more edgy. They were Shiftas, Somalian border bandits, carrying the obligatory AK-47s.

He was in the Northern Frontier District of Somalia, still a contested area. To expedite matters, Weede had come alone, owing to the antipathy between the Kenyan and Somalian governments, assuming that Somalia had any effective government. He was not a diplomat. There was no point in getting involved with bureaucratic snarls and he had a better chance of remaining undetected on his own.

Weede was well aware that *Al-Shabaab*, a loyal faction of Al-Qaeda active in Somalia, was rumored to be engaged in the aggressive purchase and sale of ivory to fund its insurgent operations. The ivory trade had become a popular funding source for several militant cadres in Africa. Now, ISIS was also recruiting local warriors and trying to expand its reach into Somalia, which its leaders regarded as the "little emirate." A presence in Somalia was coveted by ISIS due to the fact that the struggling country had Africa's longest coastline, and it was bordered by three U.S. allies: Kenya, Djibouti and Ethiopia. Devastating terror attacks were undoubtedly in the planning stages. The smugglers were taking full advantage of the instability and ineffectiveness of the Somali government in dealing with the menace on its doorstep.

Weede checked his weapons for the tenth time. He carried only his 9 mm Browning automatic, a canteen and his ka-bar, the legendary fighting knife of the U.S. Marines. No identification. None would help if he were caught.

After dusk, he would have freedom of movement again. The air was heavy and damp. He labored to breathe. The buzzing insects in combination with the heat made him feel drowsy. Weede pinched himself to stay awake.

At a time like this, he wished that Hannah Song were with him. He smiled with the memory. The F.B.I. Academy at Quantico. Some finishing school. Weede had wondered why someone so delicate was packing a Remington Model 700 with a Redfield variable scope. It was a combination historically used by Marine snipers.

She had also failed to mention in her curriculum vitae a silver medal for shooting in the Olympics. But he had asked around. Hannah was disarmingly delicate and quite suddenly deadly. Calm. Dragon appears, then vanishes. Calm again. He missed her already.

Weede took his canteen from its pouch and dropped a salt tablet in the water, swished a mouthful and swallowed. He spit out the feasting mopani flies and wiped his lips. His detached reflection was interrupted by the barrel of a rifle jabbing him in the neck.

Cursing himself for his inattention, Weede raised his hands above his head. As he started to turn around to make a wisecrack, he was slammed in the head with a rifle butt and knocked unconscious.

When he came to, he was flat on his back on the banana barge. It was moving. His head pounded. It even hurt to blink. Weede's hands were tied beneath him and his ankles were bound together. The dull vibrations of the engine did not ease the pain in his head or the queasy feeling in his gut. He rolled to one side and retched.

Feeling better, he flipped onto his back. The stars radiated in a calm sky. Insect noises reached out from the shore. Water rushed against the low bow, gently rocking the craft. Weede could feel that the ankle scabbard was minus the ka-bar. The automatic was also missing from his shoulder holster. He could hear faint voices coming from a corrugated shelter aft.

The Shifta dialect was one of many African tongues known to him. Five years as a merc in Africa had done that. It was one more skill he had to have to survive. Like field craft, sniping and hand-to-hand.

Weede could only catch fragments of the conversation. He heard the words "*waranle*," meaning spear carrier or warrior, and "*baraka*," meaning blessing. Then he heard a name that bristled the hairs on his neck and rekindled distant memories. All of them bad." Botan Niassa."

Niassa? What did he have to do with this? Weede's mind tumbled hazily a few years back to the Cabinda Province of Angola. He had been co-leading a clandestine mission mounted by the private security firm, Interban. The deep penetration raid had been planned to take out a separatist base camp supplied by FLEC (Front for the Liberation of the Enclave of Cabinda) on the border with the Republic of Congo. Weede's patrol was to have linked up with an MPLA (People's Movement for Liberation of Angola) resistance force led by Botan Niassa. Everything had gone well, until they reached the rendezvous. Without warning, RPG rockets slammed into Weede's contingent, decimating it. Everyone except Weede had been killed. It was a set up. They had been betrayed by Niassa. All those good men were dead.

The next six days had been a survival exercise for Weede, even though he was used to living off the land with an enemy in feverish pursuit. He was a veteran of the Australian Special Air Service Regiment (SASR) and had been actively engaged in operations with a task group deployed to Afghanistan in the southern province of Uruzgan. After separation from the SASR, he had joined a group of former operators with Executive Outcomes in Africa who had continued their mercenary endeavors under various flags. After surviving on snakes, insects and other indigenous delicacies, he had somehow worked his way back to an Angolan outpost to give his report. Niassa's men were later caught and executed. But Niassa escaped and was never heard from again. Until now.

Weede breathed deeply, scenting brine. They were nearing the coast. The engine slowed. He heard the deck hands shout as a line flashed by. The dark mass of the dock loomed to the left. The barge bumped once, twice, and stopped abruptly.

Several minutes passed. He strained to hear voices coming from the bow and heard the sound of someone jumping into the barge. The footsteps moved toward him with measured precision. Weede was kicked squarely in the ribs. A sudden torchlight blinded him.

"So, Sergeant Weede, we meet again."

Chapter 10

Ten thousand miles away in Ashland, Oregon, the scene was quite different. After her plane had touched down in nearby Medford, Victoria Moy had rented a car for the short drive to the U.S. Fish & Wildlife Service National Forensics Laboratory.

For years, Customs Service agents had been sending "detained" objects to the laboratory for identification. Due to the astronomical increases in ivory seizures, the laboratory had redoubled its efforts to identify and trace ivory.

Although it was illegal to import most elephant ivory, mammoth ivory taken from the permafrost of Siberia and Alaska had always been legal. Even experts couldn't tell them apart. To further complicate matters, ivory acquired before the 1989 ban was also legal. Importers habitually claimed that either their ivory was mammoth ivory or ancient ivory. It had been nearly impossible to prove the distinction between pre-1989 ivory and post-1989 poached ivory, until very recently.

Moy had read an internal memorandum about an experimental method developed by the laboratory to tell the difference between modern and ancient Proboscidea, including elephants and their extinct relatives. The latest technique to date ivory relied on radioactive isotopes released into the atmosphere during atomic bomb testing during the Cold War era of the 1950s and '60s. The method was known as bomb-curve dating. Its application allowed researchers to detect radioactive isotopes within ivory or tusks. Carbon-14 from the bomb tests quickly oxidized and was absorbed by the plants which the elephants ate. A comparison of the Carbon-14 ivory samples with the levels of the isotope in the atmosphere at various times along the bomb curve allowed the scientists to calculate the age of the ivory. The ingenious test was accurate to within a year of when the elephant had died or been killed. It was also quick, reliable and relatively inexpensive to process.

Moy had made a few phone calls and booked the first flight out. It was a cool northwest morning. A heavy mist at the airport had dampened her clothing. As the sun appeared over the crest of a hill, crystalline beads of morning dew glistened in the roadway grass. She crossed a bridge over a tree shaded brook and pulled to the side of the road to check her map. She stepped out of the car to get her bearings.

To the south, a line of snow bound mountains stood unbroken. Down the road to the east, an escarpment cut through a tilled plain. A narrow road led along its base to a cluster of isolated buildings. The Southern Oregon State College campus. Nestled in the southeast corner of the complex was a simple white building. The forensics laboratory.

She looked down into the water overflowing the embankment. Streamers of moss entangled the scattered brook stones. Moy smiled as a green speckled trout rode the currents into a waiting pool. She would have to remember this spot. Moy slid into the driver's seat, started the engine and after signaling, pulled from the shoulder. She had signaled even though there were no other cars for miles around. After all, it was the law.

En route to the lab, Moy worried that existing statutes provided too many loopholes for greedy opportunists. There were exemptions for sport-hunted trophies and worked ivory of certified origin.

Importers had little trouble obtaining phony certifications from corrupt officials. The Shih Jen matter was not the only case of this type occupying her office. There were five others working their way through the judicial process. She feared there would be many more.

Moy hoped that the new techniques, which had been developed at the Ashland lab and elsewhere, would help close those loopholes forever. Something had to, or whole populations of elephants would continue to be senselessly slaughtered. She knew that ivory was regarded as white gold in Asia, and although the commodity price of raw ivory continuously fluctuated, it now fetched about $1,000 per pound.

Moy spun into the parking lot and inched into a space marked "Visitor." She grabbed her leather salesman's case and plodded up the walkway to the lobby. After showing her identification to the security director and stating her business, Moy was ushered into an isolated, well-lit workroom. Large charts, maps and scientific diagrams were hanging on every wall. A balding technician was sitting at a lab table examining an array of ivory figurines and particles, while making notes on a legal pad. He looked up at her, smiled hesitantly and resumed work.

Moy walked past him to a remote corner of the room. A forensic specialist with her back to the door was operating a scanning electron microscope. Moy tried, but could not decipher the variegated images on the split screens. She placed the salesman's case on the floor and approached the instrument. Moy's eyes were fixed on the images. The technician did not turn around.

Her curiosity overpowered her normally reserved nature. "Excuse me. May I ask what you're looking at?"

"These are *Schreger lines*," the technician said over her shoulder.

She whirled her chair around. The technician was tiny, slender and had friendly eyes. She was wearing a tattered white lab coat over blue jeans. Her glasses were perched on top of her head. The technician fumbled with her feet for her shoes, which were under the table.

"Oh, I'm sorry. I didn't see you come in. My name is Holly Kim."
The technician extended her hand.

"Victoria Moy. U.S. Attorney, San Francisco." Moy grasped the
offered hand. It was much warmer than her own.

"Yeah, sure. You called about our new identification methods.
Let me see. Where should I begin?" Kim looked around and
selected a figurine from the table and pointed to a smooth area at
the edge of the base. "Look here," Kim said. "Notice this little spot.
These are Schreger lines."

Moy looked closely at the segment.

"If there are no Schreger lines , the piece is neither elephant, nor
mammoth," Kim said.

"But how can you tell the pieces with Schreger lines apart?" Moy
asked.

"We have examined thousands of pieces of ivory, and one thing
is consistent: the angle of intersection."

"I don't follow," said Moy.

"With ancient mammoth ivory, the angle is constantly acute,
less than 90 degrees. In a modern elephant, the angle is always
obtuse, or greater than 110 degrees. Therefore, the angle at which
the Schreger lines intersect reveals the source of the ivory."

"But that sounds so simple," Moy said.

"Really, the number of dentinal tubules is more important than
the angle of intersection. An elephant has fewer tubules than a
mammoth. It's just easier to measure the angle because it reflects
the number of tubules. The more tubules there are, the narrower
the angle."

Kim turned around and sharpened the images on the screen.

"Here, let me show you."

Moy studied the bifurcated images.

"The sample on the left is mammoth. Notice how the angles
intersect. Now look at the section on the right. See the difference?"

"Yes," Moy said. "But now tell me how you distinguish old elephant ivory from modern elephant ivory."

"That was always a more difficult question, which we have been working overtime to resolve. What we have now found is a ruler that moves with time." Kim thought for a moment and motioned with her hands. Moy leaned against the counter, listening attentively. Kim explained the new bomb curve dating technique. Then she led Moy to the lab's mass spectrometer and showed her how they measured the radiocarbon levels at the base of each tusk, comparing the results with the animals known dates of death.

Moy fought to absorb the information. "Have you made any progress as far as determining the geographic origin of the ivory?" she asked.

"You mean where did the elephant live? Yes. As a matter of fact, we have devised methods of identifying the origin of a tusk. One way analyzes DNA; the other measures ratios of certain isotopes."

Moy laughed and threw up her hands. "You've just lost me."

"Basically, ratios of isotopes in the ivory, such as strontium, carbon and nitrogen, correspond to the ratios of such isotopes in the rocks, grass and water in the given environment. Taken together, they tell us where the elephant lived, because the geographic ratios are all different."

"That's fascinating," Moy said. "But what about the DNA part?"

"Well, that technique tests genetic material from tissue found on tusk ends. It's like genetic fingerprinting in criminal cases. Marked differences in the DNA samples allow us to distinguish one group of elephants from another."

"But what standards can you possibly utilize?" Moy asked.

"Elephant tusks from every region in Africa and India have now been analyzed. We've accumulated a library of isotopic ratios and DNA markers. If we compare ratios or markers from ivory samples and match them to recorded elephant populations, bingo, we know the origin."

Moy reached excitedly for her case and opened it, withdrawing ivory figurines and a polished section of tusk. "Can you analyze these for us? We don't have much time."

Kim took the polished section of tusk. "We can begin right now."

She started a small band saw in the corner of the room. As she moved the section of raw ivory through the saw, the blade wobbled and shattered. Kim looked down and shook her head in disgust.

"What's the matter?"

"Look."

Moy picked up the section. At first she didn't know what she was looking at. Then it hit her. Embedded in the center of the tusk was a chunk of corroded metal—a bullet.

Chapter 11

Hannah Song had been doing some checking of her own. Following an extended phone call, she left her office at 555 Battery Street and drove to the Asian Art Museum in Golden Gate Park.

Before entering the museum, she wandered through the Japanese Tea Gardens. The early spring sky was veiled by a fine haze. Along the winding path, young grass shoots searched for the sun. Scented airs were stirring everywhere. She paused at a pond with a garden nook. Song had not been there in years and had forgotten the serenity of the place. No sound broke the solemn silence. Slow motion dragonflies hovered above the swirling lotus flowers. Rafts of drifting duckweed carried water insects to the far shore.

Song gazed at her own reflection in the water and suddenly felt weary. She had no one to go home to or to share life with. She wasn't getting any younger. Her enthusiasm for Customs work waxed and waned. It was becoming increasingly more difficult for her to concentrate. She was getting progressively more irritable and forgetful. Song knew enough about depression to recognize the onset of symptoms. The problem was, what could be done about it? She had to go on.

Song walked around the bend to the statue of Buddha. She flashed back to her childhood and remembered how the placid face had promised hope and offered comfort. But she had been a Christian since her teens. She stopped and whispered a prayer. After several minutes Song looked up. *"Xie-xie,"* she said, thanking Jesus for changing her life.

She felt somewhat renewed, and strolled on to the museum. When she was inside, Song walked down a narrow hallway and located a grey metal door marked, "CURATOR."

Song lifted her left fist, hesitated and rapped three times. Hearing a muffled, "Yes?," she opened the door and entered the cramped office. A slight, owlish man with strategically arranged hair was sitting behind a cherry wood desk. "Hello, I'm Hannah Song," she said quietly. "I just talked to you on the telephone."

"Oh, yes. Please do come in and shut the door." He stood and extended his hand. "Henry Wu. Pleased to meet you. Please sit down."

Song shook his hand firmly. "Thank you, Doctor Wu. I have the sample with me."

He gestured to a leather chair. She sat down and tugged at her short skirt in one motion. Wu's desk was crammed with stacks of unsorted documents and files. Artifacts and *objets d' art* served as decorative paper weights. He cleared a space on his desk and looked at her expectantly.

Song reached into her handbag and retrieved an ivory carving. She placed the borrowed piece on the desk and waited for his reaction. The work depicted four hunters carrying a boar suspended by the legs. A stylized snake was poised to strike in the background.

Wu studied the carving in place from different angles. After several minutes he reached for it. "Let's have a closer look."

Song grabbed her day minder to take notes. Wu turned the piece in his hands, astutely analyzing it. He reached behind him for a leather-bound volume of artifact illustrations. He leafed from page to page until he found what he was looking for. He traced a description with his index finger. His lips moved as he read silently to himself.

Wu reached for a pencil. From time to time, he scribbled identifying characteristics on scraps of paper. After twenty minutes, he gently positioned the figurine in the center of the desk. The curator gazed at it several minutes later before rocking back in his chair. He folded his hands over his mouth with forefingers touching his nose and thumbs beneath his chin. Wu held the pose for a minute. "This is most unusual."

Song waited for him to continue. He tapped the carving with the tip of a pencil. "This is obviously a Kainan motif, but the utilization of ivory as a medium is astonishing."

Song jotted down the word "Kainan" on her pad. "What does that mean?"

He gestured apologetically with his hands. "Oh, I'm sorry. The Kainan are an aboriginal tribe inhabiting the mountains near Kaohsiung on the island of Taiwan."

She wrote the information down and looked up. "But what is so unusual about the tribe's use of ivory as a medium?"

Wu looked pensive. "You see, Ms. Song, the Kainan are master woodcarvers. They employ ancient designs and techniques." He glanced at the ceiling before continuing. "Although they have in the past been reported to sculpt stone, I have never known them to work with ivory." Wu squirmed in his chair and flailed his arms. "There is nothing in the literature about such an occurrence. This is very strange indeed."

"Doctor Wu, do you have any explanation at all for this oddity?"

He shook his head. "No. None at all. And I find that most troubling."

Song stood and reached for the figurine. She offered him her free hand. "Thank you, very much, Doctor Wu. I've taken enough of your time. You have been more helpful to us than you may realize."

Wu pumped her hand. "The pleasure was all mine, Ms. Song. Please be sure to let me know what you find out. It's my job to know these things."

He escorted Song to the door and scurried before her to open it. As she crossed the threshold, Wu gently took hold of her arm. "Oh, and one more thing, Ms. Song."

"What's that?"

Wu looked around the door down the hallway. "The Kainan worship a most deadly serpent. It's called the hundred-pace snake," Wu whispered. "Its victims drop dead before they can run even a hundred steps. Hence, the most-deserved name. The serpent is the venerated 'spiritual elder' of the tribe. His ominous visage appears in all of their art, even the piece you now carry. I implore you, please be careful."

Song patted his arm. "Don't you worry. I can take care of myself, Doctor Wu."

Halfway down the hall, she turned and waved. "Goodbye, Doctor Wu."

"Goodbye, Ms. Song, " he said, returning the wave.

She lingered in the gardens well past dusk. As Song drove away, she thought about Weede and wondered why she had not heard from him. He had promised to stay in touch. She had called and left multiple messages, but had been informed that he was "away on business." Song had not been told what kind of business was involved. But she knew of his reverence for the SASR motto, WHO DARES WINS. She shuddered with a sense of foreboding.

Back at the office, she waded through some of the paperwork that had accumulated during her brief sojourn in Kenya. There were hundreds of import manifests, customs lot sheets, and official U.S. Government memoranda, policies and procedures to pore over.

By 11:00 p.m. Song was exhausted and ready for a hot bath and bed. She flipped off the lights, locked the door and headed for the basement. Song fumbled with her keys, which were wrapped around the artifact. Untangling them, she unlocked her car, started the engine and squealed toward the exit. She waved good night to the U.S. Marshal patrolling the parking structure and zipped down Battery.

Song arrived at her condo ten minutes later. She parked in her slot and took the elevator to Level 3, then bounced across the suspension bridge leading from the shaft to the south cluster of units. When she reached her door, it was slightly ajar. Song whipped her compact Glock 19 from her purse, adopted a combat stance and eased the door open.

Dancing light reflected from the glare of the bedroom television. Song moved silently through the unit. She crouched low in the doorway, leveled the automatic and swept the room. She gasped. A man was sprawled across her bed. He was bare chested. His mouth was wide open and he was snoring earnestly. She slipped into the room and sighed with relief. It was her younger brother, Daniel. He had left six months earlier to buy some cigarettes and had not returned. Until now.

Since the death of their mother and father in a typhoon, she had practically raised him herself. The transition to America had been difficult for him. He had been making some progress since dropping out of high school, but had fallen in with a bad crowd in Chinatown. Song looked with disgust at the drained bottle of Chivas Regal on her nightstand. Drunk again.

It was not the only thing that bothered her. The tattoo of a serpent glared menacingly from his forearm. Below the snake were the Chinese numbers, *san, wu, bah,* or three, five, eight. Song pulled Daniel up to a sitting position and tried to shake him awake. "Get up, knucklehead!"

Song dragged her groggy brother to the shower, turned on the cold tap and shoved him under the spray. He spluttered and gasped as she held his head down. "Hey, cut it out!"

He waved his arms wildly as he twisted and writhed, but she did not let him up. Finally, she turned the water off and threw a towel at him. She crossed her arms and stood there tapping her foot and glaring at him. He averted his eyes as he toweled off.

While examining his bloodshot eyes in the mirror, he noticed that she was scrutinizing his tattoo. He covered it with the towel.

"What's that?" she asked.

"What's what?"

"The tattoo. What do those numbers mean?"

He turned away. She spun him around. "Where did you get it?"

"None of your business," he huffed.

She pressed her nails into his arm. "Don't tell me it's none of my business. Out with it.

He pulled away, threw down the towel and headed for the bedroom. "I'm not going to tell you anything. I've got to go."

"You're back with that gang, aren't you?" she screamed. She caught up with him and grabbed his shoulder.

Her brother turned around in the hall and shook his finger at her. "Look. Don't nag me. At least I associate with my own kind."

Song was stunned by his callous insult. She slapped him. Tears welled up in her eyes. She reached out with a trembling hand to touch his face. "Daniel…"

He batted her hand away, teetered into the living room, spun around, and looked at her with defiance. "And don't call me Daniel. My name is Lai Wan Song," he said, smashing a fist against his chest.

He grabbed his shirt and shoes, lurched out the door and slammed it behind him. Song followed him outside.

"Daniel! Come back!" she cried in despair. She slumped in the doorway, sobbing, but he disappeared as the elevator doors slapped together. When she started back inside, Song thought she saw something move in the shadow of a black pine. She rubbed the tears from her eyes and focused on the tree. But there was nothing there. It was only the wind.

Chapter 12

It was mid afternoon in the port of Mogadishu, the capital of Somalia. A temperate breeze blew into the harbor from the Indian Ocean, but it was too weak to dispel the yellow mist encircling the city. It was one of those places where rain constantly threatened, but rarely fell.

Weede was escorted by armed guards through the back alleys of the bulk export terminal. With the country still reeling from an undeclared civil war, such sights were an everyday occurrence. None of the passersby paid any attention to him. They had learned to mind their own business.

The smell of molasses dominated the air. They passed a small freighter nesting low in a deepwater berth. It was a new, fast ship capable of forty-five knots. Weede wondered what general cargo it might be carrying. Laborers crawled about the superstructure and secured the ship's tackle. Rotating winches reeled in thick towlines. The *Lan Yu* was preparing to sail. Weede tried to loosen his hands, which were still tied behind his back. It was no use.

They approached a prefabricated metal warehouse standing catty-cornered from a dry dock. When they reached its unmarked steel door, the guards halted. One opened the door and held it as the other shoved a rifle butt into Weede's back, forcing him through the doorway. He fought for balance, but pitched forward, landing on his knees. The door slammed behind him as the guards remained outside.

Although the warehouse was dimly lit, Weede could see four men seated at a folding table in a corner.

"Ah, welcome, Sergeant Weede." Niassa's words bounced around the empty chamber. He was just as big and ugly as Weede had remembered him. The turban he was wearing did not improve his appearance, since it failed to cover his face. He knew that Niassa suffered from an exotic African skin disease. Judging from Niassa's looks, it had won the battle.

Weede struggled to his feet and staggered toward the table. The two men flanking Niassa wore threadbare military uniforms. They appeared to him to be former members of the hated NSS, the elite and brutal Somalian Security Force. Trained by the KGB, its members were completely loyal to whoever was in charge at the moment and had enjoyed broad powers of arrest and investigation. They were above the law, to the extent it existed in Somalia. The security service had been disbanded in 2013. But these were still real no-shit blokes.

But Weede was most disturbed by the presence of the remaining man seated at the far left side of the table. His downcast eyes did not prevent Weede from immediately recognizing him. Kulmie Madar, a Kenyan Wildlife and Conservation Management Department head. Another traitor had sold out for money.

Niassa made a show of shuffling a stack of papers, dropped them and folded his hands. "Sergeant Weede, it is my duty to inform you that you have been tried and found guilty," he intoned.

Weede scoffed. "Guilty of what?"

"Crimes against the security of the Somalian people, and unfortunately," sneered Niassa, "I've just caught a glimpse of your mortality."

"The only thing you're going to glimpse is the hangman's noose as it slips around your neck," Weede shot back.

Niassa sniffed through his cratered nose. "You will be returned to the border area this afternoon, and will meet a horrible fate. Your body will be located in a matter of days by a Kenyan patrol. They will conclude that you were probably shot in the head by bandits."

Weede had a barely cloaked streak of 'up yours.' He spat at Niassa to provoke him. Niassa turned away, wiped his face and arched back, pointing a finger at him. "I regret that I can't be there to see you off, but I have some rather pressing business to attend to. However, I have arranged for an appropriate escort."

"You won't get away with this," Weede said.

Niassa waved his hand in dismissal. "Oh, but I already have, Sergeant Weede. I already have."

Madar and Niassa jumped up and walked to the door. Madar kept looking back at Weede to make sure he wasn't moving. They hastily left the room.

An hour later, Weede was in the open bed of a ten-ton truck crawling through the inland dunes. The landscape was dotted with scattered clumps of scrub and grass. Five menacing looking former NSS guards sat across from him with their automatic weapons at the ready. If Africa had an equivalent to Hitler's SS, they were it.

The color of the sandy soil translated from yellow to subdued red as the truck approached a dry evergreen forest. One of the guards tormented him by drawing Weede's own ka-bar across his throat in a cutting motion.

Weede reviewed his options. They were severely limited. His people had no idea where he was. Or whether he was dead or alive. The Kenyan government would not make any inquiries. No diplomatic feelers would be sent out. That's just the way it was. Weede was entirely on his own. There was no cavalry riding to the rescue.

One thing was certain. Once the truck stopped, he would lose the ability to take the initiative. He had to act, and act now. For him, surrendering to the inevitable was impossible. But what could he do to turn the tables?

Weede calculated that he could knock the small guard off the end of the truck and use him to cushion the fall. After that, things would become measurably more difficult. He would have to run for it and make it to thick cover within seconds. The air would be filled with streams of hot lead and ricochets. How fast could he move through the bush with his hands tied? He had to get low and go. Once in the bush, he would be the master again. The pursuers would be his. Weede was renowned as an expert at war with empty hands. He had to give it a go. There was no other choice. Who dares, wins. The SASR motto still governed all his tactical planning.

Weede was careful to raise his head only slightly to take a look. They were approaching a curve. The truck would have to slow down. Thick cover encroached on both sides of the highway. He had to go now.

As the truck rounded the curve, its front end was ripped off by a ground level blast. Mines! Weede was lifted out of his seat by the explosion and tossed against the wall of the bed. What was left of the truck careened off the road and bounced to a stop. Weede lay still, feigning death.

The guards tumbled from the truck bed to take up defensive positions, but were quickly cut down in the murderous cross fire from automatic weapons. Weede's upper body was pelted by blistering splinters of metal and wood. He grimaced and drew his legs in tightly as the steady hammering continued.

After an eternity, the bursts of fire diminished and stopped. The only sound was the slow gurgle of fuel from the petrol tanks. They were going to blow! He would be boiled alive.

Weede rolled to the back of the bed and flipped off, landing on his side. He scrambled over twisted bodies and wreckage, like a crab missing a few legs. He rolled into a ditch face down and opened his mouth to diffuse the expected concussion. As soon as he did so, the truck erupted. A shower of debris rained from the sky. Something slammed into the back of his head. He lost consciousness.

When Weede came to, he heard a series of clicks coming from the ditch bank. He rolled over, and through a swirl of dust, saw a ring of AK-47s pointed at him. Bandoliers of cartridges, grenades and mixed munitions hung from torn and grimy rags of clothing. The men were poorly dressed, but well armed. These were real soldiers.

They looked emaciated, but their eyes burned with the intensity of the jungle. One of them pulled a cruel looking spiral blade from his waistband. Weede tried to inch away. Another signaled for him to remain still. The guerilla with the knife dropped into the ditch and cut Weede's wrist bindings.

The leader motioned for Weede to come out of the ditch. Weede stood and climbed out uncertainly, debating whether to try to run for it. He reasoned that he wouldn't get more than ten feet. These blokes were also masters of the bush. He smiled as they led him off the road to a hidden trail. Weede and the leader waited in the shadows while the others returned to the scene of the slaughter.

Weede kept repeating the word "*jaalle*," meaning friend in the Somali dialect. The leader ignored him, and maintained a deadpan look. They waited while the bodies of the former NSS mercenaries were stripped of useful items. Their weapons and ammunition were particularly prized, as were their shoes. The gleaners returned and the troop marched off in purposeful silence with Weede in tow.

By dark, they had reached a concealed village. Weede knew that his benefactors were from the nomadic Ogadenis clan. They were very much like him in the sense that they could not stay still either.

He was taken to the local "*abbaan*," the patron, or protector of guests. He seemed friendly enough. In this part of Africa it was hard to tell for sure. Food and water were given to him while his wounds were treated. They gave him a foul-smelling potion to drink. Weede was in no position to argue. At least not yet.

His eyes grew heavy. Maybe it was the medicine, or the strain of his ordeal. He felt drowsy. The faces of the elders began to blur in the glow from the fire. Aided by the soft notes of a flute, the distant murmur of voices and the wash of firelight across his face, Weede soon drifted off to sleep.

He awakened at first light and felt invigorated. Whatever it was they had given him to drink had worked. The tribesmen had already prepared breakfast for him. Weede's appetite was a marvel to the hovering children. At first he felt guilty eating in front of them, but decided that they probably didn't get many guests or opportunities to display their hospitality and downed the generous offering.

During the late afternoon, he crossed into Kenya, after waving farewell to his escort patrol. Courtesy of the *abbaan*. He stepped smartly to the nearest border station. Soon he would be back in action. The *abbaan* had personally returned his ka-bar to him.

That evening, a stunned Kulmie Madar was led in shackles before an impromptu tribunal. The director of Kenya's Wildlife and Conservation Management Department presided, assisted by the Kenyan Minister of Natural Resources, and Weede.

Madar stood trembling beside the solitary hardwood chair.

"Sit down, Kulmie. We'd like to have a chat with you," said Weede.

Chapter 13

Daniel Song stumbled up Pacific Avenue into the heart of Chinatown. In his drunken haze, the lights of the shops merged into a single neon image. He turned with an abrupt jerk and stopped to study the menu posted on the door of a restaurant. It featured Mongolian hot pot, a fondue of lamb and simmered vegetables and his favorite dish, chicken with hot pepper sauce. His mother used to cook it for him. She had been so beautiful and kind and proud of him. Her son had been destined for great things. But now, now...

Daniel tried to open the door. Closed. He shook and rattled it harder. A light came on within. The curtain was wrenched back. A grey-haired woman peered out at him, made a disgusted face and waved him away. She drew the curtain shut. The light went out. He slammed into the door and pounded it with his fists. He heard a muffled curse in response. Daniel gave up and staggered away laterally across the sidewalk like some shuttling crustacean. Wide-eyed passersby hastened out of his way. The vibrant noises from the street agitated his throbbing head. His mouth was dry. He needed a beer. Or better yet, two.

An hour had passed since his fight with Hannah. It would be their last. He would never call or see her again.

Daniel's sixth sense told him he was being followed. He turned in time to see a blue Acura pull to the curb. He ducked into an alley behind Old Chinatown Lane sat down and waited. After a short vigil, he became weary and rested his elbows on his knees. He strained his eyes toward the street. Nothing. Minutes passed. Still nothing. He concluded it was probably just his imagination.

He moved on, passing the lighted rear entrance to the Kai Tak Tong, a gambling and social club. Daniel debated whether he should stop and see Cindy Lee, his favorite hostess. He could confide in her. But it was more than that. He wanted to marry her. He saw nothing in the corridor of darkness ahead; the light of the club was his only comfort. He turned on his heel, fumbled with the door latch and stumbled in. The sullen doorman scowled, but let him pass.

Inside, clusters of elderly couples sat in red vinyl chairs huddled around cocktail tables. They were drinking tea and playing *mah jongg*. The glow of pagoda lanterns reflected by their faces gave them a ghostly appearance. The elders looked at Daniel disinterestedly before returning to their serious business.

Senior citizens playing *mah jongg* presented a cosmetic image of calm and innocence to inquiring authorities. But Daniel knew better. The real action took place on the second floor.

He zagged upstairs, passing a recessed wall shrine. Smoking incense sticks paid homage to a pictorial image of Kwan Kung, the legendary general. Daniel shuffled up to the bar and almost fell over mounting the stool. He looked around for Cindy. She was nowhere in sight. He tried to remember whether she worked Tuesday nights or not.

As he scanned the room again, the bartender passed him on the way to ring up a tab. "Excuse me," said Daniel.

The bartender half turned around, as if he were anxious to keep going. "Yes?"

Daniel spoke in a low voice. "Doesn't Cindy work Tuesdays?"

"Uh huh. Normally. She called in sick this afternoon. Said she had the flu. Why? You want to leave a message for her?"

"No. Thank you. That's okay."

"You sure?"

"Yeah, I'm sure."

The bartender shrugged his shoulders and continued his walk to the cash register.

Thinking of Cindy made Daniel contemplate settling down. It was nice to think about. But he had made other commitments and his personal life would have to wait.

As he passed by again, the bartender slapped a napkin in front of him. "What would you like?"

"Tsingtao, please."

Daniel noticed that the back bar was highlighted by an etched glass mirror, flanked by hand painted melon jars. He stared at his own reflection and frowned. Maybe Hannah was right. He had wasted his life.

Without speaking, the server plopped the bottle of beer on the counter in front of him. Daniel gripped the bottle tightly, savoring the coolness with his hand. With a flourish, he raised the beer, tilted back his head and guzzled a long pull. The rush of liquid burned his throat and made his eyes water. He coughed and wiped his lips.

Daniel revolved slowly on the stool, then stood with his back to the bar. Across the room, groups of youths, led by house dealers, were engaged in animated games of *pai gow*, which employed dominoes in a strategy combining elements of gin and poker. The teams of seven were separated by four-panel silk screens. He knew that, on good nights, more than $100,000 could change hands. Dealers received generous tips and the house kept five percent. No one bothered to apply for a gaming license.

To the outside world, the devotées appeared to be playing dominoes. Each hand had a combined limit of $2,100, but a game could be completed in less than two minutes. If and when the authorities came in, the money was easily hidden.

The clandestine nature of the clubs and the alluring cash had made them ripe takeover targets for associates of the Hong Kong Triads. Daniel recognized a muscular man in the group and nodded at him. The man signaled back and resumed play.

Daniel was about to return to his beer when he heard a commotion on the landing below, followed by the urgent scrambling of footsteps. Within seconds, two men in trench coats rounded the railing, swiveled and dropped into one-knee combat position.

One pulled a sawed-off shotgun from under his coat, while the other clutched a machine pistol. At first, Daniel thought it was a robbery. That is, until the hood with the shotgun opened up on the *pai gow* players without warning. He blasted one group, shifted, pumped and fired at the other. His ally followed suit, spraying the ducking crowd with the automatic.

Daniel stood by helpless, as if paralyzed by the suddenness of the attack. Two of the players twisted backward, mortally wounded. Others hit the floor and came up firing. The roar and clatter of the close-in battle was deafening. Wood chips, splinters and shards of glass spun through the air. Daniel dropped to his belly and protected his head with folded arms. When the intense firing had subsided, he looked up.

The gunner with the machine pistol back pedaled to the landing, reloaded and laid down covering fire. His accomplice wielding the shotgun whirled and rolled toward Daniel. He locked eyes with Daniel and smirked. "No! No!" Daniel cried out. The shooter laughed and discharged a load of steel shot into his face from a distance of ten feet.

The shooters scrambled down the staircase, leap-frogging each other to cover their withdrawal. They clubbed a grey-haired man from the doorway, ran down the street and were received into the night. They heard the wail of sirens nearby and ducked into an alleyway until two police cars roared past. Unnoticed, they walked casually to their rendezvous.

Three blocks later, they approached an older Lincoln limousine, parked behind a noodle factory. The electric window in the back hummed down. "Has it been done?" asked Darwin Lau?"

The man with the shotgun stepped up to the car. "Yes. He was accidentally caught in the cross fire."

Lau chuckled and tossed a bulky manila envelope to him. "Good work. Enjoy yourselves. Go!" he commanded the driver. The Lincoln lurched from the lot and disappeared into the swirling traffic of the city.

Chapter 14

It was 1:10 a.m. The regular Tuesday night poker game was in full swing when Brooker excused himself to take a phone call from the watch commander. He shifted a panatela from his mouth to his left hand and blew a smoke ring as he bellowed "Brooker," into the receiver.

"Yeah, Inspector, this is Coffey. We've had a little trouble in Chinatown."

Brooker pulled a compact spiral notebook and stubby pencil from his hip pocket. "What kind of trouble?"

"Gang shooting. Three male Asians are dead. One shot at point blank range. Coroner's on the way."

Brooker scribbled in his own version of shorthand. "Anyone else hit?"

"Uh huh. Six Asian males were wounded by shots, ricochets and fragments."

"Any suspects, yet?"

"None. Chief wants you to get right on it."

"Naturally. Thanks, Coffey."

"Hey, don't blame me."

"Yeah, right. Just gimme the address."

"Certainly. It's the Kai Tak Tong on Old Chinatown Lane."

"That's Andy Ju's old beat, isn't it?"

"Uh huh. He's over in the Mission District now."

"Well, give him a call and have him meet me there."

"Okay. Anything else I can do for you?"

"Yeah, retire."

"Very funny. You should take your own advice."

"Maybe I will. Maybe I will. But then, who'd keep you in line?"

"Hey, Brooker?"

"Yeah?"

"Be careful out there."

"Kiss my ass, Coffey."

Brooker heard Coffey laughing hilariously as he hung up. The job had already cost him his marriage. Now he couldn't even finish a lousy poker game. He cashed in his chips, gave a mock one-fingered salute to the smirking faces of the division's finest and swept through the door.

Chinatown, huh? That had been cropping up more and more lately. First Hannah Song's clue about the harbor murder. Now this.

Brooker slid behind the wheel of his battered Crown Vic, grabbed the mic and reported in to dispatch. He waited until the engine had warmed up before slicing away from the curb. Within minutes, he had left the South San Francisco suburb and was headed north on the 101.

Brooker had first been introduced to the Chinatown gangs several crime cycles before. On an otherwise quiet Friday night, gang members affiliated with the local *Wah Ching* gang had waltzed into the Black Dragon Restaurant and spritzed the patrons with Uzi fire. No rival gang members had been hit. Only innocent bystanders. A man and his five-year old daughter had been killed. Years later, locals and tourists alike would point out bullet holes in the structure which had not been patched.

That event had inaugurated a disturbing trend: the proliferation and use of automatic weapons by common street thugs. As with criminal society in general, the level of violence among young

Asian rowdies had been steadily growing. Not only that, but even the ladies were also getting into the act.

The initial radio reports regarding the social club incident were routine enough, until Brooker reached the downtown exit. Then he heard that the shooters had been Vietnamese. After attending a gang unit briefing just the week before, he knew that the Black Star gang was active in the area. It was made up of Vietnamese youths with Chinese ethnic backgrounds and was closely affiliated with the *Wah Ching*.

It was bad enough with the *Wah Ching* and *Wo Hop To*. The city didn't need any cross-cultural wars on its hands. The Vietnamese gangs usually confined their activities to protection and extortion. They used fear and reprisal to guarantee the silence of their victims.

Unlike the Chinese hoodlums, Vietnamese criminals were not deterred by prison time. The only thing they dreaded was the prospect of deportation. It was equivalent to a death sentence. Yet, that did not happen until the normalization of relations between the United States and Vietnam.

Andy Ju waved his arms over his head as Brooker pulled up to the crime scene. Ju was a wiry man with uncontrollable hair and thick, black mustache. Round, steel-rimmed glasses rested on the tip of his nose. Brooker jumped out of the car as Ju raced around to meet him. "Hey, Brooker, you old sonova...how the heck have you been?" Ju shook Brooker's paw with one hand and clasped his arm with the other.

Brooker punched Ju affectionately on the arm. "Good. Good. How 'bout yourself?"

"Hey, great. Dennis is in high school now, and the baby starts kindergarten in the fall."

"You've gotta be kidding," Brooker said.

"No, I wish I was."

Brooker looked closely at his old friend. He hadn't aged a day. Ju had been born and raised in Chinatown and was privy to its deepest secrets. Always available for the toughest assignments, Ju had been instrumental in helping the city keep a lid on the violence in the Asian community. He would know how to get to the bottom of this.

"What have you got so far?" Brooker asked.

Ju frowned and pushed his glasses back to the bridge of his nose. "Not a heckuva lot at this point." He pulled out a black notebook. "I interviewed an elderly couple. Members of this social club. They said they were playing *mah jongg* downstairs about midnight. The youths upstairs were playing *pai gow*."

He flipped the page and continued. "Two men burst in through the front door, beat the doorman unconscious and rushed upstairs. The old people heard excited shouts, scrambling and tumbling chairs. Then multiple shotgun blasts and small arms fire. The downstairs server corroborated their story. Doorman's still out of it with a concussion."

"What else?"

"The shooters ran down the staircase and clubbed the old man on their way out. He got a good look at one of the assailants."

"Any distinguishing characteristics?"

"Well, for starters, he was Vietnamese."

"Yeah, I heard on the radio."

"For another, he was wearing a black trench coat and had a purple burn scar on one cheek and was missing part of his right ear."

"The usual," Brooker cracked.

"Yeah, gang life will do that," Ju replied, glibly.

Brooker turned serious. "Did you get an A.P.B. out?"

"Uh huh."

"Victims upstairs?"

Ju nodded. There was a dour look on his face. "Yeah, but…"

"But what?"

"One of them's a real mess, man. Damned buckshot. Definitely a closed casket."

"I can hardly wait," Brooker said, opening the door for Ju.

They trudged up the stairs; Brooker heard a woman sobbing in a darkened corner of the club behind them. "We just dusted the staircase and landing areas for prints," said Ju. "Nothing."

"They didn't stick around long enough," Brooker offered. "Coroner finished?"

"Pretty near."

As they reached the top of the staircase, Brooker could see the sheriff-coroner hunched over a corpse beside the bar. It was virtually headless. Certainly faceless. Two others lay crumpled beside an overturned cocktail table. Brooker approached the coroner and turned his head to the side. "Jeez. I see what you mean," he said to Ju.

Even after twenty years on the force, he had never quite gotten used to the products of human cruelty. "Any I.D.?" Brooker asked the coroner.

"No. Just this weird tattoo. "The coroner rolled up the victim's sleeve and pointed to the forearm. "But at least this one'll have fingerprints to check."

Brooker dropped to one knee and studied the arm. Its ribboned flesh was peppered with shot and powder burns. But the tattoo was still intact. He looked at Ju. "Any ideas?"

Ju looked as if he were studying a biology specimen. "Yeah. Local gang. No doubt about it."

"You ever heard of Vietnamese and Chinese mixing it up around here?"

"Never," said Ju. "They normally stick to their own turf. Same with my Chinese brethren. Something highly unusual is going down. And this won't make the cross town boys any new friends around here."

Brooker motioned toward the other bodies. "What about them?"

"They had I.D.s," said the coroner. "Local guys. No tattoos."

"Probably just liked to play cards," Brooker said facetiously. He thought of his own interrupted poker game as he paced toward the lifeless forms. Brooker mentally photographed the scene. "Where were the other victims taken?" He asked without looking up.

The coroner paused from unzipping a body bag for the corpse. "San Francisco General."

Brooker shook his head, trudged back to Ju and laid a beefy hand on his shoulder. "Can you get over there and obtain statements from the others? I'm gonna stick around and see what I can turn up."

"Sure," said Ju. "By the way, barkeep says that some of them returned fire. Their automatics are on the way to forensics along with the shotgun shell casings and 9mm cartridges I picked up. Pretty standard stuff available everywhere from Walmart to Dick's Sporting Goods."

Ju shuttled toward the stairs. "I'll let you know if I find out what's behind this."

"Check," Brooker said.

"Take care," Ju said, starting down the stairs.

Brooker located the bartender and quizzed him. He learned that the unidentified victim had staggered into the club just before the shooting and ordered a beer. The bartender was wiping down the back bar area when the two Vietnamese had charged up the stairs. Looking into the mirror, he had seen them pull the weapons from under their trench coats and spray the far side of the room where the *pai gow* games were in progress.

There were fifteen, maybe sixteen, people upstairs at the time. The bartender had hit the floor when the shooting started and didn't see the rest. However, he told the unidentified victim was the last to be shot and that there was an interval of several moments between the initial roars of the shotgun and the final one. It seemed to the bartender that the last blast was almost an afterthought.

Brooker drove to headquarters on Polk Street, entered his private office and fell asleep at his desk. At 6:30 a.m. he was awakened by the buzzing of an intercom. The crime lab had obtained a positive I.D. from the fingerprints of the headless corpse. Brooker wiped the sleep from his eyes, mumbled something resembling "Thanks" and adjusted his tie. He tucked his coat under his arm and trudged toward the elevator that would take him to the basement. On the way, he grabbed a cup of coffee, accidentally dusting his hand with powdered creamer.

The vibration of descent almost lulled back to sleep, but the snap of the elevator doors jarred him back to reality. He signed in with the duty clerk and received a manila folder. Brooker leaned against the counter, opened it and read slowly, then lifted his eyes and rubbed his forehead. "Oh my God," he said, closing the file, "Oh my God."

Chapter 15

The natal inlet of the spring sun had opened above San Francisco Bay. It was a perfect warm morning. Shortly after 9:00 a.m., Hannah Song was at the Presidio Range, bench testing an experimental .50 caliber rifle. It was a custom big-bore gun built by Barrett, especially for special operators. Real heavy artillery. The guys at the range kept kidding her about bringing a howitzer on the line.

She had been invited to the Fifty Caliber Shooters Association regional shoot in Tucson. It was still three weeks away. Song was practicing firing shot groups at stationary targets beyond 1,000 yards. The prize she would be after was the record for the tightest shot group of five rounds ever fired in large bore competition. The current world record stood at nine and five-sixteenths inches. Song had achieved an agonizing near miss the year before by shooting a nine-and-a-half-inch group. A beastly twelve-mile-an-hour wind had made the difference.

There was a meek five- to seven-mile-an-hour wind this morning from the east. Song's first round had consisted of four shots eight and a half inches apart. Her fifth shot had impacted just to the right of the bull's eye. She tried to account for the minuscule difference. Was it perhaps a warm air current near the target? After all, the conditions might be different that far away. A minor windage adjustment ought to do the trick. She re-loaded the rifle.

Song prepared for the second round. She twisted her San Francisco Giants cap around with the bill to the rear and clamped ear protectors in place. A flock of seagulls flapped across her line of fire. She waited until they had soared to the south and took a deep breath. She exhaled deliberately and shook her arms to loosen up.

Finally fully relaxed, Song moved up to the scope and adjusted five inches to compensate for the deflection. She concentrated and waited until her heart rate and respiration slowed. She was in competition form. When she was satisfied, Song pressed the trigger with the barely detectable motion of her fingertips.

The rifle shook in its frame. In the blink of an eye, 1,300 yards away, a wisp of dust plumed from the berm behind the target. Song set herself and repeated the procedure in perfect sequence until four more shots were away.

She stood and looked over at the observation tower. She noticed Brooker walking toward her. The mournful look on his face told her everything she had to know. "It's Daniel, isn't it?"

Brooker turned his head away, then back and nodded. "I'm sorr...," he started to say, as Song interrupted him. "Where is he?" she sobbed. She covered her eyes with her hands. He gently touched her forearm, "C'mon, I'll drive you."

Thirty minutes later, they arrived at the San Francisco City and County Morgue. Walking down the corridor, Song felt the chill presence of death's dark angel.

Brooker turned abruptly at the end of the hall and held the door for her. She forced herself to walk toward the solitary stainless steel gurney. The medical examiner was standing beside it, nervously biting his lip as if waiting for her frightful reaction. When she was near enough, he tugged the sheet from the form and looked away, more out of respect than revulsion. Brooker moved behind her and stretched out his arms. He had tried to prepare her while they were en route. Song knew that he had tried his best not to be too graphic.

She gasped and covered her mouth with separated fingers. Tears surged from her burning eyes, relieving the tingling numbness in her head. Her hand trembled as she tried to speak, but only groaned insensibly. Daniel's face had been obliterated. But it was the same clothing as the night before. Then there was the distinctive tattoo.

Song spun around and pounded on Brooker's chest in a hysterical rage. "Take it away. Take it away. Oh, it's so horrible."

He nodded at the medical examiner who covered the body and left the room. Brooker held Song's fists tight and tried to comfort her. She looked back over her shoulder toward the shape on the gurney. "Who could have done this terrible thing?"

Brooker hugged her and softly patted her back. "I don't know, but I promise you, I'll bring him in."

They trudged out to the car. Slow-winged butterflies sailed among the fragrant flowers beside the walkway. The stirring of the scented air revived her. It seemed strange to Song that this dome of death was encircled by vibrant life. He broke the awkward silence. "So far, our only lead is the eyewitness I.D. of the Vietnamese shooter."

Brooker stopped and faced her. "Ms. Song, I know this must be difficult for you now, but what sort of gang activity was your brother mixed up in?"

"I don't know," she said haltingly. "He's always run with some rough crowds but he wasn't a violent type. The tattooing thing was something new and frightening, though. He wouldn't even talk to me about it."

"Did he have any enemies that you know of? Anyone who might have wanted to kill him?"

"He never mentioned any problems of that kind. Daniel was just in some minor scrapes and guilty of some petty infractions.

"Well, do you know if he ever received any threats from anyone?"

"No. I never heard of any." She sniffled and wiped her eyes. "He was basically a good kid. Just really mixed up. I blame myself for a lot of it."

Brooker put his hands on her shoulders. "Listen. You shouldn't be so hard on yourself. Anymore, this can happen to any family in America."

"Yes. But it happened to my family," she said angrily.

They did not talk all the way back to the range. Song's mood was such that she didn't want any more conversation. She bitterly made a fist and kept beating the armrest. Song dreaded the prospect of organizing the funeral and prolonging the agonizing aftermath of Daniel's death. pulled sideways into the parking space. Thunder sounded over the bay as Brooker reached across and opened her door. He looked at her and rubbed the stubble on his chin. "Maybe Daniel knew too much."

"About what?"

"That's what I need to find out. Ms. Song, if there's anything I can do…about…well, you know."

Song forced a smile. "Sure. Thanks for your help. I'll probably call you tomorrow. It's just that I…I have to be alone for a while."

"Of course. I understand. Good afternoon, Ms. Song."

She felt drained as she climbed out and walked to her car. Brooker waved as he sped from the lot. Song was about to open the driver's side door when she noticed something stuck under the windshield wipers. It was a range target with five prominent holes. Her spirits soared briefly as she read the range director's notation: "Nine and seven-sixteenths! Wow!"

Song looked up, then crumpled the target and threw it down. But it was all for nothing now. She suddenly felt cold and alone. More alone than she'd ever felt before. Song decided to take the long route home, and drove out to Lands End.

Fifteen minutes later, she parked in an isolated spot and cried from the depths of her soul. Her career had dominated her life and she had little time for Daniel, or anyone else. Now he was dead.

She had no one. There was no life for her beyond the service. The least she could do would be to take Daniel home.

Song ripped her keys from the ignition, got out and slammed the door. Standing on the promontory, she could see the Seal Rocks and the Cliff House far below. To her right, the lighted Golden Gate Bridge floated in the fog and the closing darkness.

Beyond the Golden Gate, the lights of distant ships sparkled on the open sea. She closed her eyes and inhaled deeply, drawing in the night. Minutes later, she had passed Fort Point and floored it, heading back to the city.

Chapter 16

The international port of Osaka seemed busier than usual. If that was even possible. Its swarming populace had not been deterred by an unexpected icy wind from the Arctic, which had blasted into the city. Although early spring it was a harsh reminder that winter lingered on the stage. Japan's second largest metropolis was the launch pad for its thrust into the markets of the world. It was also the site of an elephant graveyard.

Crashi Mitoma emerged from the environmentally controlled underground and approached the plaza of the Tama Building. He was awed by the flashing red and blue lights of the titanic advertisements that rolled through the Minami District in equal, successive waves. Here Coca-Cola merged with Nikon and Hennessy Cognac with All Nippon Airways. One prominent sign touted the emergence of a "New Japan."

Mitoma tucked a copy of Japan's daily newspaper, the *Yomiuri Shimbun*, under his arm and passed through the lobby. He did not know why he had been summoned to a meeting of the board of directors of Isamu Trading Company, Ltd.

Isamu was the dominant member of a powerful *keiretsu*, mutually supportive companies bound together by interlocking shareholdings. Hapless competitors were ritually slain by their combined influence, aided and abetted by institutional corruption. Graft, which oiled the gears of the island nation's economic machine. Now, even the Koreans were starting to mimic the licentious business model.

But what could the board possibly want with him? The year before, Mitoma had survived a test of fire. He had defeated all rivals in a power play and inaugurated the productive joint venture with Au. Had a sea change occurred? Were they somehow aware of his clandestine dealing with the Ainu? Had some scandal been uncovered? Mitoma could already feel the cold metal of a *katana* blade against his neck.

He passed three giggling geishas in the hallway. Mitoma rolled his eyes and sighed wearily. Too late again. They would be getting down to business now. He steeled himself for the encounter with reminders that he was a doer. A leader, not a follower. Still, he had witnessed many forced resignations in his career. Too many.

He unlatched the French doors and entered the main showroom. Video cameras scanned the premises while moisture exuded from expertly placed humidifiers. In the center of the room, a soaring ivory pagoda commanded attention. The floor was ringed by glass cases brimming with ornate objects and figurines.

The male secretary to the Chairman greeted him as he approached the double doors leading to the production facilities and business offices. Mitoma studied his face for clues. None appeared.

Once through the doors, they passed the glass-enclosed computer room. Its attendants did not look up as they eagerly tracked the movement and sale of tons of ivory.

The two men continued on to the workshop. Crates of ivory cylinders nestled beside work benches. Cream-colored dust filled the air, as artisans seated on *tatami* mats operated slow turning lathes.

Only finger-sized *hanko* were made on the premises. But since the "chops" were the largest devourer of ivory in the world, the level of production here was staggering. Mitoma knew that most of this ivory was of questionable origin. Since the worldwide ban on ivory had been imposed, false documents were the rule. "Laundered" tusks, usually poured in from Hong Kong, Singapore and Burundi. Tracing the finished artifacts was impossible.

The secretary opened the mahogany boardroom doors and Mitoma walked into the meeting in progress. He made his way toward the low, teak table littered with sake glasses. There were four others in the room, including the Chairman, Yasuhiro Nagata.

Now fifty-seven, Nagata had entered the family business at the age of twelve. His predecessors had traded in ivory for more than a hundred years. Nagata was talking on the phone with his back to the table.

Mitoma bowed to the others and waited at attention for the Chairman to finish. He looked around at the directors. Mitoma did not recognize one of them, a powerfully built man with thick eyebrows and slicked back hair. None of them was smiling. No doubt about it: Mitoma was in a tight spot.

After what seemed like an eternity, the Chairman terminated the call, turned around, jumped up and ran to welcome him. Nagata pumped Mitoma's hand vigorously. "My dear Crashi, please come sit down."

Mitoma smiled and relaxed slightly as he followed the Chairman to his place at the table. Nagata leaned toward him beaming. "You have been brought here because we wish to honor you. Last year's net revenue exceeded fifteen million dollars." The Chairman said this in a hushed tone which could be overheard by the others anyway.

"But I..." Mitoma started to protest.

"Nonsense," Nagata interrupted. "It was all due to your perseverance."

Mitoma was stunned. Nagata looked around the room before returning to him. "Thanks to you, our supply was not interrupted despite the turmoil caused by meddling conservationists."

Nagata looked at him like a father. "Crashi, I am pleased to announce that you have been promoted to Director of International Marketing. Congratulations."

Mitoma took the hand Nagata stabbed toward him western style. The others, except for the stocky stranger, broke into subdued applause. Mitoma blushed as he uttered his heartfelt thanks to Nagata and the board members. The title would be a good cover for his true profession: ivory smuggler.

Nagata motioned uneasily toward the silent man. "Oh, permit me to introduce our new member of the board, Hiroshi Zaku."

Mitoma thought he detected a momentary tremble in Nagata's voice. He bowed respectfully to the rigid man. Zaku leaned forward, grunted and bowed his head slightly, but he did not smile or acknowledge Mitoma's glance. Mitoma wondered why Nagata did not provide any biographical information, or summarize Zaku's qualifications, as was customary. Perhaps it had been done earlier for the others.

Nagata was suddenly formal. "Now there is one final item of business we must attend to."

Mitoma felt a knot in his stomach and braced himself. The others leaned forward, listening intently.

"The wholesale slaughter of elephants for profit bears the potential for a public relations disaster. Since the Nomura scandal, we Japanese must take care to guide global perceptions." Nagata paused to let the message sink in, then stroked his silver hair and continued. "We cannot be overly cautious in the protection of our industry. As you know, our trade association is the largest single contributor to the ivory unit of the Convention on International Trade in Endangered Species. But we must do more. The Chinese recently destroyed seven tons of ivory."

Nagata placed his hand on Mitoma's shoulder and spoke directly to him. "Crashi, I want you to initiate an advertising campaign to divert public attention from the ivory use issues. We must advance the perception that elephant populations are dwindling due to encroachment by civilization and competition for scarce resources."

The Chairman did not mention that Japan, as the world's largest importer of tropical timber, had contributed to the scarcity of elephant habitat, too. Nagata thought for a moment and looked up as if trying to recall the lines of his script. "The main thrust of our attack must be that people, not poachers, and population growth, not guns, threaten the elephant. Limited financial resources should be used to feed the starving people of the third world, and not to protect creatures that trample their meager crops."

He turned to the group. Mitoma could tell that the Chairman had warmed to his subject. "Furthermore, we should do our utmost to quietly support those nations that either look the other way when it comes to the trade ban, or permit trophy hunting of so-called endangered species, such as Malawi, Zambia, Botswana, Namibia and South Africa. Those enlightened countries should receive all of the assistance we are able to provide."

Nagata stood, his arms outstretched, palms resting on the table. His eyes swept from face to face, finally settling on Mitoma. "Do you understand me, Crashi?"

Mitoma was intrigued and inspired by the devious charge. It was a stroke of pure genius. Out of the corner of his eye he noticed Zaku waiting for his reaction. "*Hai!*" he shouted.

After the meeting had adjourned, Mitoma accepted an invitation from two of the others to join them in the beer garden on the roof. Nagata remained in the boardroom with Zaku. Mitoma and the others had walked out into the chill night air that had discouraged all but a hardy few.

They sat in blue plastic chairs at a Formica table and watched the breathtaking light show in the urban ravines below. Lanterns hung at intervals around the protective fence, added to the display with muted rays of orange, pink and green. Multiple rounds of beer were ordered by the enthusiastic celebrants until their alcohol-fueled voices slurred. Mitoma accepted boozy congratulations from the others. "*Domo,*" he had to say repeatedly.

Soon he was lost in his own swirling thoughts. So the Chairman wanted him to orchestrate a disinformation campaign. Well, he was the man to do the job alright. He would start immediately. Right after a final trip to Orchid Island.

Success with this new assignment would smooth the way for Mitoma to reveal what he had feared Nagata already suspected: that he intended to replace Au's network with his own. And what if Nagata should learn of his plans before he was ready to disclose them? Mitoma shuddered.

There was something else. While taking leave of the Chairman, Mitoma had caught a glimpse of Zaku's hands. The tips of his pinkie fingers had been sliced off. *Yakuza*!

Mitoma knew that the gangsters were no longer content to restrict their activities to the margins of society. They had been moving into diverse, "legitimate" businesses. Had they infiltrated Nagata's ivory enterprise, too? By doing that, they would control the head of the octopus, and all of the other *keiretsu* partners.

Mitoma remembered Zaku's cold, lizard-like eyes, and suddenly felt a chill.

Chapter 17

The 777 completed its bucking rotation as the rosy-pink light of the new dawn translated to grey. Radiant clouds chased by the wind dashed across the open sky. Electric motors whirred in the wings as the flaps retreated and advanced to adjust the trim. With a final sweeping turn, the plane headed due west toward the horizon of the morning star.

Hannah Song had booked an early morning flight to Taipei. It was a trip she dreaded having to make. Her nightmares had become reality. Daniel would be buried with their ancestors. He would have a traditional funeral. That was all she could do for him now.

Brooker had been kind enough to arrange for the immediate release of Daniel's body. Her friends at Customs had helped Song cut the usual red tape. Now they were headed home to Taiwan, for the first time in fourteen years.

Song wiped her red, swollen eyes with a tissue. The elderly woman seated beside her had her forehead pressed against the window. Her hair was tied in a bun, held in place by a tooled leather barrette. She was wearing black pants, a matching high-necked blouse and a grey button-down sweater. "*Jin-shan*," the woman said.

Song was a world away, deep within her grief. "I'm sorry."

The woman was motioning at the coastal mountains beyond the Golden Gate. Song strained to look out the window from the aisle seat. An amber light crossed with patches of shadows bathed the distant hills.

"*Jin-shan,*" the woman repeated. Seeing Song's puzzled look, she explained. "Gold mountain. The name first given by our people to San Francisco."

Song watched the hilly ravines darken under a hovering cloud. "Oh, yes, I see."

Later, the flight attendant wheeled the beverage cart up the aisle to them. She passed an orange juice to the woman and served Song hot tea with lemon. Song blew over the edge of the cup and sipped the drink. "*Jin-shan,*" the woman said again Song nodded. They watched in silence as they traversed the open sea far below. She had been mulling over Brooker's comment that there may be a connection with the ivory smuggling and the death of her brother. She made a silent vow to herself to avenge him if that turned out to be true.

The plane touched down at noon the next day. Song had managed to sleep for part of the trip. She had not needed the tranquilizers prescribed by her doctor.

After checking into Taipei's Lai-Lai Sheraton Hotel, Song called their few remaining relatives to advise them of Daniel's funeral. It was scheduled for 11:00 a.m. the next morning. Then she called the monastery to double-check arrangements.

Her sad tasks completed, Song walked through a damp fog to the police bureau. Within minutes, she had reached the building, stopped at the front desk and asked to see Detective Ku Tai Lee. She was escorted to the armory by a chatty sergeant with a roving eye. The sergeant motioned toward Lee, "That's him, there."

Sitting behind a glass partition, Song watched as Lee an attractive middle-aged man of medium build, led a group of younger men in a martial arts drill. She was fascinated by their choreographed movements. Song turned toward the sergeant. "What is that? Kung-fu?"

The sergeant appeared to welcome the opportunity to provide his analysis. "Not really. It's called *tang-shou-tao*: The Way of the Hands of Tang."

Song wrinkled her brow. The distinction had not registered. The sergeant eagerly continued his verbal lesson. "It combines the best features of *hsing-y, ba kua, tai chi* and the more difficult *shao-lin*."

Song's brow was still wrinkled. She was not tracking. The sergeant played with his mustache. "You see, there was a Tao master named Tang centuries ago. He taught that honing martial arts skills is a worthy goal, but if one's inner powers of *chi* are strong and stable, hoodlums will instinctively avoid contact. They will not dare to challenge a master."

Song nodded her head. She was beginning to understand. "I see. You mean focus on the inner power, not the outer strength."

"Yes, basically," he said. Song observed the bare-chested Lee breathe intently and ripple each muscle in his body in rhythmic sequence. There were no rapid movements associated with his exercise. He was in complete control. Her eyes lingered for a long while. Lee's command of his body was astonishing. The sergeant tried to divert her attention. "Detective Lee is a master of the soft forms."

Song turned to face him. The sergeant leaned against the glass and continued. "As a young man, he was accepted as a disciple of Master Han. To test his initiates, Master Han sat alone in a darkened room. It was lit by a single candle. The eager candidates entered the room one after another to speak to the Master, then departed. Ku Tai Lee was the only initiate to pass Master Han's test."

The sergeant glowed, anticipating her response.

"But how? What was the test?"

"He entered the room without causing the candle to flicker. Ku Tai Lee was in full command of his *chi* and Master Han recognized that."

As if on cue, Lee dismissed the group and turned to the window.

Seeing Song for the first time, he wrapped the shirt of his *gi* over his bare shoulders. Song suppressed a sudden shiver.

When Lee came through the door, she put out her hand before the sergeant could speak. "Detective Lee, I'm Hannah Song."

He hesitated awkwardly. Song wondered if he was uncomfortable because she was too forward for the old country.

But when her name registered a moment later, Lee grasped her hand. He had a light, but capable, touch. "Of course. You're with U.S. Customs, investigating ivory smuggling. I received the cablegram from your office yesterday."

They looked at each other for a long while. Neither of them said a word. The sergeant blushed, excused himself and judiciously left the room. Lee snapped out of it and wiped his face with a towel. "What may I do for you?"

Song did not tell him what was really on her mind. Instead, she remembered her mission and produced drawings and diagrams from her satchel and handed them to him. "Do you recognize any of these symbols?" She fanned them out like a deck of cards. "I think they pertain to an organization that may be involved."

Lee examined each of them closely. As he came to the last diagram in the series, a horrified look clouded his face. "This is incredible."

Song moved closer. "What is it?"

He sighed deeply. "The Ghost Shadows." Lee turned and looked through the window. His hands were clasped behind his back. "The Ghost Shadows was an ancient Triad."

Song knew that the Triads were organized criminal bands of ethnic Chinese, and an outgrowth of seventeenth-century resistance groups in opposition to the Ching Dynasty. Modernly, they were based in Hong Kong, or Taiwan. There were perhaps 100,000 members in those areas alone; nobody knew for sure. But they had branched out all over the world to commercial countries, including the United States. They were highly secretive and immersed in tradition. Their rituals were surrounded by superstition. It was a well-kept secret that they were vastly more powerful than the Mafia. And far more brutal.

"I know what the Triads are," she said, "but what is the significance of the numbers?"

Lee turned around. He appeared to be weighing the question thoughtfully. "Each member is given a number as well as a title," he explained. "For example, the leader of the Triad, or *san chu*, is given the number 489. The digits add up to twenty-one. This symbolizes the twenty-first character of the Chinese alphabet which means 'on top.'"

Song held up a card. "What about this one?"

He glanced at it and nodded. "That signifies that the wearer is a mere initiate."

She did not tell him that it was a replication of her brother's tattoo. Song flipped the cards with the tips of her nails and looked directly into Lee's eyes. "What is it about the Ghost Shadows that so concerns you?"

Lee's face clouded again. "The Ghost Shadows were involved in the global heroin trade and black market activities during the Vietnam War. They were wiped out in a raid on their mountain encampment in 1979 . . ." Lee's voice choked off. "My oldest brother was a police captain, beaten to death the year before by a Red Pole for the Ghost Shadows, named Cheng Lao Wah. Wah was known in the underworld as 'Tat Wah.'"

"I'm so sorry about your brother," said Song.

He tried to smile. "That's alright. It was a long time ago. Wah's remains were recovered from a burned out cottage. The remnants of his Triad vanished without a trace. They were never heard from again. Until now."

Lee lowered his eyes. Song put her hand on his shoulder. It was invitingly warm. "Please tell me, what is a Red Pole?"

"They are gang enforcers. Executioners. Traditionally, all are masters of the martial arts." Lee clasped her hands and looked into her eyes. "You must be very careful."

Song did not acknowledge the warning, but again reached into the satchel. "There is something else that I would like to show you."

She removed an object wrapped in tissue paper and handed it to him. "I have been told that this was carved by artisans of the Kainan tribe."

Lee removed the tissue and turned it over in his hands, examining it carefully. It was the ivory carving of the hunters capturing a wild boar. He handed it back to her. "The Kainan live in the remote mountains near Pingtung. They have never caused us any trouble. I can't understand how they could be involved. They are only woodcarvers."

"Well, perhaps it's against their will," Song suggested.

"Perhaps." Lee was unpersuaded.

"One other question. Do you know anything about a company called Dockside Export Trading?"

Lee's look was even more puzzled. "Yes. They're an established toy and novelty exporter. They started with fireworks, but the insurance costs became prohibitive. I graduated from middle school with their President, Ping Young. Would you like me to call him for you?"

Song re-wrapped the figurine. "No, if you don't mind, I think I'll just look around on my own."

"I don't mind at all."

After she packed the satchel, Lee walked her to the front door and held it for her.

"Will you join me for dinner at six tomorrow evening?" Lee asked. He had the look of an innocent boy.

"Are you married?"

Lee grinned broadly. "No. I'm not."

Song smiled. "In that case, I would be delighted. But please let's make it for later this week. I still have some jet lag and have a family matter that I must attend to tomorrow."

He nodded respectfully. She decided that she would tell him

the sad news about her brother later. She turned and gave him an interested look and slipped out the door.

Song decided to hail a pedicab for a ride to the hotel. Back in her room, she dictated a memo to Victoria Moy, until the weariness caught up with her. Song kicked off her shoes and lay across the bed, fully dressed. A distant siren echoed through the canyons of the city. She did not know if it was a hallucination or part of her dream.

Chapter 18

A pale morning sun greeted the line of mourners marching up the hill. The Buddhist monk struck a cymbal as he led the funeral procession and the casket of Daniel Song. They waded through a sea of tall grass to reach the summit populated by clusters of stunted evergreens. Their village below lay nestled in a verdant coastal valley. Few participated in the somber ceremony. Not many relatives had survived the typhoon. None had even seen Daniel since his journey to America.

The family members reached the crown of the hill and stopped beside the grave. It had been freshly cut from the overgrown ancestral plot. Clinging mosses gnawed at the inscriptions on crumbling headstones. The slope faced the prevailing winds. A gentle brook trickled from the brow. According to Chinese wisdom, burial places should have wind and water. This spot had been picked by the first ancestor of the family. It would serve Daniel well.

The consolers were clad in traditional funeral garb. Some of the mourners wore coarse burlap tunics cinched at the waist with hemp. Others, including Hannah Song, were wearing white linen robes. Everyone, including the children, wore white hoods held in place by strands of jute.

Song clutched a framed photograph of Daniel. A black ribbon and bow was stretched diagonally across the upper corners of the picture. The photograph captured Daniel in his carefree youth. He had just started his senior year of high school. It was her favorite portrait of him. Even so, his hopeful face kept breaking her heart.

They placed the wooden casket at the edge of the grave. The family formed a semicircle with Song and the photograph in the middle. Tears welled up in her eyes and streamed down her cheeks. The monk closed his eyes, bowed and chanted prayers to cleanse Daniel's prior life in preparation for his reincarnation. The others joined him in a prayer of lamentation. Song's cousin stepped forward carrying an oval brass canister. It was filled with incense and offerings of rice, tea, spirits and paper, representing money. All of the things Daniel would need in the next life. He bowed and placed the container at the monk's feet. The officiant took the paper first and burned it. Then he lit the aromatic incense sticks.

The perfumed smoke drifted around the assembly before gathering into a free pillar and slowly ascending. Another relative played a traditional tune on a *suo na*, a Chinese trumpet, as the monk scattered the offerings around the site. The soft music was accompanied by the urgent chirping of a cricket.

Everyone stood immobile while Daniel Song was lowered into his grave. The ceremony was over. Hannah Song did not linger while the others covered her brother with the rich earth. She returned alone to the family tabernacle behind the village.

All Chinese families had a *kia t'ang* containing statuettes, tablets and images of their personal divinities. At Song's family tabernacle, there were tablets honoring her father, grandfather and great-grandfather. Another collective tablet was dedicated to the first ancestor. The tablets were clustered above a perfume burner. It was filled with the ashes of joss sticks. In accordance with custom, the burner was never emptied.

Song paused to read the inscriptions dedicated to her forebears. The precepts and rituals attending the worship of ancestors had governed Chinese family life for centuries. Song had memorized the legends as a little girl. She longed for that simpler time as she lit two red wax candles and some incense.

She closed her eyes, folded her arms across her chest and prayed silently. All sense of time and space faded away. Her thoughts were clear. After a long while, an image of Daniel walking toward distant mountains entered her mind. He did not look happy or sad, just intent upon reaching his goal. The scene began to dissolve. Her attempts to hold the image failed. It disappeared with a flicker. She blinked, opened her eyes and raised them to the sky. "Be kind to him," she whispered. A feeling of warmth and reassurance enveloped her as she walked through the village. Song passed the skeletal ruins of her family home. It, along with other structures, had never been rebuilt. Children played nearby on the slab of the street. Two were kneeling and holding a multi colored string above their heads as another child tried to hurdle it. They stopped playing when she approached. Song patted the jumper on the head. "*Ni hao*," Song said in greeting them.

"*Hen hao*," the children answered.

Song told them who she was. "*Wo shì Meiguórén.*"

The children were silent. They stared blankly at her, trying to conceive of how an American could look like them. Song told herself it was true. You can't go home again. She smiled and waved goodbye to them.

"*Zàijiàn*," said the children.

Song rejoined the others at her uncle's house for the ceremonial feast. The elaborate meal was offered to the ancestors before the living could partake. This appeased the family spirits so they would not be inclined to cause mischief for their survivors.

Song ate quietly and afterwards enjoyed an enriching visit with her remaining relatives. She told them all about America as they sat wide-eyed beside the hearth. They wanted to know if she had been to Chicago and Dallas, two American cities known to every Chinese, courtesy of television and the movies. She said she had. On official business. They were clearly impressed.

Song told them how she had won the Olympic silver medal by the margin of a millimeter. They were immensely proud that one of their own had challenged the world and won. The visit ended with a wish for her to marry and have sons. Life in America was not that simple, she assured them. And daughters were just as precious and desirable.

Song climbed into the rented car and waved to everyone on her way out of the village. She could see in her rearview mirror the hillside where Daniel was buried. She watched it for a long while, now certain that he would rest easily there.

By mid-afternoon, Song was back at the hotel. She freshened up and grabbed a bite to eat before driving down to Taipei's harbor. The narrow streets were jammed with newly acquired cars, now the standard of Taiwanese prosperity. It seemed to her as if everyone in the province had taken to the roads. She regretted driving herself and debated whether it would be better to get out and walk.

Song had moved just four blocks in an hour. Not much worse than Los Angeles, she thought. By dusk, she had crossed into the harbor district. The sign for Dockside Export Trading soon loomed into view. It had been a long day.

She breezed between the open chain link fences, drove across the yard and parked in the only available slot. The facility was a modern, single-story concrete warehouse with internal offices and a raised loading dock. About 50,000 square feet, she judged.

Song made a mental note of the number of trucks in the yard and the palletized stacks of flat cardboard clogging the parking area. She knew that the corrugated cardboard could be fashioned into shipping cartons as necessary. It seemed to her that someone was poised to do a lot of packing and shipping.

She was kept waiting in the lobby by a rude receptionist who would not terminate an obviously personal call. Things were the same all over the world, thought Song. The receptionist was trying to look stylish, but her nail polish was too red for a day job. She sensed Song's irritation, and at last said her goodbyes and cradled the phone.

The receptionist glared at Song with an imposed upon look, while reaching into her overflowing in basket. "May I help you?" she said disinterestedly.

"Yes, I'd like to see Ping Young, please."

The receptionist gave her a haughty look. "And may I tell Mr. Young who wishes to see him?"

Song flipped open her badge case. "Certainly. U.S. Customs."

Chapter 19

A charging forklift hurtled past Song as she followed a painted yellow line through the toy warehouse to Ping Young's office. Its revolving light flashed with urgency as the twin forks were lowered to attack a pallet loaded six feet high with identical cartons. The operator had a scowling, determined look on his face as he elevated the forks and worked levers to adjust the incline of the load. An intermittent siren sounded as the machine ripped into reverse and dragged its kill off to a dark corner of the building. Song covered her ears and almost gagged from the stench of propane exhaust boiling in its wake.

As she approached the dock office area, she noticed that row upon row of racks and shelves stood empty. She attributed that to the reality that stateside merchants had not yet begun to place orders for Christmas in the U.S. which was still nine months away. Yet, Song was surprised that groups of grimy laborers were frantically assembling wooden crates as well as blocking and bracing devices for ocean going containers; certainly, the existing stock within the warehouse did not warrant such frenzied activity. Perhaps they were expecting a shipment to arrive. Very soon.

The frenetic hammering and sawing stopped as Song walked past the workers. She felt uncomfortable with their appreciative glances. A foreman noticed their inactivity and cursed at them to get back to work. One by one, they resumed the pace of construction. Song reached Ping Young's office and hesitated in the doorway.

A man with puffy cheeks resembling a stuffed rodent leaned against a desk as if posing for a portrait. He had obviously been waiting for her to arrive. His arms were self-consciously folded in order to display a large gold and diamond watch and matching bracelet. He was wearing a grey, pure wool suit with muted stripes. It was impeccably cut. His striped tie was conservative, even by Chinese standards. A pencil thin mustache accentuated his upper lip.

The expansive desk itself was clear. No papers or files graced the in or out baskets on the matching credenza. His trash can appeared to be empty. No message pads rested beside the multi-button telephone. There were no sales charts or diagrams in the room. He was no worker.

With a syrupy smile he swept his hand out with the palm down. "Please come in. Ping Young. And you are...?"

She clasped and quickly released his hand and stood back. "Hannah Song, Special Agent, U.S. Customs."

Young slipped behind her and closed the door. He studied Song a little too closely to suit her. She side stepped to a leather bound Queen Anne chair. "May I?"

Young slapped his forehead. "Oh, of course. Where are my manners? Please do sit down."

He scooted her chair toward his desk. Song shoved it back to its original position as he walked around and stood behind his own chair. "Now, Ms. Song, I am quite curious. What could U.S. Customs possibly want with my enterprise?"

Song crossed her willowy legs; Young's eyes eagerly followed. She waited for him to look up before explaining. "We're investigating the illicit importation of worked ivory into the continental United States..."

Young sat down dramatically and interrupted her. "But, Ms. Song, surely you're aware that we are exclusively engaged in the toy and novelty trade," he spluttered.

She gave him a resolute look. "As I was saying, we have reason to suspect that illegal ivory carvings have been shipped from Taiwan."

Exasperated, Young threw his arms wide open. "But, my dear Ms. Song, what does that have to do with us?"

Song did not appreciate his condescending tone, but remained coolly polite. "If you'll allow me to finish..."

He appeared flustered and raised his eyes with a look of resignation. "Yes, of course."

She looked at him sternly. "And we believe that one of those shipments was disguised as a container of toys."

Song watched his eyes blink and shift from side to side. He swallowed hard and rocked back in his chair. "Well, of course we wouldn't have any information about that." Young waved an arm toward the dock. "As you may have noticed, our floor stock is temporarily depleted. We haven't shipped much for the past two months and don't expect our business to pick up until June."

She bored in. "And yet, your laborers appear to be quite busy."

Young looked unsettled, but recovered. "We reward loyal employees by keeping them occupied year round. They are just making preparations for the high season. Once it begins, there will be little time available for such activities."

Song didn't say anything, so Young continued. "There are dozens of toy companies in Taipei. Any suggestion that we are engaged in such criminal commerce is preposterous. Have a look around if you like."

Song turned in her seat and switched legs. "Fine, Mr. Young. I just might. I have only one more question for you."

Young fidgeted with his hands and licked his exaggerated lips. "Oh? What's that?"

Song had a mental image of throwing a fastball at Yankee Stadium, bottom of the ninth. "Do you have any dealings with the Kainan tribe? I believe they reside in the mountains near Pingtung."

Song had zeroed in for his reaction; she was not disappointed. The blood rose in Young's face. He averted his eyes too long before engaging her again. "Well, frankly, yes. On occasion we order our wooden novelties from them. You know, they are exquisite carvers."

"So I've heard," Song said pleasantly.

A phone line lit up, followed by the buzzing of the intercom. Young reached for the receiver. "Excuse me," he said, punching the blinking button. Young turned, facing the window. "Yes. Yes," she heard him say. "Tell him I'll be right with him."

He swiveled around, laid the receiver on the desk and rocked to his feet. "Ms. Song, I hope you will forgive me. I must take this call. If you don't mind."

She stood with her legs slightly apart. "Of course, Mr. Young. Thank you for your time." As she turned to go, she added, "I won't trouble you anymore…today."

Song opened the door, walked out and closed it without looking back. She walked a few steps before rotating on her heels and tiptoeing back to his door. She opened it and poked her head in. Young was pleading for something. He saw her and held the phone to his chest with an impatient look. "Yes?"

"I'm sorry, excuse me. One more thing. Can you tell me how to get to the American embassy from here?"

Young looked like a bottled up explosion. "There isn't one," he said with a strained voice. "Your country broke diplomatic relations with us, remember?"

Song knew perfectly well what he meant. The United States had severed diplomatic relations with a friendly country for the first time in its history. It had slighted Taiwan just to appease mainland China. She feigned ignorance. "Oh, of course. How foolish of me. Please forgive the intrusion."

She smiled wryly at the receptionist on her way out.

A half hour later, Song was back at the hotel. She sent a quick cable to Victoria Moy, then returned to her room and slept until midnight.

At midnight, Song awoke and dressed in black fatigues, under a raincoat, and returned to the harbor. En route, she worked the plan over and over in her mind. By 12:47 a.m. she had parked a block from Young's toy warehouse.

Song doffed the raincoat and darted noiselessly to a building across the street from the warehouse. Unarmed, she climbed cat like up the fire escape to the flat rooftop to take her position. She began the surveillance at 1:10 a.m.

At 1:40 a.m., a single roll up door opened on Young's dock. Within minutes a cargo van backed up and was unloaded by harried workers. Two more drayage vans arrived twenty minutes apart and were also unloaded. Song kept careful notes of the intervals and associated activities. She wondered why they were receiving so much freight in the dead of night.

At precisely 2:45 a.m., a tractor pulling a twenty-seven foot container chugged around the corner and pulled through Young's lot. It backed against the warehouse dock with a loud bang. Song heard the foreman curse at the driver. He raised his hand in an obscene gesture familiar to all Chinese schoolboys. The driver responded with a churlish motion of his own.

The container's rear doors were clipped open. A steel ramp was lowered into place between the dock and truck bed. As if on cue, a steady stream of laborers with loaded and trucks raced into the trailer like ants. The loading operation continued until just before dawn. So, the cargo came in and immediately went back out. That was why the warehouse was so empty when she visited.

Song watched as the doors were slammed and locked. The foreman went down on one knee and snapped a lock through the holes in the bottom door latch. The driver scribbled something on a clipboard and handed it to the foreman. Then he climbed into the rig, started it and pulled away. It made a hard right turn and headed directly for the piers. Song did not follow, due to the rapid approach of daylight.

The warehouse roll up door cranked down and the workers filed out through the main entrance. Song waited a half hour just to be on the safe side. When she was sure it was secure, she scaled down the side of the building and worked her way across the street.

Once behind the warehouse, she searched the loading dock area. A gust of wind whirled around the building blowing dust and debris. She shielded her eyes with a hand. A scrap of paper pressed against her ankle. She picked it up and glanced at it. An export permit. Song was about to throw it down when she noticed the word "Unknown" typed under the section labeled "Country of Origin."

Chapter 20

"Tell us what you know, now, or I'll order a summary trial, followed by execution."

C. K. Peter Langdon III, Kenya's Director of Wildlife and Conservation Management paced the floor of his spartan Nairobi office. He was a tall, contentious man. His hands were clasped firmly behind his back. For this occasion, Langdon was wearing battle dress utilities. Jungle fatigues camouflaged for the tropics.

The scion of prominent East African anthropologists and himself a competent paleoanthropologist, Langdon was in the second year of an open mandate to rid Kenya of poachers. Since 1999, his militarily trained game wardens supported by air power had shot on sight 120 poachers. Many more poachers had been forced to seek refuge in Somalia.

Critics of his tactics had named him "the poaching czar." He had grabbed worldwide headlines by setting ablaze a 105 ton mound of ivory worth $105 million on the black market. Langdon knew how to make a point. Evidently he was taken seriously in some quarters. He had received countless death threats and was protected by a platoon of bodyguards. He was a workaholic and a man obsessed with time.

Ever since the price of raw ivory had rocketed to as high as $1,300 per pound, hundreds of conservation officials had sold out to the poachers. From the rangers in the field to the highest echelon administrators, the allure of easy money corrupted everyone and everything it touched.

Kulmie Madar sat on a stool facing a huge portrait of stampeding elephants. He had refused to talk at the initial interrogation five days earlier. Langdon had ordered him held in solitary confinement to give him time to think it over. Now, Langdon was losing patience. Too much was at stake. It was time for Madar to talk.

Madar gulped and cleared his throat. He blinked repeatedly as if anticipating a cuff to the head. Rivulets of sweat streamed down his blanched face onto his khaki shirt. The single rotating paddle fan above his head offered little comfort. The Kenyan Minister of Natural Resources hovered behind him. Weede stood beside Langdon. He pushed his face against Madar's and raised his hand. "Talk! You bloody…"

Weede hesitated in mid-strike as the Minister made a convincing show of staying his arm. Madar lowered his eyes. "*Wazimu*," he muttered under his breath.

In mock rage, Weede jerked Madar's head back by the hair and yelled into his ear. "Crazy, am I? I came back from the dead. Now who's crazy?"

Madar twisted his head to the left. He shifted his feet. Weede pulled him back by the chin and pinched his cheeks between a partial thumb and forefinger; they had been shot away years before. Weede was wild-eyed, "Where's Niassa?" he boomed.

Weede squeezed harder. Madar yelped in pain and tried to jerk loose. "Where's Niassa?"

"I don't know," Madar gurgled.

Weede crimped Madar's ear and twisted. "Where's the shipment being off loaded?"

Madar rasped a guttural noise and glared at Weede with hate-filled eyes. Weede pinched and twisted the other ear.

"Ahhh. Kaohsiung…!" Madar screamed. "To avoid too much attention in Taipei."

Weede clenched his teeth. "Who's behind Niassa?"

Madar tried to shake loose from the vice of Weede's grip. "I don't know. I only dealt with him."

"How many tons were shipped?" Weede asked, in a suddenly softer tone.

Madar hesitated, then shifted his eyes imploringly to Langdon. Langdon turned his back. Weede tightened the grip on Madar's hair and yanked firmly. "How many?"

"Uhhh. Two. Let go! Let go!"

Weede relaxed his hold. He looked up at Langdon and the Minister. They were shaking their heads in sadness. An average tusk weighed about thirteen pounds. That meant that more than 150 elephants had been slaughtered for just that one shipment. Since the raw ivory was worth at least $1 million per ton, that meant that the finished value of the ivory could exceed $4 million.

Langdon took over. He put his hand on Madar's shoulder and adopted a fatherly tone. "You see, Kulmie, we have an agenda here. An unlimited mandate."

Madar listened but could not stop trembling. His eyes twitched as he watched Weede.

Langdon moved to the mural and studied it. His hands were folded across his chest. He looked as if he were about to lecture a class. "The elephant has given tremendous joy to the entire world for generations. It has survived capably in the wild for thousands of years." He turned and looked directly at Madar. "Humanity simply cannot, through sloth, avarice and timidity, permit the elephant to become a relict in Africa," he said with the air of a campaigner. "Now, I really don't want to see you shot. But if you fail to cooperate, well…" Langdon faced the mural again, then whirled and jabbed his finger in Madar's face. "Do you understand?" he roared.

To some people, there was nothing more frightening than a man who couldn't be bought. Langdon was straight up. A man of his word. Madar nodded in resignation. "Good. Very good," said

Langdon. "Then you'll want to tell us everything we need to know." Weede stepped a foot closer. Madar swallowed and nodded.

He detailed for them how the kickbacks were paid and who had received them. Nearly one-third of the Wildlife Department's trusted employees were on the take. Most importantly, Madar told them to expect impending raids on the remaining herds. Kenya would be reduced to a charnel house.

Madar was just one of an estimated 2,000 corrupt Kenyan wildlife officials. Other functionaries were involved as well. Even a member of the country's parliament had been caught with 105 tusks. Illegal ivory had also been discovered in the possession of a Catholic priest, and personnel of the Iranian and Pakistani embassies. Langdon's net was finally spreading to the middlemen. Madar was not unique. Still, extraordinary measures were called for in his case.

Langdon had been looking over the Minister's shoulder as he took notes. He looked up at Madar with finality. "Anything else?"

Madar thought for a moment, shook his head and lowered it in shame.

"Then I'm afraid we'll have to decide what to do with you," Langdon said abruptly.

Madar shivered and pleaded with his eyes. Without another word, Langdon rang for a bodyguard. A solid man with a military bearing appeared and led Madar into an antechamber. Langdon sat on the edge of his desk, and puffed on a Kaywoodie pipe for a few moments. He looked intently at Weede and the Minister. "Well, gentlemen, any suggestions?"

The Minister shook his head. Langdon focused on Weede. "I don't think we should shoot him," Weede said. "He should be hung."

Langdon stood and walked over to the mural with his back to Weede. "Yes, well, I can understand how you might feel that way." He turned, sucked hard on his pipe and blew a cloud of pearly smoke. "But I have something else in mind which may help to turn the tables on this awful business."

Langdon moved behind the desk and dropped into his chair. He leaned back with his legs crossed and puffed harder, then looked up at the ceiling. "What if we announce that Madar has gone missing in a raid?"

He waited for their reactions. Weede just shrugged. The Minister looked surprised. "To what end?" he asked.

Langdon gestured with the Kaywoodie. "In truth, he'll be secretly confined in a remote camp in northeastern Kenya." He looked as if he were dictating from memory. "Our announcement will fulfill two missions: one, instill a false sense of security in the gangs of poachers; and two, preserve Madar as an informant and witness for future prosecutions. He'll cooperate, or else."

He placed the pipe in its rest and looked up at them. "Well, what do you think?"

Weede smiled and the Minister nodded. "Good, then. Consider it done," Langdon said.

While Langdon and the Minister debated the minute details of Madar's fate, Weede excused himself and picked up an extension phone in the hall. He dialed Song's office and was informed that she had gone to Taipei. He next placed a quick call to an old mate in the Kenyan Air Force.

An hour after taking leave of Langdon and the Minister, Weede was over the Indian Ocean in a jet trainer bound for the Maldives. The next morning he was scheduled to hop a military transport to Singapore. He didn't know yet how he would get to Taipei. But he would get there.

As he chatted with the pilot over the intercom, the trainer turned into the sun. Weede reflected on Langdon's solution. He thought it was a stroke of genius. But personally, he would not go to all that trouble.

Chapter 21

The "*Tien-shi*" restaurant in "Snake Alley" was busier than usual. It was just after dusk. Each table glowed in the light of a dim candle. A musician sat in a corner playing an *er hu*, a two-stringed violin. Throngs of customers lined up at open air stands in the corridor for snake bile drinks, exotic potions and medicinal drams. Song wrinkled up her face as each devotée, in turn, bolted down a miniature chalice of greenish-brown liquid. Ku Tai Lee grinned. "What's wrong?" he asked with mock seriousness.

She hesitated before responding. Her coral red lips were pursed in a cupid's bow. "There are some aspects of our culture that are hard for me to become reacquainted with." As she said this, Song looked warily at her own cocktail.

Lee threw back his head and laughed. "Well then, you probably won't care for the scorpion tail or the jimson weed either."

Song swallowed slowly as she watched the imbibers. "Isn't that stuff harmful?"

Lee had a mischievous glint in his eye. "Haven't you heard the old adage, fight poison with poison?"

She feigned annoyance and picked up a menu card. "Shouldn't we order?"

He laughed again. Song read the card and looked up. "What's good here?"

Lee raised the menu. "If you'll permit me?"

Song dropped her card. "Yes, please...but no poison," she said with a wink.

Lee signaled their waiter. He rolled up and stood by their table attentively. Lee tapped the dinner list with his forefinger. "We'll have the duck, roasted with camphor, please. Also, my friend and I would like the *ban yui, bok choy* and bean curd."

"Very good, sir," said the waiter. He poured some bronze-green tea for Song, clutched their menu cards and raced toward the kitchen. Lee tried to look into Song's eyes. She avoided his gaze and stared off into the distance. She absently lifted the tea to her lips and parted them to blow on the steaming cup. Lee touched her free hand softly and clasped it between his own. "Hannah, try to forget about business tonight."

Song didn't know what to say. Her face felt flushed. She was embarrassed by his sudden overture. Lee had a dream-like look on his face. "You know, you remind me of the legend of Hsi-tzu." His eyes flared with longing. "Are you familiar with the story?"

She breathed deeply, hoping that she wouldn't hyperventilate. "I think so," she said hesitantly. "Is that the legend about the girl who rose from a humble birth to become the wife of the King of Wu?"

Lee's face brightened like an opening flower. "Exactly. It is said that she was so pricelessly beautiful as to be capable of over-throwing a city or a kingdom."

A rush of heat drained into Song's cheeks. She tried to cover up her discomfort with a joke. "Right now, I'd settle for overthrowing a band of smugglers."

Lee smiled warmly. "Remember, no business." Without letting go of her hand, he nodded his head to summon the waiter.

"No business, huh? What else do you have planned for this evening?" Song worried that she had said this with too much of a tease in her voice.

Lee rolled his eyes, leaned back and clapped his hands. The waiter brushed against their table. "Yes, sir?"

"More tea, please."

"Right away, sir." The waiter picked up the pot and returned to the kitchen. Lee waited until he was beyond earshot. "How about the martial arts tournament at Yangmingshan Park?"

Song reasoned that it would take her mind off the case. She had always been interested in martial arts, but never had the time to devote to it. The hours, days and weeks at a time practicing at the shooting range left little time for anything else. Not religion. Not sports. And not love. She nodded her head. "Okay. Sounds like fun."

The servers brought the courses of their dinner, as the waiter reappeared with a steaming pot of tea. Song splashed hot sauce on her *ban yui* and slipped a small taste into her mouth. As she crunched down on a solid piece of ginger, her eyes watered profusely. Her ears were aflame. Gulps of water didn't put out the fire.

"Are you okay?" asked Lee.

Song fanned her mouth and tried to catch her breath. "Yes," she finally answered with a hoarse whisper.

"I should have warned you about the excessive use of ginger here." Lee pointed to the crowd. "These zealots love the stuff."

Song noticed their waiter skinning a live snake at the adjacent table. She coughed and continued fanning her mouth. "Oh, I would imagine so," she said.

They ate in silence and finished all of the courses. Song was careful to search each clump of food before tasting it.

After dinner they strolled to Lee's car. It was a late model, white Corvette. He had won it in an international tournament in Seoul, three years earlier. Song thought it was too much car for the city. It belonged on the open road, not stuck in traffic.

She was wearing an ivory-colored *chi pao*, a traditional, high-necked full-length dress with a slit skirt. It had been her mother's. Due to the strategic division of the skirt, exiting and entering vehicles involved a delicate maneuver. One which was not lost on

Lee. Song had caught him looking more than once. He looked again as she lowered into the car and tucked into the seat.

Lee pushed the door closed and sprinted around to the driver's side. Song debated whether to tell him about what she had discovered. She decided to wait until she had developed a solid theory supported by sufficient evidence.

Lee backed out and punched the gas pedal as they squealed from the lot. He turned to gauge her reaction. She obviously disapproved, so he eased off the gas. The car moved through the caverns of the city, emitting a throaty rumble. Song wanted a tuned exhaust for her own car and enjoyed the steady hum as they rode along. Twenty minutes later, they had reached the compact arena.

As they entered, the close smell of unwashed bodies overwhelmed Song. An exhibition was in progress. The crowd roared ecstatically each time a favored competitor smashed bricks and boards. Some of them succeeded in breaking two solid cement cinder blocks with a single blow. None could break three.

The Japanese promoter had noticed Lee's arrival. He stacked three of the blocks on top of one another, leaving an airspace below the bottom block. The promoter tested the stack by standing on it and then bowed toward Lee, seated in the grandstand.

Lee had a look of resignation. He clasped Song's hand. "The Japanese favor the pure drama of smashing boards and bricks."

"Can't you just ignore him?" she implored.

Lee surveyed the room. It was unnaturally quiet. All eyes were on him. His honor was at stake.

"No," he said calmly, "it is a matter of face."

He patted her hand, stripped to the waist and bounded to the floor. The crowd erupted with barbarous whistles and yells. They cheered unreservedly as Lee approached the smiling promoter and bowed. Then he turned quickly and bowed to the frenzied crowd.

Lee pointed to the stack of blocks and said something to the promoter. The man looked at the bricks and shook his head no.

Lee gestured emphatically and folded his arms across his chest. The promoter gave in. He stooped and restacked the blocks directly on the floor. Lee had made him eliminate the airspace! Breaking them all would now be an impossible feat. As the promoter shrugged and sat down, the crowd went wild again. They were so loud that Song was moved to cover her ears.

Lee bowed again to the crowd, then stood erect and silent before the blocks. His eyes were completely closed. Lee's slow, shallow breaths were barely detectable. The palms of his hands were locked at his sides. He looked like a high diver about to go off the high board, loose and relaxed. With a lightning movement, Lee drew his right fist high above his head then slammed it down with a crushing strike. It had been done between heartbeats. The cinder blocks didn't just break. They exploded.

The crowd swirled to its feet, screaming and cheering. Lee bowed to the audience and to the promoter, who ran up to him, aghast. Song hurried down and hugged Lee around the neck. He waved to the crowd as they headed for the exit. "That was nothing," Lee said. "Only an amateur would be impressed by that."

"Well, it looked pretty terrific from where I was sitting. I guess I'm an amateur."

Outside, Lee buttoned his shirt and drew close to her. "Hannah?"

"Yes?"

"What is your Chinese name?"

Song hesitated. She had not used it for so long. It was the same as her mother's. Hannah had been the name of the first relief worker to reach their village. She had sponsored them in America, and Song had honored her by adopting the Biblical name. She looked up into Lee's eyes. "Wen Mei Song," she said softly.

"That's beautiful," he said, pulling closer, "and so are you." He tried to kiss her. She pulled away, but not too far. Song wasn't ready yet, but she didn't want to offend him. "I should be getting back now; I have a big day tomorrow. Besides, this is only our first date."

Lee nodded. He did not appear to be offended and did not pressure her. "I hope so," he said.

He drove her back to the hotel and escorted her into the lobby. After they said goodnight to each other and shook hands, Song rode the elevator to her floor. Once in her room she opened the sheer drapes, then the sliding glass door. She stepped onto the balcony and leaned against the rail.

It was a clear night. The shimmering stars gathered together in the heavens made her sad somehow. Song felt cold and isolated. She wondered what was wrong with her. Was she incapable of giving love? Worse yet, was she incapable of being loved? Everyone close to her wound up dead. She was tired of it. So tired of it all.

Song returned to the room, closed the door and drapes and flipped off the lights. For a long while she stood in the darkness. Finally, she undressed, slipped naked between the sheets and drifted away to sleep.

Chapter 22

The QJ class steam locomotive thundered across the stone trestle trailing a plume of boiling smoke. A string of passenger cars chattered along behind as excess steam billowed from the engine's dual cylinders. Vestigial patches of snow glistened on the tracks ahead in the penetrating light of the train's center lamp. Its huge red wheels spun on through the night like pinwheels racing south. Soon the train would reach its destination. Very soon.

They had covered the last stretch of hard terrain. Substantial gradients and switchbacks had slowed them down. The mountains had been especially difficult to negotiate. Steam engines were used on the arduous route due to their renowned toughness. They were still the standard in mainland China and Taiwan.

Song folded up her pack of cards and leaned her head against the window. She was revived by the cold pressure of the glass upon her face. The day long rail trip had diminished her energy. She had fallen asleep twice due to the steady swaying of the car and the vibration of the churning wheels. It was the first time she had ridden on a train.

She kept telling herself that the trip south was absolutely essential to her investigation. A visit to the site may provide additional pieces of the puzzle. Without a break in the case, the slaughter would continue unabated. Song had to make something happen. Time was running out for her investigation and for the elephants.

Deep within, Song worried that she was only running away. Away from Taipei and Ku Tai Lee. She fretted that she had walked out at a critical time to avoid becoming involved. The trip was just an excuse. Her heart kept telling her that she was involved. Part of her wanted and needed a relationship. But a larger part of her was afraid. Afraid that he would die, like everyone else she had ever loved. She couldn't let it happen again. If it meant giving him up and sacrificing her happiness, that was what she would have to do. Then too, she was conflicted about her affection for Duff. Song wondered where in the world he could be and hoped for his well being.

The lonely shriek of the locomotive's whistle rebounded from the platform. It was bathed in a feeble light. Baggage handlers scurried into position. In the distance, pagoda-like structures clung to the geometric shadows. Song clutched her overnight bag as the train lurched to a stop at Pingtung Station.

An excited mother towing three animated children bounded into the aisle. One of them, a toddler, dropped her panda bear at Song's feet. She put a grimy finger in her mouth as Song stooped to pick it up. Song smiled as she handed it back to the little girl. "*Ni hao ma?*" asked Song.

The girl clutched the bear, but did not return Song's greeting. She continued to stare shyly at her. Exasperated, the girl's mother bumped her with an elbow. When the girl still stood silent, the mother bowed to Song. "*Ni tài kè-gi le.*"

"Oh, don't worry. It was my pleasure," said Song.

The mother yanked on the girl's arm. Her other children were nearly out the door. Song waved goodbye to the girl as she looked back. "*Zàijin. Zàijin.*"

The girl walked silently down the aisle behind her mother, continually glancing back at Song. She still had her finger in her mouth. "*Zàijin,*" Song repeated, as the little girl looked back for the last time and passed through the car door.

Once on the ground, Song knifed through the teeming crowd and hailed a taxi. At least it had the semblance of being a taxi. The cab was a '70s model Chevrolet Impala. Its faded two-tone paint was flecked with creeping islands of rust. Song pulled up on the moist latch and the door sprang open. She glided into the worn velvet back seat and glanced up. She noticed the driver checking her legs in the rear view mirror. With his curly hair and horn-rimmed glasses, the man looked like a Chinese version of Buddy Holly. Song tugged her skirt down firmly.

The driver slapped down the flag of his manual meter. "Where to, lady?"

Song folded her hands in her lap. "Santimen," she pronounced too methodically.

The driver twisted around with a surprised look. "You sure, lady?"

She gave him an all business stare. "Yes, I'm sure. Is there a problem?"

He studied her face for a moment. "No. No problem."

The drive from the rail station to the village at the toe of a mountain range took thirty minutes. Once they had reached open country, the distance steadily clicked away. The driver kept glancing at her in the rearview mirror. "You American, lady?"

Song nodded, slightly irritated that he wasn't watching the road. He reached into the glove compartment and pulled out an eight-track tape. "I got American music."

Before she could discourage him, he slipped the tape into the player and turned up the volume. There was a loud hiss and pop which gave way to "Surfin' U.S.A." by the Beach Boys. The driver started to sing along and gyrated to the music as they neared their exit. He turned around with a rapturous look. "I love Beach Boys, lady."

Song rolled her eyes and slumped back in her seat. Mud and snow splattered the windshield as the cab turned off the highway down a dirt road. The driver kept singing and stealing glances at her. Song ignored him and checked her watch. She kept search-ing for a landmark. It was a moonless night. Too dark to get her bearings.

When the tape ended the driver turned around again. "You like, lady? I got more American music?"

She waved her hands and shook her head. "No, no, please. It isn't necessary. I prefer the quiet."

Dejected, the driver swiveled around. Moments later, they crossed an empty wooden bridge. The tires hummed as they sped over the planks. Song could hear the thunders battle in the swollen river below. As they reached the opposite side, the flickering lights of a settlement came into view. The driver had stopped looking at her and was completely silent.

Song was absorbed in her own distant thoughts as the taxi wheezed to a stop beside a small inn. It was made of cut sheets of slate. The entire town had been constructed from locally quarried stone slabs. Subdued red, blue and green lights marked the path to the entrance. Song gave the driver a tentative look. He simply shrugged his shoulders and held up his hands. "This only place in town, lady."

She sighed and reached for her bag. "Okay. This will be fine."

Song exited the cab and shivered at the sudden chill of the mountain air. The musical notes of a *dizi*, a Chinese flute, drifted from a balcony. An evening crow cawed defiantly in a distant grove. Song looked up. Dots of flame winked from cliffside dwellings high overhead.

There was a low thud, followed by another thud. Drumbeats. They were coming from behind a grassy rise at the edge of the village. Song paid the driver, who waved and said goodbye with downcast eyes. He did not linger. The taillights of the cab soon winked out of sight.

Song checked in and freshened up. It was just after 10:00 p.m. She changed into faded fatigue slacks and slipped on a leather

A-2 jacket. After stashing her badge, passport and private papers, she left the inn and followed the sound of the drums.

The area behind the rise formed a natural bowl. An aboriginal amphitheater. Song stood on the rim. Sturdy tribesmen in ceremonial garments of embroidered black and silver chanted between rows of torches. At the base of each flaring torch was a teak wood stake crowned with a shapeless mass. Song drew closer, only to recoil at the sight. They were ghastly heads. Severed pigs' heads.

Song covered her mouth. The ecstatic tribesmen continued their ritual, oblivious to her presence. Two of them moved forward, pulled a writhing serpent from a burlap sack and placed it on a bamboo platform.

The villagers bowed to the snake in turn, then lay face down with arms extended. Song started to back away, when someone touched her on the shoulder. She froze and tensed her muscles before spinning around. It was a grey-haired woman in western clothes. She had a kind, open face. The woman pointed to the coiling serpent. "That's a hundred-pace snake. It's deadly poison."

It was the snake Dr. Wu had warned her about. Song tried to look surprised. She played along. "But why would they be handling and worshiping it?"

"Because. He's the spiritual elder of the tribe." The woman adopted a quiet confidential air and steered Song to the edge of the bowl. "You know, they used to employ only human heads in sacrifices," the woman said, motioning toward the stakes. "But times have changed. My, how they have changed. "The woman extended her hand, "Oh, forgive me. Ali Shan. I'm a cultural anthropologist with the Taipei Art Guild."

Song clasped her hand. It was warm and light. "Hannah Song. I'm a…just touring the island. I was raised near Lukang, but I'm an American now."

"Oh, Lukang. I know it well. Are you here for the weekend?"

Song nodded, keeping a wary eye on the tribesmen. Ali Shan

sensed her uneasiness. "Why don't we go somewhere quiet where we can talk?"

"Sure," said Song. "That would be fine."

They made their way back to the inn for a late dinner. Song had not realized how famished she was until she smelled the combination of foods welling from the kitchen. When the food finally arrived, Song could think of little else.

During the meal, they engaged in light conversation about sightseeing around the island and the vagaries of local politics. Ali Shan did most of the talking. She was well informed and quite interesting.

Shan told Song that she had come to the area to research ancient wooden totems carved by the Kainan tribe. Using wood culled from Taiwan's alpine forests, the tribe's artisans had carved faultless pieces for hundreds of years. The villagers also sculpted provincial stone and weaved and fashioned beadwork, utilizing traditional designs and methods. Shan invited Song to accompany her while she made her rounds in the morning. Song readily accepted. It was getting late. Her mind was starting to wander.

After saying goodnight, Song walked upstairs to her room, and without undressing, lay across the bed. The drums had stopped. With the sound of the *dizi* flowing softly in the night, she was soon fast asleep.

Chapter 23

A golden shaft of light slipped between the coral tinted peaks soaring above the village. Waterfalls draped like capes of silk etched the cliff faces. Riotous crystal cascades rushed from the mountains and mingled with the waters of the river as it plunged forcibly to the sea. Drifting amber mists girded each rocky point with a gentle gauze. In the courtyard of the inn, lotus blossoms tacked on the azure surface of the garden pond. Spring was truly at the gate.

Song sat on the balcony, sipping a cup of black tea. She waved to Shan, who was already out for a morning stroll. Shan pointed to the glorious mountains and shouted up to Song. "Now that's *chi.*"

"I'll be right down," Song yelled back.

It seemed to Song that the awareness of *chi*, or life force, permeated all thought in Taiwan. While she partially understood it, Song could not implement the philosophy in her own life and circumstances. Or could she? In softness, there is strength. After the impressive demonstration by Detective Lee the night before last, Song allowed that there was definitely something to it. She admired her people's devotion to its principles, yet lamented their absence in her own life. Maybe that void was why she felt so empty and alone in a callous, frightening world.

Song laced up her hiking boots and pulled on her poplin tanker jacket. It would be much cooler at the higher elevations. Last, she grabbed her pocket knife and a tin of waterproof matches, in case they were stranded.

Shan was feeding some flapping wild geese when Song bobbed up to her. They walked briskly to the edge of town, which was still engulfed by the early shadows. By 8:00 a.m. Song and Shan were picking their way through a river-hewn gorge to a hidden valley. Startled sand birds thrashed along the bank as they passed. Shan led Song onto a footpath that clung precariously to the edge of the mountain.

Song looked down. That was a big mistake. The height made her reel with dizziness. Rolling clouds boiled up from the bottom of the gorge. Cool wisps of moisture brushed her cheeks. She closed her eyes to regain her balance and shifted her weight to the left foot, leaning into the mountain. As she labored to breathe at the increased elevation, Song noticed that Shan was bouncing along minimal effort. *Chi* again. She decided to relax and practice her own breathing techniques. Song was surprised by the sudden surge of energy she felt.

At the far end of the gorge, a pair of marble serpents guarded the approach to a decrepit footbridge. As they rocked across, Song had the uneasy feeling that they were being watched by someone. Or something. She scanned the four compass points. Nothing there. Was it just her imagination? Or intuition?

On the far side of the bridge, the trail leveled off abruptly. Song scanned the evergreen clusters covering the cliffs. Were they ambuscades? Was she already in someone's sights? She kept tensing up, waiting for the strike. Being a sitting duck made her nervous. She hated being on the other end of a rifle scope. Song would be relieved if they could only get to some higher ground. But when would that be?

Ten minutes later, they encountered a series of rocky outcroppings. Slippery, moss-covered stones made the terrain difficult to negotiate. Fortunately, the way was familiar to the carefree Shan.

Song had continued to maintain her vigil without alarming her companion. There was no sense in worrying her for nothing. Once they had picked around a final wide bend, the expanse of a hanging valley opened to greet them.

Patches of budding sweet potatoes and taro plants carpeted the terraced slopes, like squares of a green patchwork quilt. A cluster of piled slate buildings dotted the distant clearing. Smoke trailed freely from untended cooking fires. Small children, in the midst of a mock war, battled with sticks. Barking dogs pursued them as they darted about the field from emplacement to emplacement.

Seeing the tireless children at play made Song feel much more relaxed. She grinned broadly at the memory of her own early childhood. As the road widened, Shan dropped back beside Song. "This place is called Liwu," Shan breathed out. "We should be able to catch some of the tribesmen at work."

Song nodded approvingly. She was still trying to catch her breath. Shan had forced a steady pace on them. Song welcomed the opportunity to just stroll. Or browse around.

A village elder gripping a walking staff labored out to meet them. He was stooped over so bad that his eyes were permanently fixed on the ground as he plowed ahead. The children followed cautiously a few paces behind. Their mixed breed dogs stood beside the path with tails at full alert. They lifted their heads with irregular barks and eyed the children protectively.

The elder halted a body's length away from Song and Shan and raised his head. They exchanged greetings with him. Shan explained, in the local dialect, the purpose of their unannounced visit. The children drew closer and formed a semi circle. The man grinned and patted a dingy-faced boy on the head. He turned and led them to a makeshift workshop with a wooden floor. The children tried to huddle around the door and were shooed away by an alert mother.

Shan followed the elder into the room. Song waved goodbye to the children before ducking through the doorway. Four shirtless tribesmen sat cross-legged on woven mats. They smiled at the women, but did not stop work.

Two of them cut, chiseled and filed blocks of wood. Another whittled and sanded the reduced blocks into basic shapes. The oldest carver etched the blanks with a scalpel-like knife to refine the features of a nearly finished piece. They appeared to be making statues. Sawdust and curled shavings gathered at their feet as the carvers fashioned the objects.

Song studied the room itself. Aboriginal carvings rested in one corner. Out of the corner of her eye, she noticed the familiar motif of the hunters carrying the boar. This one was made of wood. Song tried not to stare at it. There was something else that caught her attention. A fine dust resembling powdered bone meal covered the floor beneath the wood shavings. The color did not match the wood residue.

While Shan quizzed the carvers about their techniques, Song slipped outside. The children had disappeared. Song guessed that it was their mealtime. But mealtime or not, the settlement was eerily quiet. She peered around the corner. A large, prefabricated metal shed rested behind the workshop. The building looked strangely out of place. As if it had fallen from the sky. One thing was certain: it was new. There were no rust stains on the section joints and no grass growing around the base.

Song still felt as though she was being watched. She remained alert as she crept closer to the imposing structure. The door was secured by a padlock the size of a human hand. As Song tested it, a swarthy man dressed in worn khakis jumped out from behind a wall. He yelled something to her in the local dialect which she interpreted as "Get away." The man had adopted a balanced stance. He was pointing his Chi-com AK-47 at her, but his finger was outside the trigger guard. Two bandoliers filled with 7.62 ammo crossed his chest.

He frowned and yelled again as he swung the barrel of the

assault rifle toward the house. Song had not moved fast enough to suit him. She stepped back and blushed. She feigned embarrassment and made exaggerated gestures indicating that she needed to use the restroom.

The guard lowered his weapon and laughed, revealing black-stained teeth. A betel nut chewer no doubt. He motioned toward an open trench at the edge of the settlement and laughed at her again. Song pretended to be overcome with shame and shuffled toward the trench. She made it to the ditch and made a show of loosening her slacks. She looked back over her shoulder at the guard. He was walking back to his station shaking his head. Song was gratified that he did not keep watching her after she had reached the ditch. The guard had been convinced.

She waited beside the fetid, oozing ditch about ten minutes before strolling back to the work room. The putrefied smell had nearly overwhelmed her. But she had stayed in character. After that side excursion, she longed for pine-scented woods.

Ali Shan was still chattering away in earnest when Song returned. The senior carver had nearly completed a piece of statuary. He was pressing into the wood delicately with a miniature blade. The carver reverently caressed the figurine in his hands. Before Song's eyes, he fashioned the features of the face, holding his breath to steady his hands.

When the artisan had finished his work he rose with a satisfied look and offered the carving to Song. She accepted it graciously. It was the goddess, *Si-Wang Mu*, the lady Queen of the West. Song examined the face of the figurine closely. It had her own facial outline, nose, eyes, ears and mouth. The carver grinned broadly. Song was delighted. She thanked him profusely as he bowed from the waist.

The explorers checked carvings at two more hamlets that day. Shan had gathered enough resource material to keep her busy for weeks. Song had made her own discovery. The other carving centers had similar, guarded sheds. The wind was rising in the pines. A fine mist steadily descended from the highest peak. They hurried back to Santimen before nightfall.

In the morning, Song said a warm goodbye to Ali Shan, returned to Pingtung, and caught the early train back to Taipei. She had work to do.

Chapter 24

The first full moon of the lunar New Year washed the plaza in shimmering light. Joyful celebrants carrying colorful lanterns inscribed with meaningful phrases paraded through the crowd. The Lantern Festival was in full swing across from the Presidential Mansion in downtown Taipei. An annual tradition, the ceremonies insured against evil and illness in the coming year.

It was just after 8:00 p.m. The plaza throbbed with activity. In their excitement, children carrying their favorite creations brushed past Hannah Song. Her red *chi pao* hugged the silhouette of her taut figure. She was enjoying a dish of *yuan-hsiao*, a sweet dumpling served in a paper dish. Lee had promised to meet her after finishing a staff report. Song looked at her government-issued watch. He was already half an hour late.

Her train had pulled into the Taipei transportation center about 4:00 p.m. A rockslide near Chiayi had closed the track for several hours. The passengers had enjoyed a picnic lunch beside the Wufeng Temple, while maintenance crews cleared away the debris. Upon returning to her hotel, Song had checked for messages at the front desk. There had been two cablegrams. One was from Victoria Moy and the other had been sent by Brooker.

She had torn open the message from first. It read, "Positive I.D. on major suspect. More later. Regards, Brooker." Song was elated. She genuinely admired him. He was the type of cop who put his skills to good use. He didn't wait for something to break. Brooker made things happen. On top of that, he was not really bad looking.

The cablegram from Victoria Moy had been equally abrupt. It simply said, "Major breakthrough forensics. Hearing imminent. Cable results your investigation ASAP. V. Moy." The hearing was imminent. It was just two weeks away. Song had to wrap it up and get back. Her first cable to Moy had been vague. In the category of 'wish you were here.' She had wanted to wait until the investigation had peaked before reporting the results. Moy seemed anxious. Song fully understood that. Moy's career was on the line. In the legal bureaucracy, you were only as good as your conviction rate. But Song had a gut feeling that she was on the verge of cracking the case. Her report had to wait at least another day. Song would smooth things over when she returned. Moy would understand. Especially if Song had produced results.

Song tapped her foot and kept glancing at her watch. Was Lee going to stand her up this early in their romance? She rehearsed what she intended to say to him about that. She thought about Duff Weede again and how different the two men were. Distinct, yet somehow so much alike.

As she turned to dispose of her plate, Song caught sight of two well-dressed businessmen arguing in hushed tones. She coughed as she approached them. Ping Young turned and faced her. His eyes popped open. Song wrinkled her brow. She had caught him in an unguarded moment. So much the better, it seemed to her.

Behind Young was a portly, silver-haired, expressionless man. It was as if something inside of him had died long ago, but he had refused to recognize that fact. The man's eyes were hard and deadly cold. Whatever he was, the man was not a philanthropist. Song was not fooled or impressed by the silk-tailoring. He had killed and would do so again. Young's mouth twitched uncontrollably as Song just stood there waiting for him to speak.

Young switched to his public persona. He reminded Song of a

Chinese Dale Carnegie initiate. "Good evening, Ms. Song. May I present Shang T. K. Au, Chairman of Kowloon Shipyard, Ltd.?"

Au glided forward, bumping Young out of the way. The Chairman's face brightened. But his fierce eyes were locked on Song.

"I am pleased to meet you, Mr. Au," Song said, trying to shake hands with him.

He bowed stiffly, drew her offered hand to his lips and kissed it for an uncomfortable length of time. Au must have noticed her reticence, because he let go of her hand. But it was Au's continuing to stare into her eyes that gave her the creeps.

"The pleasure is all mine," Au said effusively. "Are you enjoying the festivities tonight, Ms. Song?"

"So far, yes," she said coolly.

Au adjusted his approach. "I understand that you are an American."

Song glanced at Young and back to Au. "That's right. But I don't recall mentioning that to you." Song looked back at Young. He had a sheepish look. The Chairman did not fluster so easily. "Well, you see, Mr. Young here has mentioned your name to me before. He told me about a most attractive young lady who had come into his office the other day. I thought he was exaggerating somewhat. That is, until I saw you myself."

Song detested male condescension. She was not at all distracted by strategic compliments. She glared at Young and back at Au, while she fought to keep from clenching her teeth. "And did Mr. Young also tell you the purpose of my recent visit?"

Au swept the air with his hand in dismissal. "Oh my, yes. Some sort of nonsense about ivory smuggling. You should know, Ms. Song, that Mr. Young is a reputable businessman. I can certainly vouch for that."

"And who will vouch for you, Mr. Au?" Song shot back.

Au gave her a look of repudiation, but she could tell that the remark had hit the target. "Ms. Song, my credentials are impeccable. I am known and respected by every major corporation and government on the face of the earth, including your own. So tell me, why should I be at all concerned with your approval?"

Song looked directly at him. "I'm afraid I can't answer that for you," she said with more than a hint of sarcasm.

She detected a tinge of sadness in his face. At least he was capable of showing a glimmer of emotion. Au adopted a more paternalistic air. "Ms. Song, I don't wish to argue with you. I only offer that you may have formed a wrong opinion about my associate Mr. Young here...and..."

Song cut him off. "Your associate, Mr. Au?"

Au and Young looked at each other. "Yes. You see, in addition to the shipyard, I control the ships. Mr. Young is a successful importer and hires our vessels from time to time."

Song folded her arms. "I'm more concerned with illegal exports to my country."

Au nodded. "And well you should be. But Mr. Young exports toys."

"Well, someone local has been illegally shipping worked ivory manifested as toys."

This time, Au did not look at Young. He lowered his voice in a conspiratorial whisper. "You know, Ms. Song, I am well acquainted with your boss in Washington. She represented my company as a lobbyist for many years before accepting her recent appointment as Director of Customs. Perhaps with a word from me..." Au gave her an insider's, all-knowing glance.

"What are you suggesting, Mr. Au?" Song demanded.

"Politics, Ms. Song. Politics." Au shrugged and held out his palms.

"Well, get this straight, Mr. Au. Politics, or no politics, I do my job. Someone is slaughtering the last vestiges of nobility in the wild for greed, and I intend to stop him," she said forcefully.

Au glowered at her ominously. His cordial tone had only

been an act. "Your dedication is really quite remarkable. Just be certain that you are equal to the task and that your efforts are not misdirected."

"Only time will tell," Song said icily. There was an uncomfortable, prolonged silence. Au raised his head to assess the tumult of the festivities. His tone changed again. "You know, Ms. Song, we have a much more colorful version of the pageant on my island. Perhaps you would do me the honor of being my guest."

Song looked at him with disdain. "Your island, Mr. Au?"

"Yes. Lan Yu, or Orchid Island. It's off the east coast."

Song was indifferent and remained unimpressed. "Yes, I know the place, but I'm afraid not this trip."

Au lowered his voice again. "Traveling alone can be dangerous for a woman like you. You should be careful."

"Everyone's told me that," she said matter of factly.

"Well, you should take heed. These are indeed perilous times."

Young fidgeted and bit his lip. A small girl raced up to them carrying a lantern embroidered with elegant calligraphy. Song read it aloud. Translated, it simply said, "Sleeping Dragon." It was a traditional term describing someone with enormous talent which was not yet fully developed.

Au handed the child a coin and laughed heartily. The laugh was out of place and did not suit him. It sounded like that of a hysterical monkey. "Perhaps you are a sleeping dragon, Ms. Song?"

Her eyes flashed with subdued anger. "Perhaps. But you know, sometimes it's hard to tell dragons from snakes."

Au stopped laughing and scowled. Young stepped between them. "Mr. Chairman, we're due to judge the designs entered in this year's competition. They will be waiting for us."

"Yes, of course." Au adjusted his pocket square, reached for his bifocals and slipped them on the end of his nose. "Ms. Song, I regret that we cannot finish our discussion. Goodbye." He bowed and extended his hand.

Song aimed her index finger at him and brought her thumb down like the hammer of the pistol. "I'll be seeing you."

Au looked stunned. Young led him off in a hurry as Song checked her watch. Lee was more than an hour late.

Song was playing a game with a group of children when Lee glided up a few minutes later. She gave him a curious look.

Lee held up his hands. "I know, I know, I'm late. Something's come up."

He was so calm and methodical, Song felt like shaking it out of him. "What?"

"Fat Wah was sighted this evening. Down at the harbor."

Chapter 25

The acrylic painting above the bed depicted an eagle and a snake locked in mortal combat. It was quiet in the hotel except for the muffled hum of the air conditioning system. An occasional rush of water through the walls signaled that the plumbing was being used by an early riser. The digital clock on the nightstand glowed 3:05 a.m.

Hannah Song paced the room in the dark, repeatedly looking out of the window. They were still there. Two goons stationed at the front of the hotel leaned against a late model Jaguar. Song could not wait any longer. She had to move now.

Song had been sound asleep. She had collapsed on the bed without undressing, after patrolling the harbor for three hours with Lee. They did not find Fat Wah. Young had called her room at 2:15 and pleaded with her to meet him at the warehouse. It was urgent, he had said. She was to come alone. No police. No phone calls to anyone. Only she could help him. Young would fill her in when she arrived.

He had sounded deeply distressed. Song had wondered why, but did not press him. She speculated that Fat Wah's arrival had something to do with it. Young had seemed very nervous during their encounter earlier that evening. Song had taken note of each grimace and revealing facial expression. He had tried to fool her. Had he realized that the game was over and now just wanted to make a deal?

Young's imploring tone had all but convinced her that she would not be walking into a set up. Song would hear him out. His information could lead to a positive break in the case. But first she had to get to the warehouse. To do that, Song had to make it past the nightriders posted below. That would not be easy. They were covering both ends of the street. And the street was the only way out.

Song made her way down the hall and found the service elevator. She sidestepped in and leaned against a quilted pad hung beside the control panel. Her fingers hurriedly searched the buttons, finding the characters representing "kitchen." She punched the button and the coach started its descent with a nerve-wracking jolt.

The kitchen would have a receiving door at the rear of the building. She could slip out the back, avoiding notice in the empty, glass-enclosed lobby. The double doors opened inside the spacious kitchen. A half dozen industrial-sized pots boiled and waited for chopped vegetables. The morning cook stood at a Formica counter with his cleaver poised in mid air. He yelled excitedly at Song and brandished the blade at her, instinctively protecting his territory. He calmed down when Song flashed her badge and told him that she was a sanitation inspector. She pulled a note pad from her purse and began wiping the appliance surfaces with her hand. She scribbled meaningless notes and looked at him approvingly. He resumed his preparation of the *dim sum* while she slipped out the back.

Song was not encouraged by what she saw. A twelve-foot wall with barbed wire surrounded the rear of the hotel. Was it her imagination, or were the barbs pointing inward? What did it matter? It made no difference in a skirt and high heels. She couldn't climb under the best conditions without a grappling hook and rope anyway. The front was the only way out. She would have to take the chance. Time was running out. First light was only two hours away. There was also the danger that Young might have a change of heart if given too much time to think.

Song worked around loose stacks of produce crates nestled beside the building. Her heel caught in the grate of a grease trap. She turned her ankle and sprawled forward, skinning her knees and palms. She stood and picked the gravel from her hands, wincing with each sting. There was no time for first aid. She rearranged her riddled hose, picked up her handbag and crept toward the corner. A rat scurried past a trash can, startling her. Song clutched her chest. Her heart pounded arrhythmically with the rush of adrenalin. She caught her breath to calm herself, then poked her head around the shadowy edge.

One of the men seemed to be looking directly at her. Song pulled back. Her heart hammered again. She tried to moisten her lips, but her mouth was too dry. Had he seen her? Moments passed. Then minutes. Apparently not. She anxiously peeked again. Both thugs were looking in the opposite direction. They seemed to be preoccupied with a lively argument between a prostitute and her unhappy customer.

The consort slapped the man's face and challenged his ancestry. Song had not heard most of the words in many years. Nobody could cuss like the Chinese. Every insult involved generations of relatives, or presumed relatives. Filthy as the epithets were, she could not help a feeling of nostalgia for similar characters in her own village. She even missed the earthiness. At least the communication was open and honest, not to mention highly descriptive.

Song caught herself and shelved the memories. Young was waiting. She decided that it would be best to make her move while the opportunity lasted. When one of the men marched over to shoo the love birds away, she darted for the cover of a parked delivery truck. She glanced at the guards again before launching briskly up the street.

Three minutes later, a shuddering cab crawled up beside her. The driver gestured toward the back seat. He looked almost agreeable, so she nodded and climbed in. The driver checked with her, then put the taxi in gear and roared off to the manufacturing district.

Without the bothersome daytime traffic, they reached the harbor in ten minutes. Song had the driver drop her a block south of the toy warehouse. She had decided it was best to approach the situation with caution; she didn't like surprises. Song walked along with a fearless stride. The tapping of her heels on the pavement kept time with the drip of an open sewer. She knew that the now abandoned streets would soon come to life. She planned to be long gone by then.

The façade of Young's warehouse was abysmally dark. Its right side was dimly lit by the trunk light of a late model Mercedes. The lone car was parked perpendicular to the space as though it had stopped in a hurry. Or been stopped.

Song found the closeness and density of the shadows unsettling. It was difficult to make anything out, even with her 20/15 eyesight. Yet, instinctively, she knew something was wrong. She reached into her shoulder bag for her security force. But before she could clear the flap, a stranger emerged from his hiding place and rushed her.

Song kicked off her shoes and adopted a fighting stance. She waited until he reached out before popping her knee squarely into his groin. He howled and doubled up in pain as she raked his face with her nails. The attacker thrashed and punched the air like a wild man.

Song drew back her fist. She was about to deliver a finishing crush to his Adam's apple when her head was jerked backwards. A second assailant pulled her by the hair and dragged her toward the Mercedes. The interloper clutched her hair like he was wringing a mop and repeatedly smashed her face down on the hood. Song tried to fight back. She stamped fiercely with her heel and tried to reach back to gouge his eyes. But he was a large and powerful man. And he had exploited the advantage of surprise. He grunted, and with a final flourish, bounced her head on the hood with his full force. The assailant released his grip, allowing her to sink to the pavement.

Song's head was numb. She had lost control of her muscles. Her arms were dead weight. Stunned, she rolled over face up and blinked twice before spinning into a dark tunnel.

When Song awoke, she was lying in the back seat of a moving car. Her hands were bound behind her back. The rumpled gown was gathered around her midsection. A knot of blood had collected in her mouth. She could taste warm metal and liquid salt.

Song searched for particles of broken teeth with her tongue. Her lips and cheeks were swollen grotesquely. She could not feel her hands. Her vision was blurred and her face and neck throbbed with pain. She fought to stifle a rising moan. It was no use.

Song heard an all too familiar sick laugh. Au was in the front seat on the passenger side. He turned around to look at her. "Ah, Ms. Song, welcome back." He reached back at her, trying to tug the skirt of her gown down. "We must remember our modesty."

She kicked his hands out of the way. "Get away, you bastard."

Au laughed again. "We're going to have fun, you and I. You'll see." He looked at the driver and back at her. "Oh, forgive me. Allow me to introduce my associate, Mr. Wah. He'll be our driver for the day."

Wah turned around and glowered at her. Song was repulsed by the massive balloon of his head. Wah's oversized eyes protruded like those of a puffer fish. His fleshy jowls flapped as he swiveled back to the wheel. Au laughed even harder.

They bounced along a rough road. Song cried out at the jolting pressure on her tight bindings. The car moved on at a reckless speed. Indistinguishable forms raced past the window. At times, the encroaching trees were so thick that they screened out the sun. Song had no idea where they were, or where they were going.

An hour later, they reached an open area in the mountains. The car slowed and stopped. Song felt nauseous and dizzy. The sky was whirling. Dark floating shapes gathered overhead. The clouds grew thick, but the rain did not come.

Part Two

CLOUDS AND RAIN

Chapter 26

Weede's massive transport descended through a bank of over shadowing clouds nesting above Taipei International Airport. The craft touched down hard, disturbing a group of nesting cormorants. He checked his watch. It was 3:05 p.m.

The flight had been bumpy and noisy, but on time; not to mention, free. Weede had run into a mate in Singapore who had waved him onto the C-130 loaded with helicopter parts. He had never taken a scheduled civilian flight anywhere. Too much comfort unsettled him. Weede didn't want to lose his edge. He thought of himself as a modern Spartan. Self-denial had hardened and molded him.

Before leaving Singapore, Weede had tried to call Song at the hotel. She had not answered her room phone, or the hotel operator's page. That worried him immensely. The most ruthless men in the world had gravitated to the ivory trade. Weede hoped that they had not targeted Song. At least not before he could find her. He didn't give a damn about his own safety. Everyone had to die someday anyway, and his mother had two other sons. Song's safety was another matter entirely.

Weede traveled without luggage and had nothing to declare. His ka-bar was strategically tucked away. Weede marveled that he was not searched and that he had been able to quickly pass through Customs. His passport had been in order. Sort of. In his haste, he had picked up an old Zairian passport, not his current

Kenyan papers. It had raised a few eyebrows, since Zaire, per se, no longer existed. And Weede was Australian to boot.

He had charmed his way past the harried inspector. Either that, or she had grown weary of listening to his blather. It wouldn't have been the first time he had engendered such a reaction.

Midway down the concourse, Weede kicked open the door to the gents'. He was in a hurry to relieve himself. When he had finished, Weede reached the sink and dashed water into his bleary eyes. He focused on the image in the mirror. It seemed to him that his looks had not improved. Disgusted, he rubbed the prominent strawberry stubble on his chin. Weede decided to shave after he had a shower. Whenever that was.

Weede left the restroom and raced down Concourse C into the terminal. Moments later, he hopped aboard the Lai-Lai Sheraton courtesy van. He adopted a proud, expectant air, trying to look like he belonged. The driver asked about his luggage. Weede told him it had been lost and would be delivered later. The driver looked at him in disbelief, shook his head and shut the door. Weede settled back comfortably and closed his eyes. The courtesy van darted from the airport and melted into the city traffic.

Weede had fallen asleep en route to the hotel. He was awakened by the irregular lurch of the van as it pulled to a halt at the main entrance. He rubbed his eyes and sat up. The driver refused to look at him. Weede slapped him on the back, exited with a satisfied smile and trudged into the lobby.

He brushed past the floor manager, found the elevator and pushed the button for Song's floor. As soon as the door opened, Weede rushed out and stormed down the hall. He feared that he was already too late.

Weede found his way to Song's door and rapped briskly. No answer. He rapped again. Still no answer. Weede tried the door. It was unlocked. He opened it slightly and called Song's name. He heard nothing, so he peered in. A knot formed low in his gut. The room had been torn apart, and not by the maid service. Someone had been searching for something. Drawers had been yanked out and their contents dumped. Song's clothes had been ripped and strewn everywhere. Weede picked up a silk peignoir crumpled on the floor. The scent of her perfume filled the air. Sweet smells were alien to his world.

Weede paced and cursed without restraint. He sat on the bed and dashed a fist against his forehead, trying to think. He trembled with rage. When his hand finally stopped shaking, an idea popped into his head. He left the hotel and raced to the police bureau.

Twenty minutes later, Weede was ushered in to see Ku Tai Lee. As he told the detective the purpose of his visit, Lee's faced turned ashen. Weede also told him about the ivory shipment bound for Kaohsiung. Without comment, Lee stood and faced the window behind his desk. Even just standing up, Lee exuded an easy grace. Weede sensed that he had far more than a bureaucratic interest in the case. Lee looked crestfallen. But Weede was most impressed by the fact that Lee had looked him directly in the eye.

The detective wheeled around suddenly and pounded the desk with a blurred fist. A pencil flew through the air toward Weede. He did not flinch. Lee slapped the desk for good measure, and looked up with a flash of recognition. "Young. That's it. She went to see Young."

Weede shifted his weight in the chair. "Who?"

Lee grabbed a coat draped over the couch. "Come. Let us go," he commanded.

On the way to the toy warehouse, Lee filled him in, keeping nothing from him. Including the fact that he was in love with Hannah. Weede knew exactly how he felt. All too exactly.

They parked in Young's slot and rushed inside. Lee displayed his badge to the receptionist and asked to see Young. But Young was not in. The receptionist had not seen him since the day before. The only clue to his whereabouts was an answering machine message he had phoned in to her the night before. She played it back for them. Young's vice crackled with static as he told her that he had an urgent meeting with a distant supplier and would be out of the office for at least a few days. He did not say where, and his voice sounded slightly strained.

Lee demanded to see Young's office. They hurried behind the receptionist, following the yellow line through the warehouse to Young's door. There was no activity on the floor. The workers were sitting around, idly chatting. Lee rushed inside the office and began to search the drawers and file cabinets. He was clearly perturbed by the absence of files, appointment books and telephone logs. Lee rested his fingertips on Young's desk and glared at the receptionist. She was standing just inside the door and was close to tears. "Where are your suppliers?" he demanded.

The receptionist braced against the door to steady herself. "All over."

Lee lowered his voice and shifted his weight back on his heels. "You must tell me exactly. This is urgent police business."

His demeanor was direfully serious. The receptionist put her hand to her forehead and looked at the grizzled Weede and back at Lee. She was perspiring heavily. Her voice was shaky. "Well...here in Taipei, Hong Kong, and Kowloon." She was so nervous, she could hardly form the words. "Then...there's one in Pingtung and, and...several in Santimen."

At the mention of Pingtung, Lee's demeanor changed. He had discovered something. "Any place else?"

The flustered receptionist thought for a long moment and shook her head. "No...I'm sorry...none that I can remember."

Lee's face brightened a bit. "Can you perhaps give us the addresses of those places you do remember?"

Her face told them that she would seize the opportunity to cooperate just to be rid of them. "Yes...please follow me back to the front office." The receptionist whirled and started out the door with Lee and Weede in tow.

After she had reproduced a list from the firm's mailing labels, Lee thanked the receptionist and drew Weede outside. One of Lee's men arrived just as they reached the parking lot. Lee posted him in the office and looked around before speaking privately to Weede. "Hannah went to Pintung and Santimen last weekend on a tour of the island."

"But how does that fit in?"

"Well, you see, Santimen is not far from Kaohsiung. It is a tiny farming village. Hardly a global center for toys and novelty items." Lee arched his eyebrows knowingly. "But it is known throughout the artistic world for its native carvers."

He had captured Weede's earnest attention. "Oh yeh? What do they carve?"

"Primarily wood, some stone and…ivory," Lee said with a hush.

"Ivory, eh? Right then. What's the fastest way to Santimen?"

"The police bureau's jet helicopter."

"Perfect," Weede said. "Let's go."

Lee called ahead and ordered the ground crew to fuel the craft and prepare it for immediate take-off. On the way to the heliport, Weede described for Lee the vessel he had seen in Mogadishu. Lee used the radio-telephone in his car to alert the Taiwanese Customs officials at Kaohsiung. After Lee placed the phone in its cradle, he told Weede about the ivory pieces Song had shown him the day they met. All had been carved by the Kainan masters. The Kainan tribe was concentrated around Santimen. There was an undeniable connection to the mysterious happenings and Song's disappearance.

A half hour later, they reached the heliport. The pilot had already started the engine. They ducked beneath the main rotor, and climbed aboard as the chopper lifted off with a broad sweep of its tail.

Once airborne, they turned south, leaving the city behind. The preparation for the serious business ahead began. Lee cleaned his automatic, while Weede sharpened his ka-bar. At eight thousand feet above central Taiwan, the air was cold and rough. Rolling gusts of wind manhandled the light chopper. To the left and right, dark mountains brooded over the patchwork valleys. They looked treacherous and forbidding. The incessant clatter of the rotors drowned out all other sounds.

An hour into the flight, as the helicopter dodged a peak, it mysteriously drifted left. Without warning, the pitch of the blades changed with an unearthly whine. The pilot shoved the stick forward. Lee and Weede braced themselves as the craft descended sharply. The landing lights flicked on as the copter wildly spiraled to earth. They nosed up in the final second, as the pilot "flared" the helicopter in for the landing. They somehow managed to skip-slam into a clearing. By some miracle, the craft remained upright. The pilot turned around with a grimace, acknowledging the close call. Lee and Weede looked at each other with relief. They unfastened their belts and jumped out.

Once the engine had been shut down and the rotors braked to a stop, Weede removed the engine panel. The pilot held a flashlight as Weede peered into the compartment, then cross-checked the rotor assembly. Weede turned around and shook his head. "We're lucky to be alive."

"What do you mean?" Lee asked.

"An engine nut worked loose. The main rotor shaft is cracked."

"The what?"

"The main rotor shaft. It's a miracle the bloody engine didn't explode in mid air. It'll take days to fix."

Lee turned and looked south. "We don't have days. She doesn't have days."

They climbed into the cockpit. A quick check of the charts revealed that they were near the village of Meishan. Santimen was fifty kilometers due south. They would have to travel west toward the coast, swing south, then east to reach it.

They decided to leave the pilot with the chopper and commandeer a car in the village. After radioing for a mechanic team and reporting their position, Lee reached into a duffel bag. He withdrew a Skorpion machine pistol and handed it to Weede. "Here, you might need this. It was seized from a Japanese Red Army terrorist last year in a raid. Officially, it doesn't exist."

Weede took the weapon into his hands, aimed it at the horizon and worked the action. "Then I won't officially use it." He smiled at Lee and flipped the bolt. "Who dares, wins."

"What?" Lee asked.

"Oh, it's nothing. Just an old sentiment from my adopted country."

Lee tossed him five ten round magazines. "What's our plan?"

Weede grinned mischievously. "Get the bad guys and save the sheila."

Lee handed him a heavy canvas bag. "Well, that's nice and fluid anyway," he quipped. The two warriors checked and assembled their battle gear. With a final nod from Lee, they walked in silence through the night, each with his own thoughts.

Chapter 27

Song lay on her side on a narrow cot in the corner of a window-less room. Also within the chamber were a small table, a primitive chair and a chemical toilet. The walls were blank. She rolled onto her back, vaguely remembering that a woman had come in earlier to remove the nylon bindings cutting into her wrists. The woman had helped her to use the facilities, fed her and slipped out without saying a word.

Song's vision was still fuzzy, although she no longer felt nauseous. There was still a rushing noise in her ears. She raised her head for a better look, but dropped it again. Her neck was still weak. Her head pounded with the surge of every heartbeat. She had passed out again, losing all sense of time and place. Swishing her tongue around in her mouth, Song could feel the ragged spots where her teeth had been broken off.

Song knew she was in a tight spot. She was scared and afraid of losing her head. She thought about Tim Sullivan, the high school coach who had first shown an interest in her athletic ability. He had taught her to shoot on weekends and guided her through years of amateur competition. Eventually, Sullivan and his wife had driven her to the U.S. Olympic training camp in Colorado. Song had systematically edged out the competition and made the team.

The Sullivans had also been in the grandstands when Song had suffered her first defeat. A Norwegian competing in his third

Olympics had taken the gold medal by a two-point margin. Song had been content with the silver. Now, her skill level had vastly improved. The guys at Customs kidded her about her hobby and called her the "Queen of Big Bore." No one had ever shot a higher series at Quantico. But she wondered how she could possibly deal with this reversal.

If Sullivan were with her here, he would tell her to shut out the outside world. Tune the breath. Freeze the spirit. Just become empty and quiet. When the mind is cool, clear, peaceful and light, then you focus and fire. The coaching had worked. Song had remained calm throughout the competition while others had lost the test of nerves. His methods had not worked for everyone. But they had for Song. He had told her she was special, because she had a receptive spirit. Sullivan had also introduced her to the martial arts.

His philosophy was not altogether unlike Lee's. Sullivan had never explained the origin of his system to Song; she only knew that he had served two tours with a "black ops" unit. Wherever he had been, the belief in the *tao* was prominent. Song was comforted by the memory and prepared herself for the encounter she knew would come. It would take more than a receptive spirit to master the situation she found herself in.

Song scolded herself for not providing Lee with the details of her investigation. Her independence and desire for precision had led her into this predicament. Now, she was Au's prisoner. But for what purpose and for how long? She twisted her face to relieve the pain of a swollen jaw joint. A lock and chain rattled outside the door. It flew open. Au entered with two menacing tribesmen. He covered his mouth in a gesture of mock surprise. "Oh, there you are. Come, Ms. Song, we mustn't keep our hosts waiting."

Au pointed at Song and nodded to the two men. They advanced quickly and lifted her to her feet. She felt woozy again. Her head throbbed more intensely. She started to drift to one side. The men steadied her between them before leading her from the shelter.

As they exited into a starless night, rhythmic drum beats began to pound. There was a low thud and again a thud. The beats reached far and deep. The tribesmen dragged Song by the arms down the main street. Her head was swimming, but the surrounding buildings looked somehow familiar to her. So did the fires glowing on the cliffs and the flickering lights from the dale. Santimen!

Song was led into the grassy arena filled with villagers in ceremonial dress. The aroma of death hung in the still mountain air. The Kainan swayed as if in a trance and began to chant. The drum beats intensified. Song noticed that, just as before, rows of stakes topped with pigs' heads lined the approach to the altar. But something was different.

Now, there was a center stake taller than all of the others. A swollen, distorted mass rested on its tip. At first, she couldn't make it out. Not until Au shoved her forward and pushed her down on her knees. She looked up. The impaled head of Ping Young gaped at her with a tortured expression!

Song shrieked and turned away. Au leaned over and cackled in her ear. "Perhaps the local ceremonies are too much for you."

Song fought the urge to retch. Her head pounded fiercely, blending with the pulse of the drums. Au signaled his henchmen to seize her. "She's had enough. Take her to the car."

The two tribesmen jerked Song up. She tried to wriggle free, causing them to clamp down harder on her arms. The drumming and chanting continued unabated as Song was led away.

Fat Wah was waiting in the driver's seat. He reached back and popped the rear door open. Song was shoved into the back seat. She scooted over and leaned against the door, as far away from Wah as possible. He frowned at her and tapped his fingers impatiently on the steering wheel.

Wah started the engine. Au moved away from the car and spoke briefly with the tribesmen. He handed them a manila envelope and returned their bows, before climbing in beside Wah.

Song coaxed her hand down, searching for the door latch. It had been removed. Au seemed to sense what she was up to. He whipped around in his seat. "I have taken the normal precautions, Ms. Song. Please don't test me. You wouldn't get far on foot and alone in these mountains."

He turned back around without waiting for her response. The streets of Santimen were deserted except for a lone Toyota Land Cruiser parked beside the lodge. Wah, uneasy, looked around. Au noticed his distraction. "Probably just some tourists," he offered. "Let's go; we're wasting time."

Wah dipped his head in respect and spun the wheel sharply. With a loud screech, the car sped off toward the Pingtung road. Song watched as the town grew dim behind them. No one spoke.

Five miles later, bright headlights glared in their rearview mirror. Song turned to look. The other car was hanging back a regulated distance. She couldn't distinguish its make. Au and Wah both twisted to look at the same time. Wah scowled. "We're being followed."

"Nonsense," Au said hesitantly. He continued to study the head-lights. "But do speed it up, just to be safe."

Wah's body shook as he shoved his foot down on the accelera-tor. The engine whined as the digital speedometer climbed to the 130 kilometers per hour mark. The Mercedes churned dust at it raced into the blackness ahead.

Au kept glancing backward. Soon the pursuing headlights faded and disappeared. Au looked again and smiled with satisfaction. He turned and patted Wah on the shoulder. "Fine, my friend. You've done it. They should be nearly ready for us at the airfield."

Airfield? Song wondered why they were taking her to an airfield. Whatever the reason, Song decided to regard it as an opportunity to escape. All she had to do was keep her head and she could get out of this. She would not only survive, but triumph.

When the car reached the edge of the plateau, the radiating lights of Pingtung came into view from the river delta below. There were no other cars on the road in either direction. They wound down a steep grade, reaching the outskirts of the city ten minutes later.

With a squeak of the brakes, the Mercedes pulled to a halt on the tarmac beside a Gulfstream corporate jet. It waited ominously in an isolated corner of the airfield. The jet was lit from fore to aft by portable floodlights. A tanker truck was parked beside it. The aircraft was taking on fuel. They sat in the car in silence, waiting for the tanker to finish.

After a tense interval, the loader waved to the ground crew, then detached and reeled in the hose. As the fuel truck pulled away, the pilot started his engines and motioned to Au.

An attendant ran up and opened Au's door. Wah jumped out, opened the back door and pulled Song from the car by her neck. She climbed the plane's ramp, sandwiched between Au and Wah. Song toyed with the idea of falling backwards to escape. She quickly dismissed the thought, realizing that she probably weighed one-third of Wah's weight. She probably could not even budge him.

They were greeted at the door by a black man with a pocked face. He was wearing a turban. He had deep-set eyes and clutched a string of black beads, like a rosary, in his right hand. Song reasoned that he must have come from an Islamic nation.

When they were all seated and belted in, the cabin door was sealed. The pitch of engines increased as they raced for the private runway. Song tilted back in her seat as the nose wheel lifted off the ground. She was not prepared for the short take off run. She stared out the window, seeing her own reflection in the glass. The compact jet knifed into the sky on a southeast heading. Within a heartbeat, it was swallowed by the aperture of the night.

Chapter 28

The jet streaked over a barren knoll separated from the airfield by an angular drainage ditch. The Toyota Land Cruiser was parked behind the hillock with its lights out. Lee and Weede sat next to it. The digital clock glowed 11:02 p.m. Lee jumped to his feet and slapped the dust from his pants. He switched on a pocket flashlight and kicked the dirt.

"The giant driving the car was Fat Wah," he said, gritting his teeth. "I still can't believe it. I was so certain that he was dead."

"Yeh. He was huge, alright. Who was that bigwig?"

"That was Shang T. K. Au. I can't imagine why he would be involved in this. I don't know who that was wearing the turban at the top of the ramp."

Weede already knew. It was Botan Niassa. The two men watched the craft's blinking wing lights fade and disappear as it was swallowed by a cloud. Weede shook his head at Lee. "I still think we should've rushed the plane."

"No. Too many guards." Lee held out his hands palms up as if pleading a case. "They might have killed her instantly, or she could have been hit in the cross fire."

Weede turned aside. Lee touched him on the shoulder. "If Au was going to kill her, he could have already done it. You should learn to relax, my friend." Weede did not want to learn how to relax. He was always ready.

They heard the last whines of the jet's engines as it reached the ocean. Weede spun around and threw up his hands in frustration. "Relax? How can you relax in a situation like this?"

Lee's face took on the appearance of natural serenity. "I relax in all situations," he said in a calming tone.

Weede sighed in exasperation and turned to the spot where they had last seen the plane. Lee had already begun to gather their gear.

The two had watched the loading process through night vision goggles salvaged from the downed helicopter. They had stopped at the inn in Santimen to ask directions and exited in time to see the Mercedes speed away. Acting on a hunch, they had followed the Mercedes at a tactical distance with their headlights off. Driving long distances without lights, over poor roads, was an old skill Weede had cultivated escorting convoys in Zaire. Daily ambushes had been a fact of life. Speed and daring were not only highly valued, they were a necessity. Being a merc had provided him with invaluable on the job training. The danger and intrigue of Weede's chosen career was more to his liking. That was why he had left Australia. Bloody sheep! Australia was no place for someone like him to hone his talents and specialized skill set.

Weede slapped his hand at his side and walked over to the car. Lee was sitting in the driver's seat checking a map. Weede leaned in the window. "You've already told me about Fat Wah. But who's this Au bloke?"

Lee looked up from the chart and stared straight ahead collecting his thoughts. After a moment, he turned to Weede and rested his arm on the seat rest. "Only one of the richest men in the Orient. Au has an estate on Orchid Island. He relocated there from Hong Kong to beat the rush when the Communists took over in '97."

Weede nodded and pressed down on the roof molding strip with his fingertips. "Where's Orchid Island?"

Lee folded the map. "About sixty kilometers off the southeast coast. Very isolated and well guarded." He opened the glove box and slid the map under the owner's manual. "And judging by the direction of that jet, I'd say that's where they are headed."

Weede opened the door and bounced into the seat with an expectant look.

"Well, what we waitin' for, mate?"

Lee's face was deadpan. "Reinforcements and a boat."

They both laughed as Lee started the engine and flipped on the headlights. Lee's look phased to severe. "Seriously, Au's estate is a fortress. We are going to need an incursion team."

Weede looked straight ahead. "Fine. But let's get a move on. She's waited long enough."

In minutes, they had reached the city center and turned south onto the highway to Fangliao. From there, they would head south to Fengkang, before finally swinging north to Taitung on the east coast. It was not the closest large town, but it would have everything they needed for the raid.

The two entered Taitung at 2:42 a.m. Lee had not been there in years and repeatedly turned into dead end streets. They had crossed the same railroad tracks three times. Weede was growing more frustrated by the minute, but said nothing. He could not read, or speak, Chinese and was of little help. The strange signs gliding past the window made him dizzy. After a half hour, Lee located police headquarters beside a new McDonald's. The restaurant was closed, but they were too exhausted to eat anyway.

They roamed through the police station, finally locating the duty officer. He was in the radio room with his feet propped up on the desk. The duty officer was watching a rerun of an American sitcom. Lee flashed his badge. The man looked at it disinterestedly at first, then did a double take at the name. He jumped to attention and bowed. He had apparently heard of the martial arts master. Lee explained to Weede that every policeman on the island knew his name and reputation. Weede was impressed; in his world, the respect of one man for another was something that had to be earned.

Lee told the duty officer that they were weary and asked if he could put them up for the night. The officer led them to an open cell with two bunks, and apologized profusely, while low bowing to each. After the officer had returned to the radio room, Lee smiled as Weede wedged the door open. Buildings, and jails in particular, made him feel claustrophobic. He fell asleep, longing for a canvas tent in the free, open bush.

They were awakened at noon by the province captain. He was tall and thin. Obviously nearing retirement age, his neck and arm tendons popped out like taut rubber bands. The captain was honored to meet Lee and pledged his unlimited support. Weede was mildly surprised; most bureaucrats were only interested in covering their own asses. This police captain was giving them carte blanche. When they were alone again, Lee explained why. "He's an old soldier, used to decades of Communist subversion, infiltration and espionage. A battleground philosophy still prevails throughout Taiwan. Although we have a Constitution, we operated for decades under martial law. It was only suspended a few years ago."

Weede looked at him incredulously. "Are you saying that we have license to do whatever it takes?"

Lee noticed the look in Weede's eyes. "Essentially, yes. The law here favors restriction of freedom for the criminal elements and broad operating parameters for the police."

The concept distinctly appealed to Weede. No rules. No standards. No appeals. Do what needs to be done and prevail. It was just like home. He barely concealed his eagerness. "When do we get started?"

"Right away. The captain has invited us to a social meal. We can discuss the details with him there."

The social meal proved to be more of a banquet. Local dignitaries, including the mayor, turned out to receive the honored guests. Consistent with Taiwanese tradition, repeated toasts were made with *shaosing*, a favored rice wine. A relaxed mood prevailed. Salutes were made to everything from a wish for good fortune to the arrival of the main course. Each glass was repeatedly drained at the enthusiastic command "*gan-bei*" or "bottoms up."

The mayor's immense capacity for celebrative ritual quickly became obvious. Ordinarily, Weede would be a wholehearted ringleader. But there was more important business to be attended to. He signaled Lee, who leaned toward him. "Shouldn't we get on with our mission?"

Lee nodded and whispered something to the captain. The leader shook his head yes and said something in reply. Lee smiled and leaned back, as the captain patted him on the back and raised yet another toast. Weede joined in the toast and turned to Lee again. "Well, what was that all about?"

The detective twisted his chair around to face Weede. "It seems that the captain has previously made all of the necessary arrangements."

"What arrangements?" Weede asked.

"An incursion team has already been assembled. A powerful cutter and inflatable boats will be placed at our disposal. We can leave when we are ready."

Weede raised his glass, downed it and stood. "I'm ready."

Lee and Weede thanked their hosts and left the celebration, which continued unabated. The captain's chauffeur drove them to the dock. They formulated their plan of attack en route.

The modern cutter gleamed as it rode against the dock. It was the pride of the Taiwanese Navy. Two Zodiacs with 100 horsepower engines were strapped to the foredeck. Lee and Weede were greeted on board by a six man tactical squad. They were armed like a light infantry brigade. Following introductions, Lee gathered them in a circle and outlined the plan for them, as the ship's crew hurriedly prepared to sail.

With a signal from Lee, the ship's powerful engines churned

to life. It knifed away from the dock and reached the outer break-water in minutes. By dusk, they were skipping across the open ocean toward Orchid Island.

Lee leaned against the forward mast. He pointed to a junk spreading its sails like the wings of a ragged butterfly. Black kite birds swooped and dived following it out to sea. Weede was too sick to care about the view. He spent the whole bumpy trip bent over the stern rail, spraying the fish.

Chapter 29

Au and Wah pulled Song from the servants' quarters and led her down the great hall of the mansion. Half the length of a football field, its floor consisted of square-yard sections of Connemara marble. The floor was polished to a brilliant shine. Song could see her reflection among the variegated green and black veins. Crystal chandeliers dangled from silver bases embedded in the inlaid ceiling fashioned from contrasting European woods. Massive mahogany doors with gold latches lined both sides of the corridor.

Their footsteps echoed all around them. Song was growing weary. Her legs wobbled. She still struggled, but with less enthusiasm. Song knew she had to continue fighting to deny them the dominance they sought. But the whole program didn't make any sense to her? Why didn't they just kill her and be done with it?

One of the doors rolled open. An Asian man backed from the room wearing only a towel around his waist. He was preoccupied with waving to someone still inside the room. Au coughed a warning. The man turned toward them with a start. His face flushed red as he half-bowed, dashed back into the suite and eased the door closed.

They heard a high-pitched giggle from the room. Wah grunted with a look of contempt. Au turned to Song. He was wearing a wry smile. "That was Crashi. Just one of my guests enjoying the hospitality." Au's demeanor changed. "Perhaps you would also be interested in some entertainment?"

Song pulled away in disgust. Wah grabbed her by the neck and dragged her to the far end of the hall. He threw open the last door and pushed her in. It was a combination medical laboratory and hospital. The facility was well-equipped. In the center of the room sat an operating table. It was surrounded by multi colored gas cylinders. Song's mind raced with the anticipation of what would happen next. She did not know what to expect. She spun with a surge of adrenalin and bolted back toward the door.

Wah blocked the doorway, grabbed her arm and twisted it behind her in a control lock. Song flailed at him with her free arm, until Au clutched it and wrenched her fingers. She kicked at them as they lifted her onto the table and fastened the leather straps.

With a sadistic smirk, Wah pulled tighter on the band across Song's chest. It forced the air from her lungs and made it difficult for her to breathe. Au tapped Wah and shook his head. Wah loosened the pressure a notch and dejectedly lowered himself onto a nearby metal stool.

Song could move only her head and fingertips. Au rolled up his sleeve, exposing a tattoo similar to the others she had seen. Song tried not to stare, but Au appeared to notice the flash of recognition in her eyes. He selected a hypodermic syringe from a tray and stepped toward a cabinet filled with pharmaceuticals. Au opened the glass case and studied the bottles. He reached out and picked a vial from the top shelf. Then he turned to face Song and tilted the labeled bottle upside down. He inserted the syringe through the cap and filled it.

Au set the empty bottle on the counter and tapped the uplifted syringe with his forefinger. As he depressed the plunger, a squirt of fluid arced into the air. His moves were very deliberate, as if he enjoyed her tension. He kept glancing at her in an effort to increase her anxiety. Au brandished the needle and approached Song slowly. He paused for effect for an interminable moment.

Song could now read the number tattooed on his arm. It was all too clear. 489! The digits added up to twenty-one! Au was the *San Chu* of the Ghost Shadows!

She twisted and shook the table to get away. Her efforts were in vain. Wah started to get up, but Au motioned for him to remain seated. Au massaged Song's arm, abruptly jabbed it with the needle and emptied the contents of the syringe. He withdrew the needle and laid it on a stainless steel salver. He looked over at Wah knowingly. "Now, Ms. Song, you will please tell us what we wish to know."

The stinging liquid coursed through Song's veins. She felt dizzy as burning bile rose in her throat. Her mouth was dry. Her heart rate slowed, with arrhythmic thumps. An uncomfortable tightness squeezed her chest. She fought the sensation of panic until her vision went dark.

Song heard Au's voice from a distance, as if he were shouting down at her through a long rubber tube. She sensed that she was mumbling responses. It seemed to her that she was floating in a disassociated, eternal state. She was encircled by warmth and peace. Her voice echoed within her head, but Song had no sense of what she was saying.

At last, the interrogation ceased. Au muttered something to Wah. Song opened her eyes and blinked at the glare from the lights. She felt the straps being loosened. They hoisted her into a sitting position. She tried to steady herself with her hands. Her vision, although blurry, gradually returned.

Wah pulled Song from the table and led her into an adjoining room. It was starkly furnished with an old iron bed and a painted wooden chair. Wah tied her wrists and ankles to the frame and excused himself to check the sentries.

Au stood over Song, looking down. He frowned, shook his head and rolled down his sleeve. There was an urgent-sounding knock at the door. Au turned toward it with an impatient look. "Enter!" he shouted.

The door snapped open. A servant hurried into the room, bowed and handed Au a slip of paper. Au waved the servant out before reading the note. As his eyes scanned the message, Au trembled and clenched his jaw. He pounded his fist on the wall in rage and ripped the note to pieces. He started toward Song, then turned away to regain control of his emotions. He looked at her and gestured with open hands. "It seems as though I have suffered a setback at Kaohsiung."

He spoke in a controlled manner, as if he were conducting a business seminar. "Your interference has proved very costly for me."

Song fought the urge to answer him. She could at least deprive him of the acknowledgement he craved. Au studied her for a moment. He was clearly perturbed by her silence. He sat on the edge of the bed, facing her. "It's a pity I can't keep you here to entertain my guests. They have some rather sophisticated tastes, you know."

Song prayed that he would come close enough to spit in his face. He sensed what was coming and stood. "Unfortunately, I fear that you have too much spirit for that."

Song was sick of his condescending monotone and his on again off again politeness.

At the sound of another rap at the door, Au spun around. "Come," he said.

A breathless uniformed guard rushed into the room. He wielded a rotary shotgun in one hand and clutched a burlap bag in the other. Au glanced at the sack and then at Song. He shook his head. "Yes, a pity."

The bag twitched at the sound of his voice. He bowed to Song and nodded to the guard. "Goodbye, Ms. Song."

Au nodded to the guard and slipped from the room.

The guard leaned the shotgun against the chair. He placed the bag on the floor and gingerly untied it. Without ceremony, he turned the bag upside down and dumped the contents on the floor. He caught the gun by the sling, hastily backed from the room and slammed the door behind him.

Song stared in paralytic terror at the coiled serpent lying immobile on the cold, tile floor. The snake was light brown in color, with dark cross bands. Wide segments on its sides were tinted in dull orange. Its distinctive snout ended in an upturned point flanked by large shields on the crown. It was a sharp-nosed pit viper. *Agkistrodon acutus*. The hundred-pace snake, now all too familiar to her. One bite could kill in seconds. It was the most dangerous pit viper in the Far East.

The serpent's head became alert; it had sensed the warmth of Song's inert body. The viper spiraled from its position and crawled toward her.

It paused at the foot of the bed as if sniffing the air. Song froze. Precious seconds ticked by. She knew that if the snake was alarmed, it would strike without hesitation. It inched up the bed post. She worried that a muscle would involuntarily twitch in a nervous reaction. The urge to scream or move was overpowering. The snake's head had reached the end of the mattress. Song closed her eyes, preparing for the inevitable and remembered Lee and the *chi* lesson.

Song slipped into a deep focus to control her breathing. She was initially tense, but gradually relaxed. She drew from her powers of concentration to reach a state of repose where the act of breathing was undetectable. Fog swirled around her and then cleared. She was hiking the mountain trail again with Ali Shan. Not a moment too soon; the snake had climbed completely onto the bed and was resting on her legs.

Song remained inert, although she could feel the pressure of the snake as it toured her body. It extended over her chest then passed beneath her chin and stopped.

After an eternal moment, Song felt a blast of cold air strike her face. It was coming from a vent above the bed; Au's air conditioning system had kicked on at that moment. The frigid air annoyed the snake. It moved restlessly to the edge of the bed and rappelled to the floor. Song did not break her concentration. The snake was still too close. She remained immobile, but opened her eyes.

A half hour later, the guard cautiously opened the door and stepped in. Song watched him out of the corner of her eye. He seemed to be more concerned with the snake coiled beside the bed than with her. The guard clutched the bag and approached the snake. It uncoiled at lightning speed. The guard pressed the butt of the shotgun just behind the snake's head, pinning it to the floor.

The guard fumbled with the sack and danced away as the snake writhed and curled around the butt. The tip of its tail grasped the trigger at the precise moment the guard pulled up, trying to free the shotgun. The barrel exploded with a thunderous roar, splattering the remnants of the guard's head against the far wall; his torso rocked and collapsed like a pile of laundry. The agitated snake recoiled before crawling off to a distant corner of the room.

Fortune had smiled on Song. She did not hesitate to exploit the gift. She focused her *chi* and strained at the ties. One snapped like a rubber band. Her arm was free. Song quickly untied the other arm and reached down to loosen the ties at her feet.

She leaped from the bed, grabbed the shotgun and opened the window. She straddled the sill and slipped out. As she scampered for the roof, she heard excited voices and the drum of running feet.

Chapter 30

"Before we move out, there's something I should confess," Weede said.

Lee buttoned his hip pocket laden with extra magazines and edged closer. "What's that?"

Weede stared straight ahead at the compound. "I've got a personal score to settle here."

When Lee did not respond as expected, Weede turned to face him. Tears had formed in Lee's eyes. He patted Weede on the shoulder. "As do I," Lee said, lowering his head. "As do I."

Lee slipped off noiselessly to brief the team, while the puzzled Weede kept a watch on the buildings. He studied the approaches to the target, memorizing distances, angles and, most importantly, available cover. Weede checked the time. Two minutes to jump off. He was anxious to go. Their venture had nearly ended in disaster before it had even begun.

The engines of the launch had been stopped five miles out. They had boarded the Zodiacs just after 10:00 p.m. A carburetor problem on one of the Mercury outboards had held them up. Weede had stripped off the engine cover, removed the fuel filter, unclogged and reinstalled it within minutes. He knew all about engines. In the Outback, he had to. It was a long way between corner garages.

Weede had crossed his fingers and pulled. The engine had flickered and coughed to life with a chuff of black smoke. The commandoes had all smiled with relief as they turned into the wind and raced for shore. The trip had been rough. They had said little en route. Weede's aloofness had been entirely necessary. His gag reflex was still working overtime. The roar of the surf as it pounded against the rocky cliffs had masked their arrival, 1,000 meters east of the present location.

Half the team was nearly lost in the final approach. The light inflatable had been hurled against a rock wall by a charging wave. Raiders and gear were tossed haphazardly into the air. Fortunately, the next tidal surge had lifted them onto a rocky ledge. The sea foam had glistened in the sweep of a searchlight as they secured the rafts and moved inland.

It had been a short jog to their rendezvous near the point. They had plotted the routes and intervals of the sentries. All loose equipment had been secured with duct tape. The weapons had been torn down, cleaned and oiled. Faces and hands had been blacked out.

Lee returned with the balance of the fighters and ordered a final weapons check. The team was in position. Weede was more than ready. It was time to move out.

The incursion team scurried off in defilade, with Weede taking the point. He gingerly led them around planted electronic sensors. They reached the low wall and froze at the hurried shuffle of approaching boots. A sentry advanced, paused and leaned his automatic rifle against the rocks. He fumbled in his pockets, removed a cigarette and match. When he struck the light on the wall, a dazzling flame illuminated his face, as well as the shapes of the intruders huddled behind the wall.

Weede was debating with himself when one of the men absently scraped a heel against a stone. That decided the issue. The surprised sentry hastily shook out the match and fumbled for his weapon. Too late. The ka-bar flashed from its scabbard. Weede thrust upward with one hand, dragged the sentry over the wall with the point and covered his mouth before he could cry out. The sentry tried to squirm loose, but Weede twisted the knife expertly. The sentry's fingers fluttered helplessly against Weede's cheek, as he moaned once and stopped kicking. Weede withdrew the blade and sighed. Lee nodded approval. "Good. Now you're looking more relaxed."

Weede strained in the darkness to read the other faces around him. "Everybody set?"

They all nodded. Weede kneeled and each raider followed suit. They were looking over the wall, preparing to vault it, when a side door of the mansion flew open.

Sentries carrying flashlights surged out onto the portico. Wah, forcefully blowing a whistle, hurried behind them. He was followed by Niassa, who moved to the lawn and stood, detached, watching the action. Two of the guards pointed excitedly at a movement on the roof as they hastened around the corner. The floodlights on the perimeter lit up.

Weede glanced at the dark face of Lee. Only his eyes were clearly visible; they said everything Weede needed to know. Stealth was no longer of any concern. The commotion had to involve Hannah. It was now or never. Weede gave a hand signal and scrambled over the wall.

He lifted the Skorpion to gut level, flipped off the safety and fired a long burst. Slugs sprayed out and peppered a knot of guards watching the roof. They collapsed, clutching their backs and legs as if swept under by an invisible wave. Weede skated sideways to draw the fire away from the others. Just as the remaining sentries shifted to engage the traversing Weede, Lee and the team popped above the wall, firing on full automatic.

Wah and Niassa quickly sized up the situation and bolted in opposite directions. The hapless sentries with them fell in a screaming, writhing stack. More guards raced up, went to ground and traded fire with Lee and his team. One of them opened up on the raiders with a 5.56mm light machine gun. Its biting shells pulverized the outer rocks of the wall in a shower of sparks. Weede low-crawled to the west side of the main house and reloaded. He scanned the walkways and the roof above. Where was Hannah?

He could hear the sounds of a struggle on the roof. A guard suddenly yelled out from the cupola above. The boom of two quick shotgun blasts shook the air. They were followed by the sound of a heavy object tumbling down the tiles of the roof. Weede tensed as the body of a guard fell from the edge and slapped the pavement three feet away. The man was missing an arm and part of his chest.

Weede smiled. Evidently, Hannah knew how to wield a shotgun, too. The staccato sounds of firing echoed from the east side of the house. Lee was keeping them pretty busy. They had bought Weede precious time; he had to take advantage of the opportunity. Weede leaped onto the porch, cupped his hands to his mouth and yelled, "Hannah?"

No answer. Weede changed direction and shouted louder, "Hannah?" Still no answer. He heard approaching footsteps, and dashed behind a podocarpus bush. They were looking for him. Good. They could find him, and death, too.

The footsteps drew nearer. Shotgun fire thundered again from a distant corner of the roof. Weede watched a single, crouching figure cautiously approach the fallen guard. The shadowy figure kept a wary eye on the roof as he worked his way across the open slab. He was holding an automatic at the ready. Weede noticed that the figure was left-handed and that his head was wrapped with an exaggerated turban. Niassa!

Weede didn't wait for an introduction. He bounded from cover, rolled and fired. Nothing happened. The Skorpion had jammed. Niassa was momentarily stunned, but recovered quickly. He sneered with contempt and fired four rapid shots at Weede, which were followed by a metallic click. The bolts of steel chewed into the concrete beside Weede's head. Three of the slugs had missed. But one had ripped through Weede's shoulder.

He felt like he had been struck with a baseball bat. Warm, sticky blood was already trickling through his shirt. But Weede wasn't finished yet. Niassa was out of ammo. Good. Weede would show him what damage a wounded freelance merc could do.

Weede whipped around in a blur and dropped Niassa with a stout kick to the side of the knee. Niassa buckled and dropped the gun, but countered with an upward punch to the groin. Weede doubled over in pain, but did not cry out. Niassa, savoring the moment, delivered a roundhouse kick to the side of the head. Weede threw a tentative punch to Niassa's chest, but he was growing weaker. He knew he was in trouble and Niassa was in no hurry.

Niassa would let Weede use up the last of his strength as his life's blood drained from his body. Weede leaped and missed with a final kick, collapsing face up beside the body of the guard. Weede fought to get up, but it was no use. He was too weak.

Was this how it would end? Weede was getting dizzy. He couldn't lift his head. Niassa moved a step closer. Another step. Weede heard the springing clink of a magazine being loaded. He was calm and unafraid, but did not want to die. Not yet. No, not like this.

Deep within, something pushed him, drove him on and said, Now! Weede rolled just in time. A round smashed into the pavement where his head had been. He rolled again, bracing for the impact of the next bullet. Weede was spent. Exhausted. He finished his final roll face up. Why hadn't Niassa fired again?

He was preoccupied. Weede heard the roof tiles rattle with the rush of steps. Niassa, who was looking up, suddenly dodged to his right and dropped the automatic as a shower of steel shattered the planter behind him. He started back for the weapon, but three more blasts in quick succession churned the stone path Niassa edged out tentatively for another try only to be met by more raining buckshot. He hesitated briefly before bolting around the corner.

Weede saw an interesting pair of legs dangle over the roof. Song looked down and gave him a half salute. Her eyes were still flashing. "Hi there," she said.

"Hi yourself," Weede said hoarsely. "I guess you showed that bloke. What took you so bloody long?"

Song snapped the shotgun to her side. "I should ask you the same question. I'll be right down."

Chapter 31

Some of Au's guards had made a fatal mistake: they had bunched together in the open and become perfect targets. Their frantic bursts of automatic fire had been returned by spare shots from the raiders. Lee's men had just focused on the flashes. Those caught at the edge of the lawn were selectively exterminated.

The others had split up and opened fire from the corners of the house. Lee sent three commandoes off to the right, covering them with a rain of sparkling lead. They dodged and rolled behind a bark dust berm. Once they were well in position, Lee jumped to his feet, vaulted the wall and sprinted left. The other three raiders behind the wall laid down a protective curtain of fire. Noise went wild. Lee drew himself in tightly behind a tree as automatic bursts chewed and splintered the trunk of the evergreen. He was grateful that the isolated tree was thick enough and hard enough to withstand the grinding deluge of steel.

Lee looked back at his men and waved a signal, before working his way around the tree. He sprayed the near edge of the mansion as his men surged up and rushed forward in a frontal assault. The tactical team behind the berm took the cue, leaped to their feet and raced for the house.

The two sides traded wild bursts as the firefight degenerated into a free-for-all. Screaming and furious firing erupted from every quarter. Lee dashed across the open ground toward the front of the house. Stray bullets whizzed by his head. His ears popped with the concussive pressure of a passing shell.

As Lee scurried beside a privet hedge, a sentry lunged out and sliced at him with a kukri knife. Lee side stepped and parried with a smash from his butt stock, catching the sentry on the jaw. The dazed sentry dropped the knife and reached out frantically for the muzzle of Lee's weapon. He was too late. Lee ripped his chest with a long burst. Flesh, bone, froth and gristle blew into the air. The man jackknifed backward, clawing the air as he fell.

Lee watched the silent form for a long while. He had never killed a man up close. Killing others bothered him, but not as much as being killed. The firing around him had stopped. His thoughts returned to the mission when he was joined by the three raiders who had covered him.

As they prepared to make the final push, a sentry leaped across the walkway, threw down his rifle and dashed for the front gate. One of Lee's men raised his weapon to fire, but Lee stayed his hand. "Forget it. We won't get them all."

They fanned out and moved warily to the front of the house. Lee consciously scanned all points of the compass; he didn't want any more surprises. Lee's team flanked each other in twos as they reached the main entrance.

The massive double-doors were open a notch, emitting a sliver of light. No one spoke. Lee eased the door open. The interior lights blinked out.

They crouched low and slipped inside. Lee reached out in the darkness, found the light switch and tried it. "Dead," he whispered.

He tapped each of the other raiders on the shoulders. "You men make a circuit of the downstairs. I'll take the upstairs and catch up to you later. Keep your eyes open. Good luck."

They separated without ceremony. Every man knew what he had to do. Lee moved stealthily up the staircase as the others branched off. Upon reaching the upper landing, he could see a soft light coming from the g salon at the end of the hall. He pivoted to check his back, then hunched down, swiveled and crept toward the room. Lee raised his weapon and held it ready at the hip.

He inched up to the door post and peeked into the room. It looked empty. A faint flame from a wall-mounted candle was the source of the eerie, shadowy light. He drew a single, controlled breath and side stepped in.

Lee crossed the floor with a feline grace. He was careful to watch the candle as he moved diagonally, poised on the balls of his feet. Lee stopped cold. The flame had flickered. He sensed a hurried movement to his right as it went out. He rotated and adopted a martial arts stance. Lee wheeled just in time to counter a smash to his head. He snapped back with a roundhouse kick, lashing his assailant in the face. Lee blocked a return kick to the groin, but was blindsided by a shot from the opposite direction. The force of the blow sent Lee's assault rifle spinning into the corner. There were two of them.

Lee recovered his balance, faked right and kicked left, solidly slamming one of them in the face. Then he whirled right and punched left, staggering the other with a crunching blow to the ear. Lee flipped backward, supported by his palms. A sudden sweep of his foot knocked the legs out from under one of the attackers. Then Lee vaulted upward with his head, hammering the other under the chin.

The lights flashed back on. Wah glared up at him from the floor. The turbaned foreigner he had seen at Pingtung Airfield lay spread-eagled in the corner.

Wah's stare was venomous. His eyes brimmed with hatred. Lee looked down at him with a combination of revulsion and pity. There was no rancor in his heart. Only the fierce determination to avenge the senseless murder of his brother remained. Wah staggered to his feet. Lee bowed and poised for the charge. He was calm and filled with a spirit of purpose. "Come," Lee said. "Show me what a Red Pole can do."

With an arrogant snap of his head, Wah screamed a sound from another world and drove toward Lee. Lee deflected a hard thrust with his open palm and used Wah's momentum to propel him into the wall. The turbaned assailant in the corner charged again, but was whacked flat by an arcing drive from Lee.

Wah dragged himself to his feet and lunged at Lee again. This time Lee slammed a fist under his neck, crushing the giant's windpipe. Wah grabbed his neck with both hands and collapsed, gasping, to the floor. Lee turned to face the other attacker. While Lee was occupied with Wah, the man had picked up the automatic. Lee rocketed a kick at the weapon, but the assailant fell back and emptied the weapon into Lee's abdomen, knocking him back into the frame of a low window. The attacker threw the empty weapon down and ran from the room.

Fat Wah lay still. He was already turning blue. Froth gathered at the corners of his mouth. Wah's eyes bulged even more grotesquely. Lee tried to grab the curtain to pull himself up, but slipped down, clutching his chest. He sat with his legs extended, breathing rhythmically, as Fat Wah's life ebbed away.

Lee was still breathing in a measured, relaxed manner when Song ran into the room followed by two of the team. The others were still tending to Weede. She screeched and landed on her knees beside Lee, cradling his head in her lap. One of the men opened Lee's shirt and shook his head. The blood pumped steadily from his body.

"He must be in terrible pain," said the man.

Song bent down, kissed Lee on the lips and cried, "Why? Why? Why?" She grabbed his pale hand. "Hang on. Please hang on. You can make it. Hang on. You'll make it." Her grip tightened as his grasp weakened.

Lee smiled and reached up to caress her face. "*Wen Mei*," he whispered, "*Wen Mei*." Lee gave her a long, deep look, then turned his head as the terminal breath was released from his body.

Chapter 32

The clatter of gunfire within the compound had been deafening. Mitoma's companion had run from the room in mortal terror after the first booming explosion had rolled through the house. Mitoma had waited under the covers for a few minutes before rising and wrapping a silk dressing gown around himself. When the commotion outside had not subsided, he had drawn close to the window and parted the curtains a finger's breadth.

From his second-floor vantage point, Mitoma saw silhouetted figures moving across the broad expanse of lawn. They were preceded by the soft licks of flame from their invisible weapons. The precision of their movements convinced him that the intruders were more than mere bandits. But who were they? Saboteurs? Assassins?

For the longest time, Mitoma was too afraid to move away from the window. It was as if he despaired that even the slightest movement would betray his presence to the attackers below. He heard harried footsteps and excited voices in the hall. One of them was Au's. He heard the Chairman shout instructions to his guards over the din of the firing in the yard. Mitoma had never heard Au so angry or demanding. He decided that it was of no use being a sitting duck. Fear, or no fear, he had to talk to Au. Bracing himself, he dived to the carpet, rolled to the door and opened it.

Au was storming down the hall, carrying an empty burlap bag. A look of boiling fury had risen in his face. Mitoma only intended to obtain reassurance from Au and not to confront him. He reached out his hand as Au passed and touched his arm. "Excuse me, my Chairman, but what is this awful business?"

The Chairman turned on Mitoma with a sharp glare and then remembered himself. His visage phased from irate to concerned. "Ah, Crashi, alas, we've been attacked by Communist insurgents. I have always feared that they would take advantage of our isolation, and now this . . . this . . ." Au shook his head as if he was deeply saddened by the turmoil and the inconvenience to his guest.

Mitoma trembled and his voice rasped from the dryness of his throat. "But, my Chairman, what am I to do?"

Au put his hand on Mitoma's upper arm and forced a smile. "Nothing, Crashi. Just remain in your room and await instruction from my staff. My guards will soon dispatch this gang of ruffians."

Mitoma nodded forcefully and bowed. "As you wish, my Chairman."

Mitoma shut the door and crawled under his bed. He rested on his stomach, with his crossed arms supporting his chin and contemplated the situation. He reasoned that there was no sense in getting involved. As Confucius said, *"Kúnshi wa ayaúki ni chickayóraxu,*—a wise man does not approach danger."

After Mitoma had settled in, the gunfire abruptly stopped. Good, he reasoned. The Chairman would have things under control presently. His worrying would serve no purpose. Still, he did not believe Au's statement about Communist insurgents. That was preposterous. He had the uneasy feeling that Au was not telling him everything. Could the sudden appearance of the attackers have anything to do with the shipment due to dock at Kaohsiung? Mitoma would not be sure until he questioned Au further.

One thing was certain: the time was ripe for a change. Mitoma was nearly ready to implement his coup. Tsuchiyama was in place and set to begin. All he needed was a reliable supply of ivory. Mitoma had contacted an associate in the Kenyan embassy. For the right price, the necessary arrangements would be made. Mitoma had also dealt with a low-paid bureaucrat in Botswana with access to that country's stores of confiscated tusks. The contracts had been sealed with good faith deposits and letters of credit. He had lined up a cargo carrier and bribed the necessary Japanese Customs officials. Yes, the ivory would be supplied and there would always be a market for it, despite the meddlesome international bans.

If, as Mitoma sensed, Au's network had been penetrated, his ability to continue operations would be severely curtailed. Mitoma would fill that vacuum. He would prove his capabilities and become wealthy in the process. There would be no need or desire to employ Au's agency ever again.

And what if Au had already discovered his plans? Mitoma dismissed such concerns. He had taken every necessary precaution. Au's demeanor did not reveal that he knew about or suspected the existence of Mitoma's plot. Still, Mitoma would have to be careful; Au was a treacherous man.

Mitoma did not care about the future of the elephant or the environment. There were profits to be made. Ivory was a commodity, to be bought and sold like any other commodity. Contrary opinions were sentimental nonsense. Were not men the masters of the earth? Were not its resources to be exploited?

He, at least, had done his part to divert attention from the slaughter. Mitoma's disinformation campaign had already begun. Nagata had just approved the first ad in a series created by Mitoma. It would appear in the media all over Japan, the following week. Conceived by Mitoma, the release would link the protests over the use of ivory by the Japanese to the efforts led by the hypocritical Americans to bankrupt the Japanese fishing industry because of a few, insignificant dolphins. The ad would inflame existing Japanese passions and the common perception that the so-called environmental concerns were only a cover for the jealous Americans to engage in their favorite pastime: Japan bashing.

An advertisement later in the month would offer and expound upon the premise that the real reason for the elephant's decline was over population and loss of habitation due to human encroachment, and not isolated incidents of poaching. Japan was not to blame for that. If the elephants died anyway, shouldn't the ivory be used for artistic purposes, rather than left to rot in the wilds? The Americans did not think so. Mitoma had even more ideas and could not wait to implement them.

He sighed and thought of his home in Akashi. Soon he would be wandering along the willow-draped paths that separated the houses with their ebony tile roofs. His beloved Taka would be at his side. She would be wearing his favorite powder-blue sweater and the white skirt that revealed her shapely legs. Her dark hair would be jostled by a gentle breeze from the Harima Sea. They would laugh and sing and take the afternoon train to Osaka for a dinner of *fugu* and *tempura*.

With one month's profits from his planned venture, Mitoma would be able to buy his own restaurant in the fabled Osaka underground known as "Rainbow Town." He would treat his friends and become an important man in his town. The ivory trade would make it all possible. It would save him from a life of mediocrity. But first, he had to attend to business. Mitoma listened for signals of activity beyond the door. The sound of muffled gunshots reached him.

He strained and heard a rustling sound coming from the floor vent beside the bed. It was probably just the expansion of the metal duct, he told himself. Mitoma strained to hear. There was that sound again. This time it was louder. And closer. He wiggled his leg. Something had touched his slipper. He moved his foot as a precaution. Mitoma reasoned that he had just imagined a touching sensation. His nerves were on edge. There was nothing in the room. Or was there?

Mitoma felt around with his other foot. It touched a firm object. Had some careless workman left a coil of rubber tubing beneath the bed? He pressed harder, as if denying the evidence. He screamed in depraved anguish as something clenched his ankle, snapped needles into his flesh and injected him with a stream of fire. Mitoma scrambled from under the bed, rushed to the door and threw it open. He staggered down the hall, screeching at the top of his lungs. With heavy, spastic steps he fell into the arms of Au and collapsed.

Part Three

EAGLE AND SERPENT

Chapter 33

Au did not have time to ask Mitoma what had happened. He did not need to, anyway. There were no visible marks on him. Yet, he was already dead. The violent convulsions, the swollen tongue, the incoherent gurgle and the rapidity of death were all he needed to know.

Mitoma's sudden, horrible death could present messy complications for his business. His operation had already suffered a serious setback due to the seizure of the shipment at Kaohsiung. Au would personally explain things to Nagata. He did not wish to offend his primary trading partners. Au knew that Mitoma could be replaced; legions of boot-licking vice presidents waited in the wings. Still, he would have to personally smooth things over, once his present difficulties were resolved.

Song had escaped. Her agents were even now swarming over his grounds. She had disrupted a single shipment. Au would be inconvenienced, but she would never stop him. He regretted with every fiber of his being that he would have to destroy her.

Au had heard successive shots echoing from the ballroom. His guards were nowhere to be found. Wah had not reported in. Au could not allow himself to be seized by the infiltrators. It was time for him to go.

He left Mitoma's body in the hall and slipped into his private study. After barricading the door, Au started for a carved mahogany desk in a corner of the apartment. Doors slammed along the hallway. He heard rushing footsteps. Song's rescuers were already searching room to room. There was not much time left. He had to hurry.

Au pulled a bulging manila file folder from the top drawer, lit a match to the contents and dropped the flaming mass into a tin wastebasket. He watched with satisfaction as the flames flared and consumed the records. Au looked up. Niassa stepped from the shadows, holding a curved knife. "I believe we have some unfinished business."

Au was momentarily caught off guard, but rallied quickly. "Let's discuss it later, shall we? Right now, we have some more pressing concerns upon us?"

He tried to move around him, but Niassa blocked his path. Au backed up. Niassa glared at him and raised the knife. "There is no need for that," implored Au. They both turned to look as someone shook the study door. The shaking was followed by excited shouts. Niassa's eyes twitched nervously. Au motioned toward an ornate fireplace. "Come," he commanded.

Au pressed a button hidden behind the marble mantle. An adjacent wall panel swung open to reveal a dimly-lit staircase. There was a sonorous boom as someone tried to kick down the door. "Hurry," Au said.

Once they had cleared the opening and were standing on the staircase, Au touched a button under the lip of the third step. The panel closed and sealed behind them. Au ripped the switch wires so that the portal could no longer be opened electronically. He led Niassa down to a rock chamber with a high ceiling. A walk-in vault with a massive stainless steel door had been cut into the far wall.

An armed guard leaped out at them from an alcove. He pointed his AK-47 menacingly at Niassa. He scowled at him with a look that said he would not hesitate to pull the trigger if Au willed it. Niassa closed his eyes and began praying to Allah.

Au tapped the barrel of the rifle. "It's alright. He's coming with me."

The guard relaxed his grip on the weapon and lowered it. Niassa opened his eyes and breathed with relief. Au stepped to the vault. He twisted the dial left and then right at precise intervals. The door rolled open with a sharp pull on its chromium handle. He glanced back at Niassa, who had not moved. The guard was still eyeing him with suspicion. Au wagged his arm. "Well, come on."

Niassa hesitated for a moment then brushed past the guard. As the guard kept a vigil outside, Niassa walked with Au into the vault just as Au flipped the light switch. Niassa stood in profound amazement. Shelves were stacked with all manner of currency, bank notes and bearer bonds from at least fifty nations. Au noted the blaze of greed in Niassa's eyes and reached to the top shelf. He pulled down two canvas mail sacks and tossed one to Niassa. "Here, help me with this, will you"

Ten minutes later, the satchels were filled. Au looked anxiously at the staircase. "It will not take them long to find the entrance. We must go." He gestured toward a low opening in the rock wall. They worked their way along a narrow passageway the length of an airport concourse. It was lit by recessed lights. In places, water had collected and formed puddles along the floor of the tunnel. They splashed each other accidentally as they ran. They soon reached a ladder stretching up to a wooden door.

Au climbed the ladder as the other two followed. The door opened through the floor of the gatehouse, which was 300 meters from the mansion. They ran from the sentry station and climbed into an idling Rolls Royce. Au tapped the driver's shoulder. "Alright. Go!"

The car sped down a gravel road to a waiting helicopter. It was a Bell Jet Ranger.

As they approached the landing pad, the driver flashed the headlights twice. The chopper's turbine whined as the rotor blades began their leisurely swing.

Slugs ripped through the trunk deck and rear window as the Rolls fishtailed to a stop. The driver dived for cover. Au, Niassa and the guard bolted from the car and slammed into the ground. They jumped up, stooped over and raced for the helicopter. Clumps of sod kicked up all around them. The whine of the engine increased to an ear-splitting level. Au and Niassa fought to hang on to their precious bundles.

The guard wheeled and returned the fire. He was cut down by a buzzing swarm of steel. From the door of the chopper, the co-pilot laid down a covering fire with an Uzi. The compact automatic spat rounds at the pursuers, as he helped Au through the door with his free hand.

But the raiders were not to be denied. Bullets tore into the fuselage and tail boom as Niassa stumbled and fell. Au hesitated for a second, debating whether to leave him, until he remembered the other satchel. Au stretched out for Niassa's hand. Niassa dug his nails into Au's palm, and pulled himself forward. He landed in the chopper on his belly. His legs frantically kicked the struts as the helicopter lifted off sharply and clawed sideways through the air.

The craft skimmed low over the grey water, until it arrived at the airfield north of coastal Taitung. They landed in a far corner of the field beside a private hangar. Au made expedient arrangements with a charter operator. By dawn, the Lear jet carrying Au and Niassa was in the air, headed for the South China Sea.

That evening, Au was seated at a baccarat table in the casino of the Hotel Lisboa. The governor of Macao joined him in placing a wager. At an adjacent craps table, an exuberant player threw the dice erratically. The dice tumbled across the table and landed in front of Au. Each displayed a single dot. The governor laughed so hard he shook. "Snake eyes, Mr. Chairman. Snake eyes."

Au slowly picked them up and studied them. They were made of ivory. He looked into the distance before handing them to the croupier. "Yes. Snake eyes."

Chapter 34

The sound of the monastery drum floated down the mountain and enveloped the fishing village of Tai O. Hermit monks were being summoned to the dawn service. Shivering waves rolled through the stilts of the frame houses stacked high above the water. Fleshy purple crabs scuttled among the pilings searching for scraps of dross. Stirring voices welled from beneath the matting of restrained sampans as seagulls flew off to gather fishes from the bay.

Yasuhiro Nagata and Hiroshi Zaku wandered through the quaint town searching for the mini-bus that would carry them to the brooding peak. Their destination was the Chihpen monastery, which overlooked the anchorage on the northwestern tip of Lantau Island, Hong Kong Territory. The ferry trip from Victoria Harbour had taken just over an hour. Nagata hoped their business would be concluded quickly. "Do you see it?" he asked Zaku impatiently.

"*Hai, soko desu,*" said Zaku, pointing toward a stone wall. Nagata saw a colorful vehicle parked halfway up on the curb. They hurried across the street, so as not to miss it.

The early morning frost pressed down on the roof of the mini-bus. Its engine rocked at idle, warming up for the first trip of the day. "Good morning," Nagata said to the driver, as they stepped aboard.

"*Ni hao,*" replied the driver cheerfully.

Nagata sat by himself toward the rear exit. Zaku grunted and lowered himself into a seat behind the driver. The driver waited for an elderly couple to climb aboard, then made a U-turn and headed for the high road. Nagata checked his watch and drowsily gazed out the window. Wildflowers added by a natal spring rain graced the byway. Soon, their swelling buds would burst with the flames of the sun. Nagata was mesmerized by the soft swirl of color.

They pulled into the monastery courtyard just after 7:00 a.m. Nagata paid the driver as Zaku brushed past them. The elderly couple stood still beneath an ancient evergreen, preparing to meditate. Male and female elephants cast in white plaster stood at the foot of the steps leading to the ascended shrine. Gnarled pine trees leaned against each other beside the terrace wall. Beyond it, a tea plantation reposed in the fresh light of the new day.

The temple square itself looked tranquil, and vacant. Nagata started after Zaku, as a monk clad in peach-colored robes descended the steps to greet them. He treaded softly as he led them to the detached templar quarters. They were shown into a narrow, windowless cubicle with a low ceiling. The glow from the candles played with the shadows on the wall. A hard wooden bed rested in a corner. In the center of the room huddled a wicker table and three chairs. The chamber was devoid of any other objects. Zaku tried to make himself comfortable in the undersized seat. Nagata stood facing the entry. There was an abrupt knock on the door. It opened, admitting a vertical ray of light and Shang T.K. Au. But Zaku temporarily stuck, remained seated. Au hurried over to Nagata and bowed. "Nagata-san, I am sorry to have kept you waiting. Welcome. Welcome."

"*Domo arigato gozaimasu*," Nagata said, returning the bow. "May I introduce my associate, Zaku-san?"

Au spun toward Zaku. He studied the ruthless eyes of the brooding man and instantly did not like him. "I am very pleased to make your acquaintance, Zaku-san."

Zaku struggled up and made a half-hearted attempt to bow. He said nothing. Au turned back to Nagata. "And how is business, Nagata-san?"

"My dear Au, that is what I have come here to find out," Nagata sniffed.

Nagata's abruptness was uncharacteristic and very un-Japanese. Au wondered what sort of pressure Nagata was under. He decided to drop the little pleasantries and get down to the point in question. "Since the tragic loss of my dear friend Crashi, I have had to embark upon a certain restructuring of my operations."

Au slipped a look at Zaku to gauge his reaction. There was none. The large man remained impassive. Nagata lifted his eyes and shook his head. "Ah, Crashi, poor fellow. Horrible! Just horrible."

"*Hai, so desu*," agreed Au.

Nagata appeared more conciliatory. "Tell me, what is your plan?"

Au drew back where he could watch both men at the same time. "Due to the officious meddling of a U.S. Customs agent and her band of ruffians, I am presently not welcome in the Republic of China. Consequently, I have made an arrangement with my good friend, the Governor of Macao, to develop my business under the umbrella of his providence." He smiled coyly at the memory of the nature of the arrangement. $10,000,000 had been deposited in a bank in Zurich that morning.

Nagata pressed the issue. "What about your distribution system? Is it intact? Can you continue to guarantee a reliable delivery schedule?"

Au did not hesitate with his response. "Yes, Nagata-san. Many, many years ago, my vessels were transferred to a holding company and placed under Liberian registry. At least on paper, they are not traceable to me, although I control them. If any should be seized, I can simply lease or build more. Please do not let that concern you."

Nagata looked over to Zaku. "Au-san, may I remind you that one shipment has already been seized. I view any interruption of my business most unfavorably."

Au studied Nagata for the flash of a moment. "Yes, of course, and I predict that no further obstructions will occur," he said slyly.

Nagata checked for Zaku's reaction again, and then nodded his approval. "Very well. But tell me, what of your production facilities and your African acquisition team? Have they been impacted?"

"My master carvers and their families have been relocated to Macao and will receive sizable bonuses for their sacrifices. And due to the civil strife in Somalia, a favorable climate now exists for the expansion of our operations there. In fact, our stockpiles grow steadily, and are well-secured."

Nagata shifted his weight to his right foot. What about the Kenyan situation? Is it under control?"

Au swept his hand through his hair and sat on the edge of the bed looking up at Nagata. "This Langdon fellow is guarded night and day. Fortunately, lesser Kenyan officials still need to feed their families. He cannot match our resources and his elite team is poorly equipped. If it were not for the meddlesome Americans, he would not have any air capability. But that advantage will soon be neutralized."

Nagata did not appear to be interested in details, only results. "And tell me, Au-san, what of this prying American Customs agent, Song, I believe? I hear that she is very beautiful."

At the mention of her name, Au could feel the faint, warm flush of blood rising in his cheeks. He remembered the lustrous glimmer of her eyes and fought to control his subdued yearning. "Yes, she is pricelessly beautiful." Au looked through Nagata into the distance. "A beauty capable of overthrowing a city or a kingdom."

Nagata looked puzzled by his morose tone. He glanced over at Zaku, who merely shrugged. Au quickly recovered with a snap of his head. "All the more the pity. Beauty will not save her. My associates will see to it in short order."

Zaku rose and walked to the bed. He fixed Au with an intense stare. "Tell me, Au-san, were any documents of an embarrassing nature seized from your headquarters?"

Au knew that the discovery of Mitoma's body and his identity would confirm Japanese involvement in the illicit trade. He had taken care to destroy as many records as possible in the limited time available to him. But he could not be sure that he had eradicated them all. Still, now was not the time to give rise to doubts about his competence with clandestine matters. He decided to lie. "No, of course not," Au snapped. "Records of a compromising nature were kept to a minimum in the first place and were centralized. I personally destroyed them all during the raid. What do you take me for?"

Nagata moved in to soften the impact of the provocative question. "You understand, Au-san, that we prefer to remain inconspicuous. What with this business of the whales and dolphins, we Japanese can ill afford the publicity."

Au said nothing, but waited for Nagata to finish. "I am an old man. Sense comes with age. Crashi was actually employed by another company in our *keiretsu*. I have taken the precaution of having him retroactively discharged. Sadly, his employment records were destroyed in a warehouse fire. They cannot be reconstructed. He will not be traced to us in any case."

Zaku snorted and stepped aside. Au was uneasy. The Neanderthal-looking man was still within striking distance. Nagata put his hand on Au's shoulder. "Tell me, when may we anticipate our substituted delivery?"

Au warmed to the prospect of continued business. "Within the next moon. The raw tonnage has already been consolidated for movement and will leave for Mogadishu on the morrow."

"Splendid," said Nagata. He motioned to Zaku. "We must go."

Au walked with them outside. The nearby peak of Chihpen stretched up into the clear, pure color of cold. In the harbor below, dauntless sails were already spreading wide. A matronly sparrow guided her chicks from their path. The promise of an early Spring had come to the gate. It would be a beautiful day.

The mini-bus had returned bearing a fresh load of pilgrims. Once the bus had emptied, Zaku lumbered aboard without looking back. Beside the steps, Nagata turned to Au, covered his mouth and whispered, "Can you do it?"

Au asked himself why he had become involved in smuggling ivory in the first place. He certainly did not need the money. It carried no prestige. Was it the intrigue? Excitement? No, it was none of those things. Perhaps what spurred him on was the gamble. The risk of losing it all. Regardless, the thing had progressed too far to turn back. He filled his lungs with the crisp air and drew to his full height. *"Hai, dekimásü."*

Chapter 35

It was getting cold behind the slag pile. Dawn had taken too long to arrive. That seemed strange to Song, since the African nightfalls were so sudden. Dark clouds streamed over the hills and marshaled in a leaden sky. It threatened to rain. Now, in the middle of a drought, during the operation.

A faint sun appeared on the eastern horizon. Song peeked over the outcrop again to check the locations of the guards. She studied her potential targets. Three were still standing beside the entrance to the cave; two others crossed the compound and entered a bunker. They were all heavily armed.

Razor wire ringed the perimeter. A mortar tube jutted up at an angle behind carefully arranged sandbags. Beside the front gate sat the Russian BTR 152 armored personnel carrier Weede had warned her about. Its twin stingers were pointed directly at her.

She backed down the face of the mound and looked to her left. Weede's *abbaan* was smiling at her with yellow, broken stumps of teeth.

"*Jaàlle*, he said.

Song smiled back. "*Jaàlle.*" It was the only word she knew. Weede had told her it meant "friend." She hoped so. The *abbaan* was still staring at her. He had probably never seen a Chinese woman before, much less a lady warrior. Women did not carry spears in Somalia. Not even high caliber ones. "My, are you in for a surprise," she said.

The *abbaan* smiled even more profusely and nodded his head up and down. "*Jaàlle. Jaàlle. Jaàlle.*"

"*Jaàlle*," Song said again. She made a note to expand her vocabulary. Although his immediate attention made her feel uneasy, she was comforted by the presence of the *abbaan* and his ten hand-picked warriors. They would need all the help they could muster.

Trained fighters were a precious commodity in heavy contact situations. Weede had routinely enlisted their assistance. He had not been joking about his claimed specialization in cross-border transactions. Damn him! What was taking so long? Song tugged anxiously on her fingerless gloves.

They had crossed into the province of Gedo just after midnight and followed the Juba River north. Song was grateful that it had been a moonless night. By 0315, they had reached their present position, five kilometers west of the Bhardeere hydroelectric station.

Weede's informants had tipped them to the information that twelve tons of raw ivory would be delivered to this NSS stronghold at daybreak. After they had moved into cover, Weede left to reconnoiter the area. That had been two hours ago.

The eerie calm was breached by the drone of truck engines along the river road to the southeast. They were warily inching along with headlamps still burning. Skirts of dust gathered about their wheels. On they came, carrying a cargo of death. Song could make out three covered lorries sandwiched between two ten ton stake beds loaded with security forces. If they had not been outnumbered before, they certainly would be now. Where was that Duff?

As if on cue, he low-crawled up beside her and turned over on his back. A Stoner assault rifle was nestled in the crook of his arm. He was perspiring and breathing hard. Song thought he was still feeling his wounds. Weede averted his eyes and looked up at the swollen sky. "Yeh, going to be a dazzler of a day."

"What are you talking about?" she asked. "It's going to rain."

He shook his head confidently. "Nah. Not here." Weede's expression turned grim in the blink of an eye. "It's going to be murder city when our guests arrive in a few minutes. When it starts, remember that the most deadly thing on the battlefield is a single well-aimed shot."

Song was almost offended by the patronizing tone of his advice. "What are you trying to say?"

"Don't fire until you've got a target. Hit the easy ones first. Decide on your own rate of fire."

Song huffed. "Thanks for the tip. Anything else?"

Weede did not take her hint. "Yeh. Aim low. Ricochets can do more damage than rounds sailing high."

Song raised her arms in mock surrender. "Okay, you're the expert."

Weede was starting to get the point. He kissed the Stoner and patted the drum magazine. "That's right, lovey."

The *abbaan* and one of his men crept up to Weede. They spoke quickly in hushed bursts. Weede nodded and gestured with his hands in a manner familiar to all infantry men. He faced Song and touched the *abbaan* on the arm. "Ahmed here is going to take half the team and hit that ten ton." Weede pointed to the other warrior. "And Jama's group will get the rear guard."

"What about us?" Song asked.

Weede started to say something, then changed his mind. "I'll take out the bunker boys. Think you can off the BTR crew and the cave sentries?"

Song swallowed hard and nodded. The trucks were less than a kilometer away. "Alright then," said Weede. "Time for the mad minute." He gestured to Ahmed and Jama and they rose and slipped off in opposite directions.

Weede took a deep breath, closed his eyes and pursed his lips. He appeared to be meditating. After a few moments, he slowly opened his eyes. "Okay, Hannah. This is it. Wait for the signal," Weede said as he started to move out.

"Hold it," she whispered. "What's the signal?"

"An exploding truck," he said under his breath. He patted her arm and was gone.

Song flipped the bolt of her Remington and tried to collect her thoughts. How long should she wait before setting up? At this range, the intermittent breeze would not be a factor. And she had the advantage of plunging fire. Should be easy. But would it? Her hands trembled. They had done that periodically since the night of her rescue from Lan Yu Island. The night Lee died. She wiped her eyes and reached for a spare bandolier of cartridges.

The drone of the engines had become much louder. Metal clanked and groaned as every pothole received a wheel. One of the drivers blew a shift with an annoying grind, followed by a racing engine and a final ringing clank of the gears.

Song cradled her rifle and kicked up the scrabble to the crest of the rise. The sharp, jutting rocks scraped and poked her stomach and breasts. But the weapon was protected. When Song reached the top, she gently laid the rifle down and pulled a foot-square kerchief from her back pocket. Lifting the weapon, she placed the cloth beneath the tip of the muzzle. It would prevent any dust from being kicked up and giving away her position.

She started to sight in on one of the guards at the cave entrance. Take the easy ones first, Weede had said. Without warning, the air erupted with the chatter of automatic weapons along the route of the caravan. The exchange of bursts sounded almost musical. Song tried to sight again. Something was wrong. Her vision had blurred.

One guard ran through the gate, while the other scrambled into the cave. Song wiped her eyes and tried to follow the runner. She sighted in and hurried her fire. She missed. The guard ducked. Song fired again. This time he rocked backward.

Song corrected to her left and took aim on one of the two men in coveralls racing for the BTR. Rounds began cracking over her head from the vicinity of the bunker. She heard a howling whoosh followed by a roaring boom fifty meters away. Jagged shards of hot metal and rock flayed the air. The acrid, sharp stench of cordite rolled over the landscape. The mortar! They were just getting the range. The next round would fall right on her.

She sighted in on the pit and picked off the loader before he could drop a second shell. Another mortar man scrambled to take his place. Song quick-fired and he tumbled over, still clutching the mortar round.

The furious fighting along the road continued unabated. The *abbaan's* men were laying down a curtain of enfilading fire. But Song had problems of her own: the BTR men had reached the carrier and activated the guns. They moved the mount slightly, stopped and unleashed the pounding fury of two antiaircraft cannons. The rocks to Song's right were pulverized by the solid stream of crashing fire. She tried to melt into the rubble and only managed to slice her face.

Sparks careened by as the red hot torpedoes slapped and skipped over the rocks. One shell struck the stone beside Song's hand. She snapped her hand to her body and curled into a fetal position. Her head was buzzing. Her mouth was drier than it had ever been before. All too abruptly, the BTR firing stopped.

Still shaking, Song edged back to the top. The BTR was rolling out of the compound toward the fighting down the road. A thunderous shock convulsed the air. Balloons of flame and debris rumbled into the sky. A truck had blown. It was the belated signal.

The intense hammering of automatic fire preceded a second eruption from the rear of the column. This time, a solid orange bolt flared above the road and fled into the air. Scratch another truck. Song could see men running toward the burned-out shells of the guard vehicles. The *abbaan's* men. They were on a dead run, shooting at any movements in the brush. Red and green tracers were flying only about the battlefield. Caustic, coal-black smoke from the flaming tires filled the air.

Song gasped and felt her heart in her mouth. The *abbaan's* men could not see the BTR headed their way. They would be caught in the open and slaughtered. She saw a furtive movement by the road and sighted in. It was Weede! She positioned her finger outside the trigger guard and watched him through the scope.

As the weapons carrier rounded the curve, Weede rolled from concealment and vaulted onto the BTR. Once mounted on the rear deck, he pulled the pins on two grenades, but held the spoons while he kicked the hatch door open with his foot. In their haste, the crew had not locked it down! Weede released the spoons, hesitated for two seconds and tossed the grenades down the hatch. He slammed the hatch cover and bailed into the bushes, just as the BTR shuddered and rocked with the internal explosions.

Red flames stabbed out from the viewing ports. The carrier careened from the road and smashed to a halt against a boulder. It brewed up as Weede retrieved the Stoner and headed for the bunker.

Song heard the now familiar whoosh of the tube, then a cracking detonation on the road. It was followed by another. And another. A creeping barrage of pinpoint blasts walked toward the *abbaan's* followers. The mortar was back in operation! But not for long. Weede maneuvered skillfully toward the emplacement.

He scampered through a hole in the wire and hit the ground just in time. Fusillades of machine gun fire raked the outer wire at his crossing point. Weede was in trouble. He had been caught in the open in a crossfire. There was no cover. Song saw him look her way. Could she help him?

Song's hands were shaking and clammy. She was still trembling as she loaded a cartridge and tried to sight in. Song tried to relax. Breathe, breathe, she kept telling herself. It was no use. Her vision was obscured. She couldn't focus.

Song panicked at the thought that something might really be

wrong with her. Was it a brain tumor, or a stroke? Or was she just losing her nerve?

Weede attempted to roll out and was met by furious volleys of searching fire. He couldn't move. The mortar crew kept up the rain of shells pinning down the *abbaan's* warriors. Song had to do something. She had to do it now.

Song aimed at the muzzle flashes of the blurred silhouettes on the right and fired. They moved. She fired again. They stopped peppering Weede. She traversed the yard and fired at the gun crew on the left. They, too, ceased firing at Weede and ducked. Song fired again, forcing them to adjust position. Her covering fire was shaky, but effective in buying Weede valuable time.

He bounded forward, zig zagging left to right. Fifty meters from the mortar pit, he cut loose with the Stoner. The mortar men were ripped by the lightning fast 5.56 mm rounds. Scratch one mortar.

Weede skidded to his left as the machine gunners tried to finish him off. Song fired again at both emplacements. Weede ducked behind a pile of sandbags.

Song could see knots of NSS men maneuvering toward Weede. She fired unceasingly at the advancing groups. They stopped, ducked and then moved forward again. Song raised the rifle to fire again and heard an empty click, which sickened her. She was out of ammunition.

She looked on in horror as they neared Weede. He raised up and loosed a burst from the Stoner. Three of the attackers dropped. A string of others rushed Weede as he was trying to reload. Dirt kicked up all around him.

Suddenly, the advancing NSS men were cut down in a hail and stream of fire from the rear of the compound. It was some of the *abbaan's* men. They had circled around from the east. The rest of his warriors poured over the wire and quickly dispatched the remaining NSS skirmishers. Weede ran up to the *abbaan* and embraced him. His men milled about, cheering and clapping.

Song trudged into the compound moments later. Her hands had stopped trembling and her sight had returned to normal. Pools of blood moistened the sandy ground at her feet. Spent cartridge cases littered the yard. She felt sorry so many had to die in such a brutal way.

Two of the *abbaan's* men emerged from the cave, dragging the cowering guard. They threw him to the ground at Weede's feet. One raised an AK-47 and prepared to fire into the back of his head. Song noticed Weede looking at her as if requesting a verdict. She shook her head, weary of the killing. Weede waved his arms at the guerilla. "No, wait. Maybe he'll talk."

The *abbaan's* men jerked the guard to his feet.

"Where's Niassa?" Weede asked sternly.

The guard spat at him. "Okay, take him," said Weede.

A terrified look crossed the man's face. "No, I'll talk."

"Where's Niassa?" Weede demanded.

The guard looked away, then back at Weede. "On his way to Kenya."

"Where in Kenya?"

"I don't know, but it involves business."

"Tie him up. We'll take him with us," Weede ordered. "C'mon, let's have a look around."

As they walked to the mouth of the cave, Weede softly touched Song's shoulder and took her aside. "What happened up there?"

She looked away, toward a stand of barren trees. "I wish I knew. Everything just went blurry."

Weede nodded in compassion. "Well, no worries." He clutched her hand as they entered the sepulchral cave. A narrow passageway opened into a gaping cavern with a concrete floor. Palletized ivory was scattered about the room, along with crates of rifles and ammunition. "Look," said Weede, pointing to the far wall.

The entire length of the rock face was covered with ancient petroglyphs. Enigmatic rock carvings. There were snakes, crocodiles, ostriches and elephants. All in procession. Song gestured at the cavern filled with ivory. "What are we going to do with all of this?"

Weede did not hesitate with his response. "What Langdon would do. Burn it."

The *abbaan's* men retrieved the undamaged lorries and stacked the ivory in the center of the encampment. They found an ancient forklift in a maintenance shed and were soon shuttling in and out of the cave, adding the palletized tusks to the pile. The automatic weapons and ammunition were saved for Langdon. He could use the help.

Weede had them dump a hundred litres of petrol on the massed mound. When everyone had moved back a safe distance, he hurled a crudely fashioned torch at the pile. As it rotated through its final arc, the air erupted with a surging wave of crimson flame. Murky smoke billowed from the heap and encircled the compound in a belt before flying off toward the climbing sun.

While the fire raged, the *abbaan's* men moved the dead into the cave and laid them in line. Weede and Song set C-4 charges at the entrance while the others moved down the road a half kilometer. After fixing the final charge, they retreated to the sandbags. Weede held up the electronic detonator. "It's time to blow and go. Cover your ears with your hands and open your mouth wide," he instructed Song. "It will help to diffuse the concussion."

Song complied as Weede opened his mouth, touched the digital button and cupped his hands over his ears. It seemed as though the entire mountain lifted in a thunderous rumble of swirling earth, then pressed down and swallowed the cave.

Strange birds screamed in abject terror as the team marched down the dim road. They made it to the trailing lorry as the searching rays of the sun pierced the lowered veil of the jungle.

Chapter 36

It began high above the South Pole, still engulfed in frigid seasonal darkness. A mass of super-cooled air rode a river thirty miles aloft, destined for the equator. The polar night jet stream flew relentlessly north, picking up force and velocity as it advanced.

Just beyond the horse latitudes, it merged with a warm equatorial front. The temperature differences gave rise to extreme pressure fluctuations, which caused violent whirling eddies. As the system arrived over the South China Sea, it began to spin inward to a low pressure center, creating cyclonic winds. By the third day, it covered a vast area of the sea. The system gyred north, drawing up moisture from the ocean.

By dawn of the fifth day, it was bearing the world's mightiest winds. The *tai-fung*, or "great wind," was sixty kilometers off the northwest tip of Taiwan. The forecasts said it was expected to turn out toward the open sea. Still, its arrival had been preceded by high winds and torrential rains. On the west coast, the tiny village of Lukang was besieged by blustery winds and covered by a grey cloak of gloomy clouds. It was Tuesday, May 9, 2000.

Wen Mei Song took a bath, scrubbing her head with perfumed soap, and then rinsed under the dribble of the rusting faucet. She stepped out and dried her body with a soft towel, then dried and combed her shoulder-length hair. As she drew past the mirror, Song turned and studied the profile of her developing body. It did not quite please her. She was fourteen years old and at the awkward stage, when the figure of a woman begins to emerge from the body of a child. In two weeks she would be fifteen and everything would be different.

She lived in a four-room brick and wood cottage with her mother and father and a six-year-old brother, Lai Wan. Song had to share sleeping quarters with her brother, which inconvenience she detested. Her father had promised her that when she turned fifteen, he would build for her a room of her own. That would be glorious. She could finally have the privacy she craved.

Song's father was a kindly, slender man with faded grey hair. He was the town mayor and a taro grower. He was much older than her mother, who was a young thirty-three. Song's mother still retained the vibrancy of her adolescence and a little figure, owing to her work as a dancer at a lakeside resort. Song's father was from an aboriginal family, whereas her mother had emigrated as a child from the Chinese mainland in 1973 via Hong Kong. Song loved them deeply, and even her brother, when he wasn't in the same room with her.

Now, Song's mother had begun to train her to dance in the local festivals, a prelude to employment at the resort. Her very first competition would take place that afternoon at Sun Moon Lake, fifty kilometers to the east. Song dreaded that her mother would not be there to watch her perform. But her father had to receive visiting dignitaries that afternoon and her mother had traditional dishes to prepare for the guests. Lai Wan would make the trip with her, however.

The traditional dance steps required agility and natural grace. Additionally, each dancer was expected to signify intense feeling, in her own individual way. Song practiced her moves, whirling in front of the mirror, arms uplifted, as she tested the range of facial expressions which would convey her moods and emotions. She rehearsed her favorite, a slow spiral, and smiled with satisfaction.

Today was a very special day. Song's mother had said that she could wear her new ceremonial costume to the contest. She slipped into her underwear and meticulously donned the outfit.

It was a striking combination. The woven costume consisted of a full-length skirt, brilliant red in color, and slit to the region of the upper thigh. A matching bodice was trimmed with a diamond pattern, embroidery stitched with white thread, upon a coal black sash. The skirt was contrasted by an apple-green coat, embellished with golden bands that ran horizontally on the fluted sleeves and vertically on the front and back of the tunic.

Something was wrong. The mirror shook, distorting her image. Song felt the fierce wind quake the house and rattle the fragile roof. It terrified her. But Song's mother had told her not to worry. The news reports had confirmed that the typhoon would sweep far north of the island and move out into the Pacific Ocean, where it would wane and die. Only the north island areas were in the path of danger. Still, the previous day's heavy rains had lashed the coastal village, despite all predictions to the contrary. Experts were often wrong. Song did not know whether to trust the reports or not. But she trusted her mother, and her mother was calm. Her mother would not allow them to go to the distant competition if there was any possibility of real peril.

Song sat down to breakfast and ate quickly. Her mother was stooped over, tending the cooking fire. Lai Wan had already finished his meal and was waiting impatiently for her. "Hurry, or we'll miss our ride," he said. Song knew that he didn't care about her dancing and that he just wanted to ride on the double-decker bus.

"Hush," she said with a self-important air, "I'm the one who will be doing the dancing." Her brother scoffed as only a skeptical six year old could, "Not if you don't hurry." So young, yet so precocious. Song clenched her teeth, but did not reprimand him further. She didn't need to. Her mother turned around and looked at Lai Wan, with flashing eyes. Whenever she was angry or upset, the telling glint appeared. Lai Wan knew the look and its meaning. He glanced down at the table.

They heard the sound of a horn coming from the road outside. Lai Wan jumped up and ran out the door.

Song stood as her mother rushed over to adjust the costume. She fretted as her mother tugged on the coat and brushed it. The sleeves were too long. Song tried to extend her fingers. Her mother stepped back to look, as her eyes enveloped Song with a mother's love. "Wen Mei, you are pricelessly beautiful. You are much better than I was at your age." They hugged each other with tears in their eyes. Her mother patted her back gently. "I know in my heart that you will do well today."

The horn sounded again. Song's father shuffled in from the bedroom. His copper-colored eyes studied her tenderly. He gave her an encouraging smile as she opened her arms to hug him. Her mother tugged her away from the embrace. "Come, Wen Mei, you must hurry." They kissed each other, as Song opened the door. Her mother touched Song's cheek with delicate fingertips. "Dance, my daughter, dance."

Song walked down the pea-gravel path. The cold slap of the wind almost knocked her off her feet. She pulled the coat tight against her and bounded aboard. There were seven other contestants on the bus. And Lai Wan. He had already climbed to the upper deck, which he commanded alone. From her seat, Song could see her mother standing in the window and waving to her. Song waved back. She would always remember her mother's proud, tear-streaked face as she said goodbye.

Two and a half hours later, the tram pulled up to the pavilion at Sun Moon Lake. There were not many people milling about. While they were en route, the weather had grown progressively worse. Now, the wind velocity had risen to gale level. The pelting rain stung Song's face as she exited the tram, pulling Lai Wan behind her. Once in the lodge, they learned that no competition would be held that day. It would have to be rescheduled, as the weather had delayed both judges and contestants. That was not all; the *tai-fung*, named Tara, had caromed off a temperate cold front and shifted direction. It was now headed straight for the island. The great wind would make the landfall in an hour, in central Taiwan near Lukang!

Song was gripped by fear and anxiety. They had to get home. What about her parents? No, the bus driver had said, it was too dangerous. He was not about to cross the suspension bridges in the middle of a typhoon, or risk passage through historic mudslide zones. It would be safer for them all to wait out the storm in the lodge, which was sheltered on all four sides by high mountains. Then the lodge owners herded the children into the basement, where they were provided with lunch and warm blankets.

At 2:20 p.m., the full fury of the *tai-fung* entered their lives. The building vibrated with the roar and rumble of the wind. They heard uprooted trees smash into the walls, as water rocks and natural debris rained down on the building. The pounding torrent of the deluge soon drowned out all other sounds, as if they were standing under a waterfall. Song huddled in a corner with Lai Wan. The little boy was clutching the front of her coat, with wild fear in his eyes.

They endured the onslaught of terror for nearly five hours. By 8:00 p.m., the wind had died down to isolated gusts. But it was too late to return. No one knew the condition of the roads, or what areas had sustained the most damage. Their lodge had lost the best part of its roof. The great wind had passed. They would be able to return home in the morning.

It was three more days before they returned to Lukang. By then, their worst fears had been confirmed. It was the village hardest hit. As they rounded the curve, they could see that few buildings remained standing. Relief workers were still prowling among the ruins searching for the living and the dead.

Song's own house was at the edge of the village. The relief workers had not gone that far yet. She ran toward it, half-carrying, half-dragging Lai Wan. Song gasped and stood in the road with her hand covering her mouth. She wanted to scream, but no sound could escape from her throat.

The typhoon had shattered her house. It was an indistinguishable, exploded pile of lumber and bricks. She fought back tears as she left Lai Wan crying at the edge of the yard and began to pick through the mass of rubble.

She dug and lifted with unrequited fury. An hour later, Song uncovered a frail, grey hand. Her mother! She frantically ripped away timbers and chunks of debris. With a surge of adrenalin, Song threw over a final sheet of wood and collapsed, sobbing uncontrollably. She had uncovered them. They were clinging to each other. And they were dead.

Song stumbled from the wreckage in shock and worked her way down to the road. With the sound of Lai Wan's cries ringing in her ears, she began to twirl and spiral, arms uplifted, in a trance, moving to her own music.

When they found her at twilight, she was still dancing in the road with a lost expression and lifeless eyes.

Song awoke from the vision shrieking in agony. It was 2:20 a.m., in San Francisco, and the dance and the dream had ended.

Chapter 37

A mood of expectation settled over the courtroom as the hearing entered its third hour. It was almost time to wrap it up. Victoria Moy had completed her rigorous cross-examination of the witness seated in the box beside Judge Mallison. She had been in no hurry. With every probing question, followed by another pointed question, Benson Wicklow had squirmed lower in his chair. He had been trapped.

Defendant Shih Jen had fared no better. By utilizing the additional documents obtained by Song from Taiwan, Moy had destroyed the credibility of both. Brick by brick. The defense attorney had made the over confident mistake of having his clients testify. He would not repeat that error for a long time. All you need now is to bring in the closer, Moy told herself.

As Wicklow slumped in his seat with downcast eyes, she turned her back on him, displaying obvious contempt. No, loathing was a more appropriate word, she thought. "No further questions of this witness, your honor."

Moy walked back to the counsel table and noticed for the first time, the dark circles under Song's eyes. Her heart was broken for Hannah. The death of Ku Tai Lee, coupled with her brother's murder only weeks before, had clearly taken a toll. Hannah seemed world-weary and distant now. Her lively spark was gone. Song was still professional, but somehow distant.

The attorney for the defense jumped up to argue a point of law. Moy almost tuned him out. "And so, your honor, none of what we have seen today proves that the ivory seized from my clients was illicit elephant ivory," he said.

The attorney digested his notes before continuing. "I grant your honor that Ms. Moy has made some interesting arguments. But what she says is not evidence." With that, he started to sit down, surrounded by an air of finality.

Moy climbed to her full height, trying to contain her eagerness. "If it pleases the Court, may I call my last witness, your honor?"

Mallison glanced at Moy over the tops of his bifocals. He had an amused look. "Why, certainly, counsel."

The defense attorney dropped down, deflated.

Moy took a deep breath. "The Government calls Holly Kim, your honor."

Mallison's formal gaze swept the gallery. "Is Holly Kim in the courtroom?"

The petite raven-haired woman stepped into the aisle carrying a chart case. "Yes, your honor."

"Please step forward, Ms. Kim," Mallison said.

Holly Kim passed through the bar gate with a swing of her hips. She placed her chart case beside an easel and approached the clerk. After the oath was administered she stepped up to the platform and eased into the chair. She tugged at her skirt. Kim looked confident, personable and relaxed. A perfect witness.

Moy waited while Kim slipped her glasses on. Kim adjusted the microphone and looked up at Moy, poised for the first question.

They reviewed her qualifications as an expert witness and her background as a wildlife forensic specialist. Using her charts, Kim outlined for Mallison the distinction between mammoth and elephant ivory. Moy slipped an insert into the overhead projector. It was a split screen view of the two sections of ivory. Kim walked to the screen, holding a pointer. "Here, your honor. These are Schreger lines." She pointed to the bald spots on each image. "One of these is mammoth and the other, African elephant." After a dramatic pause, Kim nodded to the prosecutor.

Moy slipped a highly magnified view of the separate Schreger lines into the projector. Kim pointed to the image on the left. "Measurement of the angle at which the Schreger lines intersect reveals the identity of the ivory."

Kim paused again for theatric effect. She was an old hand at giving expert testimony. "In this sample, the angle of intersection is less than ninety degrees. Ancient ivory from mammoths tends to be consistently acute like this. Therefore, this tusk sample came from a mammoth."

She allowed Mallison time to absorb the information and pointed to the right segment. "In the modern elephant, the angle is obtuse—usually greater than 110 degrees. In this sample, the angle is 120 degrees. Therefore, the tusk came from an elephant."

Mallison leaned back in his chair and looked at the ceiling. Kim rested the pointer against the wall and returned to the witness chair. Moy flicked off the projector and picked up the ivory figurine. "Based upon your examination of Exhibit Five, have you formed an opinion as to whether it is elephant or mammoth ivory?" Moy asked. Mallison tipped forward to gauge Kim's demeanor and her response.

"I have."

"And what is that opinion?"

"It's elephant ivory."

"Same question for Exhibit Six."

"Same answer. Elephant ivory."

Moy smiled at the defense counsel. "Your witness."

He approached Kim with a condescending air. His hands were clutching his suspenders. "Now, Ms. Kim, do you mean to inform this Court that you can tell the difference between an elephant and a mammoth merely by the way some little lines intersect inside a tooth?"

The lawyer sprawled backward against the jury box, waiting for a response. His legs were crossed.

"Yes," Kim replied instantly.

With a smug look, he paused before springing the trap. "Well, then, perhaps you can tell the Court the difference between old elephant ivory and modern elephant ivory."

Moy and Song both tensed. The whole case turned upon the defense position that the ivory was more than one hundred years old. That could be legally imported. If the Government could not prove the age and origin of the ivory, its case would be reduced to a simple one involving a mislabeled commodity. The defendants would go free. All eyes were on Kim. The defense counsel nodded triumphantly to Moy and turned to go to the counsel table. He only made it two steps away.

"As a matter of fact, I can," Kim said, looking at Moy. "If I could see Chart Seven, please."

Moy leaped out of her chair and pulled the chart from the case. She almost forgot herself. "Your honor, may I approach the witness?"

"You may," intoned Mallison.

Moy handed the chart to Kim. Ignoring the defense counsel, Kim spoke directly to Mallison. "Your honor, as all living things age, their protein starts to degrade. That's just a fact of life. This chart depicts the rates of protein degradation in sampled elephants over a one-hundred year period."

Mallison gave her a reassuring look. Kim continued. "The rate of protein degradation in the tested samples was negligible. Based upon that evidence, I can say that each of the segments tested came from an elephant killed within the past two years."

The defense lawyer wasn't finished yet. "Excuse me. But how can you honestly say that this tusk came from an African elephant?"

Kim asked for Chart Eight. Moy produced it with an assured flourish. Kim allowed Mallison sufficient time to peruse the graphic display and data. "Two tests have been devised for identifying the origin of a tusk. One method analyzes DNA; the other, ratios of certain isotopes."

She pointed with her index finger to the upper corner of the chart. "The DNA test uses genetic material from tusks. Like genetic fingerprinting, this method uses telltale differences in DNA to discriminate one group of elephants from another. Elephant tusks from all over Africa have been analyzed to create a library of isotopic ratios, or DNA markers. Based upon this analysis, Exhibits Five and Six came from Africa. They belonged to African elephants." The defense attorney started to open his mouth, but Mallison silenced him with a perturbed look. Kim pointed to the right side of the chart. "The remaining test involves ratios of carbon, nitrogen and strontium isotopes appearing in elephant tusks. The ratio of strontium depends upon the ratio in local minerals and geologic features. The ratio of carbon is proportional to the percentage of vegetation that comprises the elephant's diet, and the ratio of nitrogen isotopes is related to the quantity of water in the area. All of those factors considered point to the origin of Exhibits Five and Six as the Amboseli National Park area of Kenya."

A hush fell over the courtroom. The defense counsel was finished. His spirit had left him. "No further questions of this witness, your honor." Mallison didn't allow any time for second thoughts. "Very well. The witness is excused. You may step down." Kim winked as she passed Moy and Song. Mallison stacked his papers and thumped his knuckles on the stack. He had made up his mind. "The Court is now prepared to make its ruling."

Mallison looked directly at the defendants. "The Court finds that the Government has met its burden of proof as to the issue of the origin and age of the ivory samples in question. There is no doubt in the Court's mind that we are dealing with a vile case of smuggling contributing to the decimation of an endangered species. A most noble species. The defendants are ordered bound over for trial."

He glared at the defendants for a long while, shook his head and swept from the bench. Wicklow sniveled. Shih Jen sat with his mouth hanging open. The defense attorney buried his head in his hands.

Song embraced Moy, then both shook hands with Kim. They had won another round in the ongoing fight.

"Congratulations, both of you," Kim said.

"No. Thank you," Moy emphasized.

Song was suddenly pensive. Moy noticed her abrupt withdrawal. "Hannah, what's the matter?"

"I...I just need to be alone for a while."

Fighting back tears, Song rushed from the courtroom.

Chapter 38

Song listened to radio reports concerning renewed fighting in Somalia. Insurgents were active once more. The president had fled into the countryside, protected by an armored battalion. Armed might prevailed everywhere. Bandit groups had controlled Mogadishu for years and were fighting amongst themselves once more. Tribal godfathers had controlled the bandits and each vied for primacy. Now Al-Qaeda and ISIS were draining the fragile government's security resources. The entire country was propelled by fear and rumor. No one was certain of anything. It was ultimate chaos again.

Song pushed the off button at the news of the latest ISIS atrocity. The world had gone completely crazy. People were dying of hunger, while others were awash in plenty. Beheadings were on the evening news. Death and destruction ruled the planet. Did anyone really care about the elephants?

Song rolled down her window and punched the Charger down Van Ness. The breeze softly tumbled her hair as the landscape whizzed past. Old Saint Mary's Cathedral came into view as she turned right on Grant. Drawing to the curb at the intersection with California she parked and started toward the front entrance. As she started up the steps, Song saw movement out of the corner of her eye and turned to face it. Nothing was there. She scanned the area and shook her head. Must be imagining things, she thought.

Song was not Catholic, but felt compelled to enter the church. In the sacristy, she was drawn to the statute of the Virgin Mary, with its serene face, half-lidded eyes and the palms of the hands outstretched toward the seeker. A priest emerged from a side room, acknowledged her presence and hurried out. She marveled at the perfect silence within chantry. Song lit two votive candles, knelt, clasped her hands together and prayed.

She gathered her breath, trying to shut out the external world. Become empty and stay quiet, she told herself. Harbor no unnecessary thoughts. Soon, she pictured herself sitting on a high mountain. Before her was an infinite vista of mountain peaks cut by the convulsing veins of icy streams. All was tranquil. But was it really?

Something was wrong. In an instant, nightfall descended with a whirling wind. The ridges turned red, then black. High overhead, the lonely moon faded, then darkened and tumbled in the heavens. She felt the gnawing fear of her nightmares. Song cried out, opened her eyes and fell on her face, gasping for air. She stumbled to her feet and ran from the church, sobbing.

As she ran down the walkway to her car, a man with a shotgun appeared from behind a stunted tree and fired. Song dodged left and felt the shot pellets rip through the tail of her coat. She tumbled erratically to improve the odds. The assailant fired again. The wad of shot struck right in front of her, kicking shattered concrete into her face.

Song reached down into her purse for the Glock. It wasn't there! She had left it in the car in order to go into the cathedral unarmed. The gunner ran after her, cranking the pump and firing. A flight of pellets whizzed past the left side of her face. Song dodge-hopped sideways. She had to make it to the car. It was her only chance.

As she reached the passenger's side door and fumbled with her keys, the gunner fired again, shattering her windshield. Song ducked, shoved the key into the door lock and turned. It snapped off. Her pursuer fired again, rippling the hood with shot. Breathless, Song slid under the car as he reached the pavement. Song heard his footfall and closed her eyes.

She heard the scuffing of his shoes and the rustle of his pants as he stooped to look under the car. The man laughed and calmly reloaded the shotgun. Song winced with the click of each shell sliding in.

The roar of an engine and the squeal of braking tires startled her. Song heard a car door open and a man yell, "Drop your weapon" She saw the attacker back away from the car, go down on one knee and fire. Six shots, in quick succession, answered him. The assailant collapsed face down, with the shotgun wedged cruelly between his legs. He lay bleeding and moaning as she crawled from beneath the car.

"Lord, did you ever give me a scare," Brooker said. "Are you alright?" He slapped his automatic into the leather shoulder holster. Song touched her forehead and nodded. She felt faint. Brooker helped her to the curb, sat her down and went to check his suspect.

He walked down to the man and kicked the shotgun out of the way. Brooker cuffed him as he screamed in pain. The man had been shot through the shoulder and arm, but he would live.

He was Vietnamese. There was something else. He had a purple burn mark on his face and was missing a piece of his ear. Brooker looked over at Song. "I was tailing this character and lost him an hour ago. I thought he might try to make a move. Good thing I heard the shots."

Song noticed that the shooter was sweating profusely and grimacing with the pain. Brooker grabbed the man's chin between his thumb and forefinger. "How about it, bud, you want me to call for an ambulance?" The man nodded and closed his eyes. "Then tell me who you're working for."

"Go to hell, white devil," the man cursed.

Brooker was nonchalant. "Okay, pal, suit yourself. I got all day.

In fact, I have some errands to run. Bye. Bye" He waved to the suspect daintily.

As he started to walk away, the man screamed after him. "No! Wait! I'll talk! I'll talk! But I need protection." Brooker wheeled around and whipped out a book and stubby pencil. He wet the lead on his tongue. "Go ahead. I'm all ears. Who hired you?"

The man coughed. "His name is Lau. Darwin Lau."

Brooker laboriously scribbled the name in his book. "Lau, huh? Where's he at?"

The suspect struggled to breathe. "Warehouse...behind Sansome Street...Call, will you?"

Brooker folded the book and stuck it in his pocket. "Sure, pal. Take it easy. Oh, by the way, you're under arrest for Murder One. You have the right to remain silent. Anything you say can and may be used against you in a court of law. If you can't afford an attorney, one will be appointed by the Court to defend you." Brooker touched the man on the shoulder. "Now, do you understand all of your rights?"

The shooter turned his head away and gritted his teeth."Good," Brooker said, "I'll make that call." He winked at Song and reached into his car for the mic.

Ten minutes later, while the paramedics were loading the assailant into the ambulance, Brooker briefed the shooting investigation team that had just arrived. Song leaned against his car with her arms folded. The Glock was comfortably resting in her hand. She was anguished by the damage done to her car, but happy to be alive. Brooker finished his briefing and rumbled over to her. "Care to go for a ride, Ms. Song?"

She dropped the automatic into her purse. "Where to?"

Brooker smiled demurely as he held the door. "Why, Chinatown, of course."

Song looked expectantly at the investigating team. Brooker waved his hand with disdain. "Oh, don't worry about them. They'll get your statement later. Hop in."

While they were en route, Brooker had the dispatcher patch him in to Andy Ju. After prolonged static, followed by musical beeps, he came on. "Lieutenant Ju."

Brooker cranked the wheel with one hand and manipulated the mic with the other. "Hey, Andy, that tip you gave us just panned out. Thanks a helluva lot, pal."

The radio crackled when released the talk button. "My pleasure. So you collared the shooter, huh?"

"Damn right we did. I even read him his Miranda rights." There was a long pause and Ju chuckled, "No comment. Anything else I can do for you, ?"

"Yeah. Matter of fact. You know of a warehouse behind Sansome Street?"

"Sure do. Novelty store up front. Used to play in the alley next to it as a kid. Why?"

"Just meet me in that alley in about fifteen. That's one-five. I'll explain it all later."

"Okay, Brooker, I'm out. Bye."

They rolled down Clay in silence. Song cleared her throat and turned to him. "Why did you tell that suspect back there that he was under arrest for Murder One?"

Brooker flushed at the question. His throat noticeably tightened. He looked straight ahead. "Because, Ms. Song, I believe he was one of the men who shot your brother."

Song turned and pressed her face against the glass. After an uncomfortable moment, he accelerated over the speed limit and rolled down his window. The air rushed in. Piles of paper in the back seat blew around the interior. Song turned around to fix the stacks. Brooker gently touched her arm. "Oh, don't worry about it. That's just my filing system. Who knows, it might be an improvement."

Song faced the dash and covered her mouth, trying hard not to laugh. Brooker's demeanor changed to serious. "That punk didn't do it on his own," he said in a low voice. "I want the guy who hired him."

Brooker wheeled sharply left, taking the corner on a high angle. Song took a deep breath and stared into the depths of Chinatown. "Me, too," she whispered. "Me, too."

Midway down Sansome Street, Brooker pointed to an ancient brick building on the right. "There it is."

They turned down a side street and slipped into the alley. Brooker stopped and slammed a fresh clip into his automatic. He had a funny look on his face. "Say, I've got a bullet proof vest in the trunk. Want to see it?"

Song checked her Glock and took a practice aim out the window. "No, thanks. It might hinder my movement."

Brooker smiled teasingly. "What about this joint operation of ours? Isn't there a federal form we're supposed to use?" Brooker reached into the back seat and pretended to search. "I think I have one back here somewhere."

"Same answer," Song teased back.

Brooker laughed as they raced down the alley, scattering leaves and debris in their wake.

A car was parked with its nose out behind an adjacent restaurant. "There he is," Brooker said, flashing his lights. They stopped right behind the warehouse as Brooker answered a call from the dispatcher. "Brooker here."

The radio buzzed with an electronic hum. "Yeah, Inspector, this is O'Connor. Just thought you might like to know that shooter just copped to the name of his accomplice."

"Good work, O'Connor. What is it?"

"Guy named Trinh. Nguyen Cao Trinh. Vietnamese. Five feet, five inches...Slight build. Thirty years of age. Affiliated with a local gang, the V Boys. We'll bring him in for you."

Song and Brooker looked at each other. He raised his eyebrows. "Thanks, O'Connor, I owe you one."

Brooker clipped the mic into its bracket. "Let's get their boss."

They got out of the car and Brooker introduced Song to Ju and filled him in. The three of them walked abreast to the rear entrance. A Lincoln Town Car was parked in the only reserved space. Song and Brooker flanked Ju as he pounded on the door.

"Police. Hurry up!"

After a few seconds, Ju beat on the door again and repeated the message in Chinese, *"Jing chá. Gan kuài!"*

"Hai guan" shouted Song.

"What the hell's that?" Brooker asked.

"Customs," said Ju.

"Hey, don't confuse 'em," Brooker joked.

A muffled curse came through the door, followed by the sound of scrambling footsteps. *"Jing chá* shouted Ju, as he kicked in the door.

They ducked through the door, covering each other. The place looked deserted. Empty pallets were stacked in rows. Each column was marked by numbers within yellow circles on the floor. There were no novelties. It was too dark for comfort.

Fanning out in an inverted V, they whirled at irregular intervals to check their backs. Ju worked his way up the stairs, while Song checked the dock office. Brooker searched among the stacks of pallets.

Song walked through the office on her haunches. As she poked her head around the desk, she heard the spat-pop of an auto rifle on the floor above. It was followed by return fire from an automatic. Ju!

She raced to the door and heard a sharp crack to her left, followed by a series of cracks. Stacks of pallets crashed to the deck, adding to the din. The blasts above were deafening, but it sounded like Ju was holding his own. Song low-crawled across the floor to check on Brooker. "Brooker," she called out. "You okay?"

A groan escaped from a scattered stack. "Sort of."

Song heard running upstairs followed by scattered bursts from automatic weapons. She reached around an anchor pier and touched flesh. She recoiled, but the body did not move. She put her fingers to the throat, checking for a pulse. Finding none, she moved on. Brooker was pinned face down nearby. A cluster of pallets lay across his back. "Can you get these damn things off me?" he groaned.

"You got it." Song tugged them off one by one. She was careful to look around from moment to moment. Brooker winced as she helped him to his feet. "What's the matter, are you hit?" she yelled. "Oh, I'm so sorry. I should've got here faster." Song grabbed his arms and looked at his torso, "Where are you hit? Talk to me."

Brooker gave her a sheepish look and grimaced as he placed his hand on his right buttock. "Coffey always said I was half-assed. Now he's right."

Song cringed as she examined his posterior. "Well, it looks like a flesh wound."

Brooker winced. "You're tellin' me."

She started to fuss over him, but waved her away. "Uh, I'll be okay. Why don't you go help Andy?"

Brooker limped to the pillar and supported himself on it. "Okay," she said. "If you're sure."

"I'm sure," Brooker said.

They looked at the body of the henchman. Brooker was embarrassed. "Sorry. I don't know the Chinese word for freeze."

Song shook her head in disbelief and reached the base of the stairs on a dead run. She looked back at Brooker. "*Dòng*!" she yelled.

"Thanks," he answered. "I'll have to remember that."

Song moved up the steps one at a time. The furious bursts of fire above made her duck, although they weren't aimed at her.

Upon reaching the upstairs landing, Song suddenly felt dizzy and had to drop down on one knee to keep from passing out. She took a deep breath and tried to clear her head. Her palms were sweating. Even worse, her vision was blurred. She was gripped by an overwhelming sensation of panic. What was wrong with her?

Recent medical tests had proved inconclusive. Her vision was still 20/15. Heart and brain functions were normal. Song's doctor had frankly told her that she had ruled out any physiological disorder. In the doctor's opinion, Song was suffering from acute anxiety and stress reaction.

Song had always been so confident that nothing like that could ever happen to her. But, anxiety or not, she had to get a grip. Ju needed her help. She was his only back up now. Song willed herself to her feet and adopted a combat crouch.

Her vision regained its acuity. Song swept the room with the leveled automatic. She saw a muzzle flash from beneath some loaded storage racks. Another flared out across the room. Their combined fire ripped through some packing crates in a far corner. A head popped up behind the crates and returned fire with three quick shots, followed by a metallic click and another click. It was Ju! He was out of ammo and trapped in a crossfire!

Song moved into position, just as the two started to rush him. "*Dong!*" she yelled. Startled, they stopped in their tracks, wheeled and fired at her. She took the smaller one on the left first, squeezing off three rounds. He spun backwards, clutching his throat. The other, a portly man, rolled out of Song's line of fire. Noiselessly, she shifted position.

He popped up where she had been and sprayed the surrounding crates. Puzzled, he looked around, then turned. Song pointed the Glock at his forehead. "*Dòng,*" she commanded. He dropped the AK-47 and raised his hands. Song kept him covered as Ju hustled over, proned the suspect out and cuffed him. "Good work," Ju said, leading the perpetrator downstairs.

A back up team had arrived and the paramedics were already patching up Brooker as Song exited the building. He was lying face down on the stretcher, with his buttocks exposed. He was complaining loudly and shaking his head. "Twenty years on the force, never wounded, and I have to get shot in the ass. Me, shot in the ass."

Ju waltzed over and winked at Song. "Don't worry, Brooker, we won't tell anyone where you got it."

The paramedics snickered when Brooker swiped at Ju's leg. He just danced away as Brooker flinched with pain. "You're only making it harder on yourself," Ju giggled.

Ju gestured to Song and took her aside. They walked over to his car. The suspect scowled at them from the back seat. "Congratulations, Ms. Song," said Ju. "Looks like you nailed the big fish. May I present the great Darwin Lau? He says he'll cop for the right deal."

Song looked directly at Lau. He turned his head away. "Look at me," she ordered. He complied, obediently. "Good. Get this. No deals!" she shouted, loud enough for everyone to hear.

Ju reached into his coat pocket. "Oh, by the way, I found something upstairs which may tie into the motive for your brother's homicide."

He withdrew an object and placed it in her palm. "*Xiàng-yá,*" he said.

Ivory. A miniature motif of a Chinese god. It was in the Kainan style.

Song turned the artifact over in her hands. So that was it. Daniel had been killed just because they were afraid he might talk. Not because he had talked. It was only a precautionary measure. They must have discovered his connection to her, a U.S. Customs Agent.

Song coldly stared at Lau. A Ghost Shadows tattoo was prominently displayed on his arm. Her eyes flashed with unleashed fury. She reached through the window and grabbed Lau by the neck. "You bastard!" she screamed, whipping his shocked face with the carving again and again.

Ju tried to pin her arms. "Hey, take it easy." Song quickly spun him off and dropped the piece at his feet. She marched over to Brooker, still fuming. Song was even more angry at herself for losing control.

The paramedics were loading Brooker into the ambulance. "Hey, it's alright," he said. "I probably would've done the same thing."

Song nodded her head. Brooker allowed her a moment to calm down. "Where you going from here?" he asked.

"Africa," she said.

"Well, take care of yourself."

Song clasped his hand. "Aren't you going to wish me luck?"

"No," Brooker said as they started to close the doors. "The bad guys are the ones who are going to need it."

Song leaned against the building and watched until the ambulance was out of sight. She calmly cleaned her pistol while she waited for the police crews to finish. The twilight mist had thickened over the city by the time a patrolman dropped her back at her car.

Chapter 39

It was dawn now, and there was a light breeze gliding over the tarmac of Nairobi's Wilson Airport. Langdon's single engine, Cessna Station Air was parked beside the Customs shed. Resting directly across from it at the edge of the runway was a hunter-killer. The Bell AH-1G Cobra gunship. She had heard a rumor that they would soon be receiving drones to help fight the poachers. But right now, she was comforted by the fact that the Cobra would be flying top cover.

The ship's wide chord, door-hinge main rotor, and trim fuselage distinguished it from the original Huey helicopter, the workhorse of the Vietnam War. That, and the fact that it was designed to do one thing well: attack. The ship's stunted wings sported rocket pods, while the chin turret toted a grenade launcher and an updated version of one of the most feared weapons on the modern battlefield: an electric 7.62mm mini-gun. The cockpit configuration was also different. In the Cobra, the pilot and co-pilot/gunner sat one behind the other, jet fighter style. The gunship could attain a top speed of 219 miles per hour, and then stop and hover right on top of any target and destroy it with accurate and concentrated fire. It was Langdon's most versatile weapon of war, and the newest tool in his arsenal. The U.S. had them to spare, since its war inventory now included Apaches and Blackhawks.

Song ran her fingers over the six barrels of the mini-gun, while Weede was loading the rocket pods. "How would you like to be on the receiving end of this thing?" she asked.

Weede snapped a rocket into place and looked up. "I wouldn't. In fact, we have a saying about that. 'Don't try to run, you'll only die tired.'"

Song grinned as Weede went back to work. Walking around to the side of the gunship, she noticed the name "Margie Mae" freshly painted in white below the gunner's canopy. As she stared at it, she was more apprehensive than she wanted to admit to herself. "Who's Margie Mae?" she asked with a tone of innocence.

Weede was wrestling with a stubborn lock. "Huh?"

Song repeated her question louder. "I said, who's Margie Mae?"

Weede looked at the name and at Song. His face turned scarlet as he coughed. There was no way out. He had to answer. "It's my mum," he said at last.

Song raised her eyebrows. "Your what?"

He lowered his eyes. "You know, my mum, mother."

She laughed and looked at him incredulously. "You mean that you named a hunter-killer gunship after your mother?"

Weede looked like a schoolboy as he scuffed his toe on the asphalt. "Yeh, well, you haven't met my mum."

His look told her that he was only half-joking. Weede jiggled the assembly and reached for the final rocket. "Here, give us a hand, will you?"

Song cradled the miniature missile while he coaxed it into place. Her breasts brushed against the back of his arm as she helped push. Weede pretended not to notice. "Duff, do you have anyone?" she asked.

He stopped working, but did not turn around for a moment. When he did, he had a quizzical look, but there was a flicker of understanding in his eyes. "What do you mean?"

Song's mouth was dry. Her heart skipped a beat and her voice tightened. "You know…anyone in your life."

Weede caught on and nodded his head. "Oh, you mean sheilas." He abruptly turned his back to her, as he tried to act busy. "No, not anymore. I used to, but it didn't work out." His voice was tinged with an overriding sadness.

Song said, "I'm sorry," although she really wasn't. Her curiosity urged her on. "What happened?"

Weede fussed with a part he had already tightened. "Oh, you know, the usual story...I said I'd come back from the war, and didn't. She said she'd wait for me, and didn't." Weede turned to face her and gestured with a crescent wrench in the general direction of Australia. "I think she's married to the owner of a sheep station now." He kept looking at the horizon. "Probably got a couple of kids terrorizing the Outback."

Song gave him a warm smile. "And I thought I was the only one with a messed up love life."

Weede shook his head solemnly and looked deeply into her eyes. "No, you're not the only one."

They started to move closer together, but each hesitated awkwardly at the critical moment. It was too late. "I'd better get those guns loaded," Weede said in self-disgust. "Langdon will be along any time now."

In unbearable silence, Song helped him uncrate the ammunition. She thought about the first time they had met. He still needed a shave. There was still an intense air of danger about him. And yes, he was cocky, but he was far more complex than she had realized. Beneath that self-confident, man-of-action posturing, was a human spirit capable of loving and of being loved. He had allowed Song to see that he was vulnerable after all, just like her. Within her being, Song knew that her feelings for him had passed far beyond the professional level and even beyond the mutual esteem of close friendship. Their relationship had entered a new dimension. They had been bonded together by the circumstances of their lives and had reached a fragile turning point in their interaction with each other. She was strangely attracted to him and wary of getting involved with him at the same time. Physical attraction was not enough for her.

For a long time now, Song had yearned to share her life with someone. Not just anyone, but that someone resident in her heart of hearts. Duff was not just anyone. But was he the one? Did he feel the same way about her? He had treated her with respect. But could the deadly warrior also treat her with love?

Song was paradoxically eager to proceed, while remaining reluctant to commit. She might be hurt again and she had experienced enough heartache for one lifetime. Song did not want to be hurt again, or go on alone anymore. Then there was the black cloud of death hanging over her head. She didn't want him to die, too. Song shuddered at the possibility that it could happen.

Sometimes she wished that she could think about absolutely nothing. It would be a welcome relief to just let life happen and not have to worry about what each new day would bring. But her empty feeling was no good. Change had to come. How long could she wait?

She worried about her nightmares and attacks and wondered if she was suffering some neurosis. They seemed to occur at regular intervals, and when she was under extreme stress. They had become so severe recently that they left her exhausted. She had no relief, night or day. Would Weede understand and be sympathetic to her problem? He had been more than kind in Somalia. And since returning from San Francisco, Song had been feeling a little better. She longed to once again experience deep delight in the movement of life. Song hated being a bystander. She wanted to dance again.

Song watched Weede systematically prepare the guns. He was all business now. The mission was about to begin. She wondered if he had busied himself to keep his mind on the sortie and not on extraneous concerns. Like her. Couldn't he see how important this was, too? Didn't he care? Maybe she hadn't given off the right signals. Maybe things would be different after Au's ring had finally been broken. Maybe he was as afraid as she was. She didn't know. She just didn't know what to do.

Her thoughts were interrupted by Langdon's approach. The director was carrying a roll of maps and sipping plain soda water. "Well, then, all fit this morning?" he asked her. Song forced a smile. She wasn't feeling chipper at the moment. "Yes, and you?"

"Good, good," Langdon said. He waved to Weede in the cockpit as he signaled with a rolled map. Weede nodded, dismounted and pulled on his flight suit. Then he scrambled up to them on the double."Mornin', sir."

"Good morning, Duff," Langdon said. "Where's your pilot?"

"Oh, he had to run into town to pick up some spare blades. He should be back in about a fortnight."

The attempted humor bombed. Langdon did not laugh. In fact, he frowned, choosing to ignore the remark. Langdon was not in a joking mood. Song turned her head, slightly embarrassed for Weede. "Uh, I mean, any minute now," Weede added quickly.

Langdon looked at him seriously. "Good. Then you can brief him when he arrives. Let me tell you what has transpired within the past twenty-four hours." As he said this, Langdon unfurled one of the maps. "We received a report that a sizeable band crossed the Somalian border last night, in this sector." Langdon pointed to a position at the southeastern corner of the map. "Our source was only able to confirm that they are Shiftas and that they are heavily armed."

Song inhaled sharply. She was glad that Weede would be in the air where it was safe and not on the ground. The Shiftas were no match for the Cobra. It was airborne terror and would make short work of them.

"We don't know their destination, or what mischief they might be up to," Langdon continued. He looked straight at Weede. "We'll have to cover the entire eastern section of the park. And that's where you come in." Langdon unfurled another map. "We want you to fly this specific pattern today." Langdon's brow furrowed. "And shoot anyone out there you can't readily identify. They aren't tourists."

Weede and Song looked at each other intently. Both realized what had to be done. Langdon pointed to a red mark on the map. "There's a large herd in the vicinity of this waterhole. It must be protected at all costs. Ms. Song and I will set up our station there. We'll be in radio communication and our ranger patrols will be out. Their Rovers and lorries will all be clearly marked with a light blue X on the roof." Langdon grimaced at the Cobra's firepower. "So no mishaps can occur." Langdon rolled up the maps and handed them to Weede. "Any questions?" He looked from Weede to Song and back to Weede. They both shook their heads. "Good. Then let's get started, shall we?"

The pilot arrived as Langdon went to call for his Rover. Song waited while Weede filled him in. The pilot climbed into the cockpit and slapped on his helmet as he started his pre-flight check. Song saw Weede signal him that he would be just a moment. He walked over to Song with a tender look in his eye and took her hand. "Well, I guess this is it."

She did her best not to look apprehensive. "Guess so. You be careful."

Weede scoffed. "Me? I'm always careful." His face clouded. "Don't take any chances out there in the bush, okay?" Song shrugged. "Promise me," Weede insisted. Song looked away for a moment and back at him. "Okay, I promise. You better get going."

"Good," said Weede, walking away backwards. "We'll have to finish our little chat later," he said with a devilish grin.

Song just shook her head and smiled. Weede slipped into his seat, donned his helmet and strapped himself in. As the pilot started the engine, Weede gave her the thumbs up sign, which she returned. Song backed well away from the craft to avoid the backwash. The twin blades kicked to life and turned lazily at first, before whirling to terminal velocity. With a blast of wind and dust, the gunship lifted off.

As they started to bank away, Weede leaned over and blew Song a kiss, which she returned.

Chapter 40

The afternoon was warm and cloudless. It was early March, Kenya's dry season. The iron-rich soil was parched and dusty. Fissures spread through the terrain, severing the irregular tufts of yellow-green grass. Water was scarce. The few grassland sources available attracted an array of beasts, including nature's most unfathomable one: the elephant. Song prayed that it would not also attract nature's most cunning predator.

She scanned the spreading savanna below her position on a rocky plateau. She estimated that a herd of about 70 elephants was feeding at the edge of a river. Young elephants frolicked among their patient elders. Some of the older elephants painted their backs with the brick-red mud of the shore, to ward off the sun's rays. Song marveled that elephants were susceptible to sunburn. Nearby, Hunter's antelope bounded around baobab and wild fig trees. The plain beneath was peaceful.

Song grieved that the herd contained few mature adults. There were no big-tuskers. Male or female. She knew that, in Kenya, it had become the norm. Most of the herds now consisted of orphans and adolescents. They were leaderless bands of refugees. Nomads. Continually moving, with poachers in relentless pursuit.

When the big-tusked bulls were slaughtered to near-extinction, the poachers began to shoot the females. The reproductive capabilities of the herds had been decimated, along with memorized behaviors, and the knowledge of migratory courses and locations of water reservoirs in times of drought. Within a few short years, the entire social fabric of the African elephant had been destroyed.

It was rumored that a few poachers even shot juveniles for the stubs of ivory they had managed to grow. They had to kill twice as many juveniles and females to net the same amount of ivory derived from the bulls. Most of the plunderers viewed the elephant as nothing more than a walking gold mine. Song and the Langdon coalition had done their part to foil the poachers' plans. Inroads had been made. Corrupt officials, wardens and rangers given up by Madar, had been arrested. Now, they were finding fewer and fewer .303 caliber bullets in elephant carcasses. Only rangers still used the pre-World War I .303 caliber, bolt-action Enfield rifles. Perhaps most telling was the fact that Somalian Shiftas were so desperate for currency that they had resorted to robbing safaris and tourist caravans. Only the craftiest poachers continued to operate without fear. With the deployment of the loaned Cobra helicopter gunship, soon to be supported by drones, Song hoped that would soon change as well.

She laid her field glasses on a boulder and looked over at C.K. Peter Langdon III. Throughout the day, they had waited for Weede's gunship to return. It was long overdue. Langdon was alternating between reading a report and watching a dung beetle roll balls of foodstuffs for its larvae. Song beat the red dust from her fatigue pants and wandered over to where he was sitting. "Do you really think that we can preserve the remaining herds?" she asked.

Langdon dropped the report in the dust between his feet, and looked over the rims of his bifocals at her. "We've got to. We're at the bloody brink now."

The familiar whap whap of rotor blades reverberated through the dry still air. The field radio crackled from Langdon's Rover. He jumped up to answer it. Song ran back to her observation post and pressed the binoculars to her eyes.

The speck of the gunship came into view. She judged that it was five miles out. The chopper had nearly completed its day long sweep of the eastern park. They would touch down on the plateau to confer with Langdon before returning to base and refueling. The daylight patrols would continue until the organized bands of poachers were apprehended or obliterated. They could have it either way, but they would be out of business.

Song continued to watch as Weede's gunship drew closer and closer. It was now about two miles out. She was about to relax and turn away, when she saw the brilliant white tail flare of a surface-to-air missile streaking toward the chopper.

The craft surged with a power thrust and a rolling dive in an effort to evade the oncoming missile. But it was too late and too close to the ground. The tail rotor was sheared off by the blast. "They've been hit." Song screamed.

She watched in horror as the gunship rotated helplessly like a wounded quail and plummeted to the earth. t crash-landed on its side. The main rotor churned the dirt, as if fighting to stay aloft. One blade snapped off. The other was imbedded in the soil. Precious seconds ticked by. Song breathed a sigh of relief when there was no fire.

Song felt utterly helpless. The formidable gunship had been blown out of the air before her eyes. She was terrified and fearful for Weede and the pilot and kept her focus glued to the downed craft for signs of life. She hardly noticed Langdon standing beside her. "What in bloody hell was it?" he asked.

"A missile. Some type of portable SAM," she said. "Probably a courtesy loaner from Al-Qaeda or ISIS."

After an interminable minute, the figure of a man emerged and staggered from the wreck. He fell face down in the dust and lay motionless. Since the man was still wearing a helmet, Song could not determine whether it was Weede or the pilot. She kept switching back to the gunship, anxiously hoping that the remaining crewman would climb out. There was no movement in or around the craft.

She was horrified to see a grey lorry roll from cover and advance on the fallen gunship. Song dropped her glasses, ran to the Rover and seized a six foot aluminum rifle case. "Grab the base, will you?" she shouted to Langdon.

Langdon complied and scuttled behind her. "They're much too far out. That's an impossible shot," he protested.

Song ripped the monster .50 caliber rifle from its slot and held it up. "Not for this."

Langdon's jaw dropped. The oblong attachment on the end of the experimental Obermeyer barrel looked like the muzzle brake on a tank gun. Song screwed the new Leupold & Stevens 48 power scope into its mounts and test sighted her field of fire.

She had to hurry. The lorry would be on the downed crewman in less than thirty seconds.

Song hefted the weapon. Langdon fastened the mahogany support block to the aluminum tripod and set it near the cliff edge. Song deftly inserted the barrel into the base and drew back the bolt, exposing the stainless steel chamber. She reached for a canvas bag and opened the flap, displaying a row of ten wickedly stream-lined shells.

Langdon sputtered. "Those look like machine gun bullets."

Song loaded the rifle with what looked like a small artillery shell and slapped the bolt closed. "They are. With a little extra powder." The match loads would propel the bullet the improbable distance. She tossed a handful of dust into the air, testing for wind speed. To be sure, she repeated the ritual and looked at Langdon. "At this range, I have to compensate five inches for every mile an hour of wind."

The lorry pulled up just beyond the downed man Song lay prone with her eye against the scope. The image was bright and clear. Wind conditions were nearly perfect. She cranked in the correct windage and made sure the bolt was clamped down. Song could see two men exit the lorry and approach the gunship crewman. She got a good look at their distinguishing characteristics as they kicked the crewman in the ribs to roll him over. She gasped, backed away from the scope and looked up at Langdon. "You'd better call for back up."

Langdon ran to the Rover, released the whip antenna and began broadcasting for help. Song heard excited voices crowding the radio net. She slipped back down behind the rifle. She eased the scope to her eye and vowed not to rush her shot. More than one chance would not likely be afforded. One bullet had to count. She had to do it.

Scratching a toe hold in the uneven scrabble, Song took a deep breath. Her vision blurred as she fought a spinning sensation. No. Not again. Not now. She looked anxiously through the scope. The field of view was completely obscured; or was it just her? Song pulled back and rubbed her eyes. Could she really do it? This was no time to lack confidence. But they were more than a mile away. Song reeled off the arithmetic in her mind. 1,760 yards. 1,609 kilometers. Song had never hit anything beyond 1,500 yards. She had never even fired at a stationary target beyond that range. How could she expect to hit a moving target beyond any range she had ever tried before? At that distance, the wind and surface conditions were probably different. No one could make a shot like that under ideal conditions. But she didn't have perfect conditions, and something had to be done.

Her sight still faded in and out. She could hear Langdon calling all around the radio net for help. They would arrive too late to save the crewman. It was up to her and the big bore.

Song pressed her eye against the scope and lined up the crosshairs. Her thoughts kept returning to Ku Tai Lee. And the essence of *chi*. Could it help her overcome this affliction and do the job she had to do? She had mixed feelings about employing a life force to take life. Song abhorred having to kill human beings. Still, it seemed like a compelling necessity to protect and preserve innocent life from greed and predation. Whether it was Weede or the gunship pilot in mortal danger, she had to act. Now.

Song closed her eyes and relaxed her body completely. Next, she adjusted the rhythm of her breathing and waited until she felt balanced and synchronous. The voice within compelled her to press on. She opened her eyes and inched up to the scope. The crewman was now sitting up with the two standing over him. He removed his visor and helmet. Song saw a shock of blond hair. Duff! He was alive!

Song's vision cleared. Her body worked in harmony with her spirit and her will. She was ready. She shifted the rifle slightly left and found her target. It was lined up. With a final controlled breath, she rested her finger on the trigger and thought only of the *chi*.

Chapter 41

Weede stared up into the faces of Au and Niassa. For the first time since this bloody business had started, he felt truly alone. He was a prisoner again. At their mercy. Weede knew that they would not make the same mistake twice.

He had been prepared to die his entire adult life. As a warrior, he had to expect that his luck would run out someday, and he would die. Some day. But not today. Not like this. Cornered and cut down like some cowering dingo. Weede determined that he was not going to die. And not by the hands of these scum. He would overcome and live. Somehow. And if they tried to kill him, they would pay a terrible price. He would fight back, and they would know it. There was no true glory in dying. But if you had to go, it was best to go out right.

Niassa was covering Weede with an Uzi sub machine gun. Au patted the stinger rocket launcher he was carrying. So that's what had brought down the gunship. Efficient American weaponry diverted to the wrong people.

"Wonderful gadgets these," said Au. "I obtained this one from an Islamic envoy." He gave Weede a look of mock pity. "Well, perhaps not so wonderful from your recent perspective."

Niassa laughed so hard his turban nearly tumbled from his head. Weede studied them for an opening. He started up, but Niassa kicked him in the ribs and sneered. "That's far enough, Sergeant Weede. It would not please me to have you on your feet."

Weede winced, but did not cry out. Au dropped the stinger launcher and produced a 9 mm Beretta 92 from his safari jacket. Weede debated whether to trip Niassa, then stomp his trachea and take his chances with Au. He reasoned that even if Au was more cruel, he was also softer, fatter, older and slower. If he could just make it to the bush, he would soon leave Au behind, and return to deal with him on his own terms. It was time for a change. And time to make a decision. They would not toy with him too much longer.

Niassa kicked him again. Weede's eye shift must have given away his plans. "Don't try anything. You'll die soon enough. Why rush the inevitable?" Niassa stepped on Weede's hand and ground it into the gravel. "Your pilot is dead and you soon will be, Sergeant Weede. Niassa worked the bolt of his weapon and weighed it in his hand.

A stake bed truck scrambled from the bush and roared past them. It was carrying ten Shiftas armed with AK-47s. They were heading for the herd watering along the river. Weede sneered at them. "Bugger off. Bloody bastards. Slaughtering elephants with automatic rifles."

Niassa kicked Weede in the face and glared at him. "I've grown weary of your insolence and your interference."

Smiling coyly, Niassa laid the Uzi on a nearby flat rock. He ripped a cruelly curved blade from his waistband. It had a jewel-encrusted hilt, like a ceremonial knife. "I don't like automatic weapons. They are much too impersonal. I want to kill you with my own hands and enjoy it." He flashed the knife at Weede and did a sloppy pirouette. "Maybe I will go easy on you and just cut your throat, like a pig."

Au trained the automatic on Weede. Weede edged back. He wasn't going to allow Niassa to work his will. Niassa stepped forward and turned to Au with a condescending look. "If you'll permit me?"

Au laughed. "Of course," he said genteelly.

Niassa wiped the blade on his tunic as if cleaning it. The knife sparkled with the mid-afternoon light as Niassa took a slow step forward. Au stood ramrod straight like a statue, silhouetted against the sun. Just as Niassa started to bend down in a crouch, there was a sickening sploosh sound. Au suddenly pitched forward. At least, what was left of him pitched forward. The top half of his head had disappeared in an explosive shower of liquid, bone, grey-matter and cartilage.

Startled, Niassa stopped in his tracks to look, before launching at Weede. That was all the time Weede needed. He had his opening. Weede snapped the ka-bar from its ankle scabbard and rolled over to his knees. Niassa lunged in desperation as Weede shifted left and jumped to his feet. It was only then that the rolling crack of a gunshot echoed across the plain. Hannah! And she had fired from an incredible distance! Weede tried to maneuver Niassa to the same point where Au had been standing. But Niassa was too clever for that. He kept dancing and feinting behind Weede.

The sound of automatic weapons' fire broke from the river bed. Weede could hear the elephants trumpet in panic as they tried to flee. But it was strange. The firing sounded like it was coming from two different directions. More like a boiling fire fight than the constant hum of slaughter.

Weede bided his time. Now he had all the time in the world. Niassa had some dues to pay. He waited for him to blunder forward and thrust again, thereby exposing a vulnerable part of his body. Weede watched his eyes to predict the angle of his next attack. Niassa flinched, faked right and then committed with a violent shove. Weede was ready. Something deep inside urged him on and said, now. Now. He moved lightning quick to the left. As Niassa overshot the kill zone, Weede whirled and slashed down and sideways at the exposed neck, using the momentum to cut with his edge.

Niassa howled as dark blood pulsed from the freshly opened gash. He thrust again at Weede with increased defiance. This time, Weede kicked the blade from his hand and drove the ka-bar deep into Niassa's throat. He buried the tang from point to hilt. Niassa's eyes rolled back. His head dangled in a curious way, like that of a pinned insect. "The Law of Compensation just caught up with you," Weede said. Niassa rocked and withered as Weede twisted the blade and, with a final snap, withdrew it. Niassa dropped face down, like a limp doll, as Weede clutched his turban.

Grabbing an AK-47 and a pouch of banana-shaped magazines from the lorry, Weede ran down to the river. He surveyed the battlefield. Park rangers had set up a skirmish line and were pouring fire into the poachers. The Shiftas were pinned down and Weede was behind them. Their truck was ablaze beside a sand berm. They had no way out.

Weede was a one-man bunker. He found a natural fox hole, settled in and assumed his blocking position. Waves of heat radiated from the ground. The air was heavy and stale. His body was drained of sweat and he felt light headed, but he loved a good fight. And this would be a good fight. To him, it was just like any other day at the office.

Weede set the selector switch for semi automatic fire and drew a bead on one of the Shiftas in the brush. He was a hundred meters out with his back to Weede. The slamming jolt of the AK-47 almost caught Weede off guard. It had been a long time since he had fired one. He knew it to be one of the sturdiest weapons in the field. It was also coldly effective. The Shifta staggered forward, raised a dust cloud as he hit the ground, and lay motionless. Dead.

In a fire fight, Weede had one cardinal rule: you show yourself; you die. He squeezed the trigger as a Shifta's head popped up. This time the target lurched to his feet, buckled at the knees and toppled over. Weede saw hand signals from the other Shiftas. They were pointing in his direction. He had been spotted quicker than he had wanted to be. The Shiftas were going to rush him and try to break out. Good. Weede's job would be that much easier if they came to him. They could try to break out, but they would meet death in the process. Military school was in session. He would teach them a lesson in combat tactics.

Weede laid four of the thirty round magazines on the lip of the hole. As a five man squad disengaged and moved toward him, Weede flipped the selector switch to full automatic. It was time to rock and roll.

Weede caught a glimpse of a face and shot it to pieces with a quick burst. No argument there. He saw a flurry of movement to his right. He waited until he saw a patch of fatigue cloth. There it was again. Weede fired a long controlled burst and heard an anguished scream. Weede's senses were on high alert. Nothing moved for several minutes. But he knew that they had to be getting closer. He kept sweeping the battlefield from right to left in a wide arc, waiting for the charge.

Thirty meters out, a bush swayed unnaturally. Weede popped up and sprayed a burst into the ground in front of the target. A Shifta lurched backward, flailing his arms. Ricochets can kill, too. Now there were two left. Weede reasoned that they would try to take him simultaneously from opposite directions. They probably believed that he would not have time to react. He might get one, but not both. But the Shiftas were wrong. They had broken the primary rule of warfare: never underestimate your enemy.

Weede lifted himself out of the hole and crawled to a position ten meters away. He loaded a fresh magazine and waited. He didn't have long to wait. Both men jumped up twenty meters out and rushed forward, firing long bursts on full automatic. Hot slugs chewed the dirt around the foxhole. But Weede was no longer there.

Firing from a rifleman's squat position, Weede loosed a two-second volley at the closest Shifta. The bullets stitched him across the chest like a sewing machine. He folded backward as Weede rolled to take on the remaining man.

Weede surprised the second Shifta by firing a burst while he was still on his back in mid-revolution. The bandit screamed, clutched his abdomen and collapsed into the foxhole.

Down by the river, the fire fight between the rangers and the remaining Shiftas had intensified. Weede selected a bandit on the line, aimed, fired and dropped him. The others, seeing Weede's reactivation and realizing that there would be no escape, raised a white flag. The rangers quickly overran and captured them.

Weede walked down to the shore and looked across the river. Only one elephant was down. Two young bulls stood on either side of the carcass. As Weede watched, they rocked anxiously from side to side. The rest of the herd had scattered. And yet, the stalwart juveniles were trying to lift the massive body with their own miniature tusks. They searched and sniffed the carcass with their trunks, finally pausing at three bullet holes across the beast's forehead. Their trunks loitered for a long moment, interpreting the wounds, before the young bulls raced off to join the herd.

Weede was not surprised at this behavior. It was even said that elephants could shed tears when stressed. Some believed that they could even die from grief.

Song arrived with Langdon ten minutes later. There was no direct route to the river from the plateau and they had blazed their own trail. Song ran up and hugged Weede tightly without saying a word. "Oh, I thought you might be about," said Weede. "As you Americans say, 'That was some pretty fancy shootin', ma'am'."

Song's face was red with chagrin. "There's something I have to tell you, Duff."

"What's that, love?"

She hugged him tighter. "I missed."

Weede looked dumbfounded and extended his arms, trying to grasp what she was saying. "What?"

Song looked up into his eyes. "I was aiming for Niassa, not Au. The shot traveled."

Weede threw back his head and laughed until he was nearly convulsive. He coughed and patted her on the back. "I'll sure say it did. But, hey, no worries. No worries at all."

Chapter 42

The gleaming 767 came in low over Osaka just before dawn. Song straightened her seat back in preparation for the landing. Weede clasped her hand and squeezed it twice. The diminutive flight attendant smiled sweetly as she passed through the cabin on her final check. She reached for Weede's cocktail glass. "May I take that for you, sir?"

Weede had a severe look on his face. "Only if you promise to bring it back full."

The flight attendant hesitated in mid reach. "But, sir, we'll be landing in a minute." Song elbowed Weede in the ribs. He broke into a wide grin. "Sure, take it, love. Say, what part of Ireland are you from, anyway?"

The flight attendant was Japanese. Song elbowed him hard again. "Stop flirting." Weede smiled and looked straight ahead. He was starting to enjoy flying commercial.

The flight attendant blushed. Bowing politely to them, she clutched the glass and headed for the bulkhead jump seat to strap herself in.

Song looked over at Weede. He was tapping his fingers on the seat back in front of him. "Why do you do that?" she asked.

"Do what, love?"

"You know, tease people."

Weede reached overhead and fiddled with his ventilation knob. "Heck, I don't know. Just my digger heritage, I guess."

Song nodded in mock understanding. "Oh, I see, it's a cultural thing, huh?" She shook her head. "I think you're just incorrigible."

"Yeh. Not housebroken. That's one of our national characteristics, too," he joked. "We have to do something in the Outback to entertain ourselves." Weede squeezed her hand tighter as the jumbo airliner bumped, skidded and settled on the runway.

It had been a good trip. Weede had not gotten airsick. As a precautionary measure, he had taken two Dramamine before boarding in Nairobi.

An hour after landing, they had cleared Japanese Customs, and were in a taxi rolling through the narrow streets of the industrial city. Song had been forced to wait while Weede explained certain irregularities attending his passport. His photo didn't look at all like him. In fact, it wasn't him, as he later explained to Song. She had just rolled her eyes.

Although he had refused to show the expected deference to the officials, Weede's facility with the Japanese language had won them over. He was charming, if not polite. Weede had been thoroughly searched. Fortunately, he had not been armed. At least he hadn't appeared to be. Weede was in the front seat of the cab, bending the driver's ear. "That's what I get for traveling with a ruffian," Song said unintentionally.

Weede stopped chattering to the bored but courteous driver. "Huh? Did you say something, love?"

Song looked out the window. "No. Nothing. Just talking to myself."

"I thought you were over that, love," said Weede. "And I'm not a ruffian. I'm a rogue. There's a vast difference."

Song grinned sheepishly as Weede resumed his animated one-way conversation with the driver.

A cold mist hung over Osaka Bay as they left the city, headed toward Kobe, and beyond: Akashi. They had come to investigate Mitoma's involvement with Au and the Triad. Japan's National Police Agency would not be contacted, just yet. Not until they were ready. The Japanese police would move too slowly and be handcuffed by political considerations. Everything was all very unofficial at this point anyway.

There was another reason for Song and Weede to visit Japan. Au's billfold had included a number of business cards, including one from Yasuhiro Nagata, Chairman of the Isamu Trading Company. It was the country's largest purveyor of ivory products. The implications of Japanese involvement in the illicit ivory trade highlighted for Song the international scope of the tragedy. She rested her head on the cool glass. The vibration from the road was soothing. Coupled with the drone of Weede's voice, it soon lulled her to sleep. She awoke with a start a half hour later. The cab had lurched to a halt in front of a frame cottage with a blue slate roof. It sat among well pruned willow trees. "*Koko desu,*" said the driver, pointing to the bungalow.

"He says this is it," said Weede. "Let's go."

Weede stretched out and opened the back door for Song. He casually paid the driver and asked him to wait.

A pebbled walkway curved up from the street to the front step. In a shallow pond beside the house, a white crane stood alone and motionless. Weede tapped lightly on the door. There was a sudden movement inside, but no answer. He waited a moment, rapped again and called out, "*Mitoma-san, kikoemásu ka? Mitoma-san?*"

If she could hear him, Taka Mitoma did not answer. The bang of a shutter on the side of the house sent them scurrying around the corner. A hooded figure crouching beneath the window lunged up and sprinted for a stone wall. Weede grabbed the trailing leg as the runner tried to vault the fence.

The runner caught hold of the wall with his hands and kicked Weede full in the face, loosening his grip. Song reached up and grabbed the hood, yanking it off along with a section of hair. As the man yowled and reached up to touch his scalp, a black, leather-bound book dropped from his sash. He reached back in a futile attempt to recover it, as Weede cracked his arm over the stone ridge. The man tumbled over the wall screaming and writhing in agony. Weede wiped the blood from his nose. "I wonder what that was all about."

Song picked up the book. "I don't know, but this probably has something to do with it."

She thumbed through it. The characters and entries were hand written, entirely in Japanese. Song passed the book to Weede. He opened it to the first page. "Here, let's have a look." He read the page, then another. Weede hurriedly thumbed through the rest. His eyes suddenly opened wide. He closed the book with a low whistle.

"What is it?" Song asked excitedly.

Weede looked as if he were thinking about what he had managed to read. "Some sort of daily journal. Mitoma evidently wanted a record of his business successes and aspirations. It's a self-motivational technique. Real big in management circles. It gives names, dates, places, tonnages, everything."

Song glanced at the wall and looked back at him. "No wonder our friend wanted it so bad. C'mon, we better check on Mrs. Mitoma."

They found Taka Mitoma bound and gagged in the kitchen. Her face was swollen and bruised, but she was otherwise unharmed. The attacker had ransacked the house and threatened to kill her. She had just opened the floor safe for him when their cab had pulled up.

Weede questioned her at length. However, she knew nothing about her late husband's business affairs, except that he had traveled frequently to Hong Kong and Taipei. Just to be sure she was not seriously injured, they took her to a local hospital before heading back to downtown Osaka.

The National Police Agency was housed in a modern, imposing building on the edge of the Minami district. Song and Weede were ushered into a meeting room by a nervous-looking adjutant. Throughout the day, they had waited. From time to time, an officer would poke his head into the room, apologize, bow and leave.

A digital clock on the wall read 3:10 p.m. They could hear the strains of a heated argument through the wall. The discussion stopped with a final angry outburst. A weary-looking captain entered the room, carrying a sheaf of loose papers. He was stooped over and his eyes were downcast. The captain didn't have far to go to bow. "Welcome. I am Captain Yoshida."

"*Komban-wa*," said Weede.

The captain looked him over warily. Song smiled. "Good afternoon, I am Hannah Song, and this is...my associate, Mr. Weede."

Yoshida flapped his hand. "Yes. Yes. Please sit down." He sat and refolded his papers in a neat stack. Yoshida cleared his throat and spoke as if choosing his words with discreet care. "I have reviewed your accusations with my superiors."

Song sensed what was coming next. She cut him off. "Accusations? What do you mean accusations? We have brought you hard evidence."

Yoshida waved his hands to calm her. "As I said, I have reviewed the charges with my superiors and they have advised me to assure you that they will study the situation."

Weede jumped up, seething with indignant fury. "Study the situation? Don't you realize what you have here, man? People have been killed over this. Good, innocent people too. And all you can do is offer to study?"

Yoshida held up both hands. "Please. Please. This is not helping anything. This matter has international implications. Our foreign office must review the situation before anything else occurs. No precipitous action may be taken."

Weede jabbed his finger in interruption. "Look. You know as well as I do that this is a brush off."

Song folded her arms and tapped her foot. "Please..." Yoshida started to protest. Weede turned his back in disgust.

"Look here," Song said, "you must tell your superiors that if they don't raid that place right now, and seize the evidence, we'll handle it ourselves. Not only that, but we'll contact Greenpeace and the World Wildlife Fund and then we'll give the whole story to the press. They'll all be interested in knowing how you've handled this endangered species case." She moved closer to him. "You will not be able to sweep this under the rug. This will not be covered up. Do you understand me?"

Yoshida nodded in shame and hurried from the room. Weede smiled and applauded. Song was still fuming when Yoshida returned ten minutes later with two polished looking men in grey silk suits. After the introductions were made, the sterner looking man, named Tazuko, focused on Weede. "Now see here..."

Song stepped between them. "No, you see here. We've presented you with an open and shut case. That ivory must be seized for testing before it disappears. You must arrest the perpetrators of these vile crimes against man and nature." Song was close to tears with emotion. "Don't you understand? You must act now. Not later. It'll be too late. Too late for us, and for the elephants."

She sat down and looked at them hopefully. "Won't you please help us? It's a matter of honor."

They appeared to be mortified that a woman had to remind them of their duty. The police force would suffer a loss of face if they did not act. Tazuko gave her a favorable look. But the other supervisor, named Ajiro, had not softened. "My dear Ms. Song. These men are respected businessmen. We can't just barge in and..."

"Like hell!" Weede shouted. "Respected businessmen, my..."

Weede caught himself, knowing of the Japanese disdain for profanity. "Listen, an incident like this will solidify worldwide opinion against your innocent countrymen. If this story gets out, your agency and your government will lose face." Weede paused, then played his trump card. "Can your honorable land afford even one more scandal?"

The final appeal to their sense of honor and nationalism appeared to have worked. They huddled by themselves, talking in whispers and keeping an eye on Weede to insure that he could not overhear and interpret their remarks. At last they all nodded with finality. Ajiro looked up at Song and Weede. "Very well. We go tonight."

Song broke into a smile and thanked them profusely. Weede breathed a sigh of relief and bowed with respect.

By 5:15 p.m., on the strength of Mitoma's diary, they had secured a warrant from a magistrate and swooped down en masse to the showroom of Isamu Trading Company. Computer records, raw ivory and finished samples were seized. Despite his vehement protestations, Nagata was taken into custody for questioning. So was another trader present in his office at the moment of arrest: Junji Tsuchiyama.

The police agency seemed to have everything under control, so Song and Weede went up to the beer garden on the roof. They were seated across from one another at a table resting on the edge of the downtown overlook. An officious waiter suddenly appeared to take their order. "Do you want anything in particular?" Weede asked Song.

"Uh huh. I'd like the *teppan-yaki.*"

The waiter wrote it down without waiting for Weede's labored interpretation. "Anything else?" the waiter asked Song directly.

"Yes. Tea, please."

Their waiter scribbled the character for green tea. "And you, sir?"

Weede studied the menu for a long time, then folded it and placed it on the table. "*Biiru.*"

The waiter scratched the symbol and walked away shaking his head.

"All that deliberation for just a beer?" Song asked.

Weede leaned back in his chair. "Yeh. Well, that's just for starters."

They looked out over the energy-charged city. Billowing clouds chased the rapidly fading sun. "Oh, thank goodness it's all over," said Song.

Weede said nothing. He had a wary look on his face. Why was he so tense? She noticed that he kept glancing uneasily at two men who had entered the restaurant through a private door. One of them was Hiroshi Zaku. "What's the matter?" asked Song.

Weede tried to act nonchalant. "Oh, nothing."

She continued looking directly at him, while his neck continuously swiveled. "Well, then, why are you keeping such close tabs on those two characters in the corner?"

"I'll let you know," he said. "In the meantime, try to look as if you're enjoying yourself. Laugh out loud when I tap your foot."

Weede inched his foot forward. Song laughed as if he had just told a hysterically funny story. He guffawed, and slapped his knee, all the while watching the men out of the corner of his eye. Weede stopped laughing when he detected a sudden movement. "Duck!" he yelled.

The men were running at them. They both dived under the table as shots from automatic pistols peppered the wall. The other patrons screamed and crowded through the exit. Song scrambled behind a planter as Weede rolled into the aisle and kicked the legs out from under one assailant. Weede grabbed him by the collar and stood him up, just as Zaku fired, stitching his accomplice across the chest. "That's one way to get a tattoo," Weede quipped, dropping the man.

Zaku glared and fired another burst, as Weede rolled left. Song tried to cut to the right as Zaku reached around the planter and dragged her out by the hair. The assassin grabbed her behind the neck and clamped down on her carotid artery. She fought to keep from blacking out. He aimed the automatic at her head, point blank, and squeezed the trigger. Song shut her eyes. The magazine clicked like an unwinding spring. Empty. Zaku scowled and threw the weapon across the room. He reached beneath his overcoat and produced a gleaming tanto blade. Song writhed to free herself from the meaty hand. Zaku had just snapped her head back to expose her soft throat when Weede slammed into him with a cross body block. As Zaku released the deadly vise, Song fell to her knees, gasping for air.

Zaku recovered, and with one iron arm, bent Weede over the ledge. Weede dug into Zaku's other arm holding the blade and kicked him in the groin with a steel-reinforced boot. It had no effect. Weede knew he was up against it now. Zaku pressed the tanto blade forward inch by inch. Weede felt the angular point against his throat. Then he remembered who he was and what he had to do. He decided he didn't want to die in Japan either.

With a final surge of strength, Weede rolled the hulking Zaku to the right and reached into the lining of his boot for a needle pointed stiletto. With an abrupt thrust, he rammed the dirk into Zaku's belly. The porcine face of the professional killer convulsed and erupted in an unsettling scream as Weede twisted and rocked on the hilt. Now in shock, Zaku stepped back, looking curiously at the stiletto still protruding from his gut. He gurgled and made a spastic lunge at Weede. As Weede side stepped the desperate thrust, Zaku's momentum carried him over the edge.

Weede and Song looked over the side to the street below. A crowd was already gathering around the lifeless form lying in the gutter. Song heard a whirring noise like a gentle wind. A mated pair of swallows flying north wheeled by. They were going home. Weede wrapped his arm around Song and pulled her close to him. "Now it's over," he said.

Chapter 43

Along the Tsavo River, lowering clouds stained the twilight sky an ashen grey. The soft yellow wafer of the sun perched in the crown of a barren acacia tree. Nearby, an adult giraffe dined on a whistling thorn bush clinging to the shore. Its prehensile tongue grasped branches and searched among the needles for the sugary pulp of young shoots. He was accompanied by vervet monkeys, baboons and ground hornbills, as they gleaned kernels and hard-shelled bugs from the scattered pyramids of elephant droppings. The wild beasts moved about the reserve peacefully, in the heavy calm.

Song and Weede picked their way around a crop of stones and continued walking up river. It stretched through the park like an uncoiled snake, bearing the sustenance of life to the reserve's inhabitants. The river was a foot below the traditional low-water mark. It had not rained in the park for months. On the opposite shore, a Kamba warrior stepped from behind an isolated granite kopje and waved to them. They waved back as they entered the trail to the Salt Lick Lodge. Weede had on his long-sleeved uniform. Song was wearing khaki slacks and a white t-shirt with rolled up sleeves. It was imprinted with the simple message: "BAN IVORY."

The previous week had been restful. Langdon had ordered Weede to take a break and Song had accrued too much unused vacation leave. But there was more to it than that. They needed the time for themselves. And for each other. Their stay at the Salt Lick Lodge had been arranged by a grateful Kenyan government. Everything had been provided for them. Their only obligation was to rest and recreate.

Long walks together had nourished their relationship. They had grown closer. And closer. Even though Song had caught more fish than Weede, both times they had ventured to his "secret" spot. She did not tell him that her grandfather had been a fisherman and had schooled her well in the art. Song hoped that they would fish together again. She had never seen him so relaxed and at peace with the world. The impression was so out of character, with his war-like image, that it both intrigued and attracted her. They had both been lonesome for years and were now lonesome for one another.

When they reached the trailhead, Weede steered them to the right. Painted white stones marked the dirt paths within the complex. A windowless Quonset hut stained with bird droppings rested on the perimeter. They walked past it, but Weede turned around as if he had forgotten something. He walked back to the hut and opened the door. "There's something I have to show you." Weede's ordinarily chipper voice was laden with dread.

Song looked at him quizzically, as they passed through the entrance. It was lampblack inside. Weede searched the wall with his fingertips and flipped the light switch. The entire building was filled with elephant tusks in various lengths and degrees of white. Rows of blanched elephant skulls rested on the floor. Certain specimens were stacked on bolted-together metal shelves. One shelf held the most distressing display of all: miniature, blood-stained tusks of baby elephants. Hundreds of them. Most no longer than a ball point pen.

Song clasped her hand to her mouth and ran outside. Weede followed her and shut the door. "I think Langdon is going to burn it all as an example. He's flying a film crew in tomorrow to make a documentary."

Song's eyes brimmed with ready tears. She turned away, shaking her head. She anxiously studied the horizon above the distant Taita Hills. "Looks like rain."

Weede moved up beside her. "Don't you know that it never rains in Kenya in March?"

Song looked into his eyes for a long while. "We'll see," she said.

They strolled on, arm in arm, and encountered some orphaned elephants playing in a drainage pool. The scrappy juveniles stumbled as they tried to spray each other. More often than not, they missed. The bigger ones accommodated the smaller elephants by standing still from time to time and allowing them to attack. A ranger was feeding the smallest one from a bottle. It sucked greedily, pulling in the sweet formula along with the fingers of the attendant.

Weede and Song were captivated by the unfolding progress of the mock battles. In its own way, Nature was preparing the elephants for the struggle to come. "At least they'll be safe," offered Weede.

"Yes, but for how long?" asked Song.

Lau and the other members of the Ghost Shadows had been indicted by a federal grand jury. In Japan, Nagata and his associates faced fines and forfeitures. The National Police Agency had even launched a crackdown on the *Yakuza*. Gang bosses had become too bold. They had expanded beyond their usual criminal enterprises, such as prostitution, loan sharking, and protection rackets, and infiltrated legitimate businesses. Most unforgivable of all was the *Yakuza's* recent disregard of its traditional "understanding" with the police. Previously, if a serious crime was perpetrated, the *Yakuza* would present the felon and his weapon to the police within a matter of days. But they were no longer doing that and the police were angry. Song did not care why they were stopped, as long as they were stopped for good.

Au's organization and its nefarious offshoots had been destroyed.

But others waited in the wings. And due to the enormity of the slaughter already, elephant breeding patterns would be disrupted for untold generations to come.

Still, within the heart of the precious refuge, the species had an unfettered opportunity to thrive. These playful youngsters were proof of that. Song knew that the modern elephant traced its lineage back fifty-five million years. It was an adaptable survivor. Given the necessary room to live, free of human predation, the elephant would survive to delight the world to come. Song realized all too well what was at stake. If humankind could not rescue the earth's largest land animal, how could it hope to save a host of lesser creatures from the threat of extinction? And what would that failure portend for the human species itself? No, the valiant efforts of a few could not and would not fail. Song was certain of that now.

Weede stretched out a hand to pet one of the babies standing ankle deep in the water. "Hello, little fell…" Before he could finish, it stepped back, raised its trunk and sprayed the front of his pants. Song tried not to laugh, but she could not contain herself once Weede's face turned a shade redder than the shore. Raindrops splashed only on his forehead, adding to the indignity of the moment.

A passing ranger turned away and covered his mouth to stifle a snigger, lest he offend Weede. Song stopped laughing and grabbed Weede's arm. "C'mon, bwana, let's get you back to the lodge before you get any wetter."

As they plodded up the rise, a moist breeze tossed her hair. She did not bother to brush it back, but just allowed it to drift free. Weede stopped her in mid-stride. "You know, you're beautiful in disarray."

Song smiled tenderly and spoke a timeless message with the brightness of her eyes. She traced the outline of his stubbled chin with her index finger. "And I think you're an itinerant rogue."

Weede sighed and mopped his forehead with a jacket sleeve."What a bloody relief. For a while there, I thought you didn't like me." He wrapped a long, firm hand around her waist as they trudged up the last few steps.

When they reached their hut, Weede slipped inside to change. Song stood on the veranda, watching the approaching storm. It was blowing in wingedly from the northwest. From the mountains. Arcs of lightning traded places in the electrically charged sky. Distant pillars of smoke rose from the villages on the valley floor to join the tempest in the heavens. A primal, turbulent sensation saturated the air. Song breathed deeply, drawing in the unspeakable beauty of the earth and the power of life. She felt inspired, refreshed and renewed.

Song twirled around the deck, practicing the steps she had learned as a girl. Her hands floated gracefully above her head as she danced and swept into her favorite spiral. Soft and round. Soft and round. The dance her mother had taught her. The dance of life. She looked skyward and wheeled to the edge of the deck. She wiped joyful tears from her eyes and leaned against the rail.

A dark, heavy cloud covered the last rays of the vanishing sun. The rain increased its drumming tempo as Weede drew up behind her. She could feel the fullness of his thighs pressed against her. Song turned to face him and noticed his Cheshire grin. "Why are you so happy?"

Weede stroked her hair tenderly. "I watched you dance." Song lowered her eyes, then raised up on her tiptoes and kissed him quickly. He pulled her back to him and kissed her firmly and deeply. Song's hands trembled as she caressed his arms. "Dance with me," she said.

Weede stepped back as she slipped her arms around his neck. He fanned his fingers over her hips as she started to sway. Weede swayed in time with her, until they locked together in a waltz, moving to a music that no one else could hear. Song rested her head on his chest as they slowly reeled around the deck. Weede murmured her name and kissed her again, while the two danced on through the lively drops of rain.

When they brushed against the railing, they stopped and stood for a long while, clutching each other and looking out over the storm-drenched valley. Campfires winked out in the villages below. It was spring. The night was rainy. And they were together.

Song looked up into Weede's golden green eyes. "There is a story my people tell of an ancient emperor who, having journeyed to Mount Wu, became weary at mid day and fell into a deep sleep. As he slept, he dreamed. In his dream, a beautiful woman drew near, identified herself as the Lady of Mount Wu and said, 'Having heard that you have come here, I wish to share pillow and couch with you.' As the lovers parted, the lady told the emperor, 'I live high on Mount Wu. At dawn, I am the morning clouds; in the evening I am the pouring rain. Every morning and night, I hover about these hills.'"

Weede brushed her cheek with a gentle hand. She glanced toward the hut. Water cascaded from the roof and splashed the deck in a torrential wash. They were soaked and did not care. Weede entwined his fingers in hers as they moved inside. Without looking back, he reached behind him for the switch and flicked the lights off. The rain continued to fall as if it would never stop.

After the rain had come, the clouds dispersed.

Nature's great master-peece,
an Elephant,
The onely harmlesse great
thing; the giant of beasts...

—John Donne, 1612